Cora Linn Daniels

Sardia, a Story of Love

Cora Linn Daniels

Sardia, a Story of Love

ISBN/EAN: 9783744708135

Printed in Europe, USA, Canada, Australia, Japan

Cover: Foto ©Andreas Hilbeck / pixelio.de

More available books at **www.hansebooks.com**

BY

CORA LINN DANIELS

BOSTON MDCCCXCI

LEE AND SHEPARD PUBLISHERS

10 MILK STREET NEXT "THE OLD SOUTH MEETING HOUSE"

NEW YORK CHAS. T. DILLINGHAM

718 AND 720 BROADWAY

S. J. PARKHILL & CO., PRINTERS
BOSTON

I DEDICATE THIS, MY FIRST NOVEL, TO

My Dear Mother,

WHO, IN HER LIFE, UNWITTINGLY FURNISHED ME WITH THE
TRAITS FROM WHICH I HAVE DRAWN THE
CHARACTER OF HELEN.

CORA LINN DANIELS.

"*Devise, wit! write, pen! for I am for whole volumes in folio.*"

CONTENTS.

SARDIA: A STORY OF LOVE.

CHAPTER I.

"Thrift, thrift Horatio ! the funeral baked meats
Did coldly furnish forth the marriage tables."
Hamlet.

IT was the evening of their marriage day. It had been a singular wooing and as odd a wedding. The bridal party had made the little trip from the old homestead to the seaside villa, and the ladies had retired to their rooms. Ralfe Fielding, the groom, and Guy Thorne, his groomsman, hurriedly entered the library. "I really don't know what to do about it!" exclaimed Fielding. "The telegram is imperative! I cannot let this business go! It is of the utmost importance. And besides, my uncle's old partner calling me to his deathbed! How can I refuse ?"

"You cannot, in common decency," said Guy, decidedly. "You will be obliged to go! Let's see!" consulting a guide-book. "You can leave here at eleven o'clock and get there to-morrow morning."

"But Helen ?" queried Ralfe, impatiently. "I suppose she must be told ? And on our wedding-day, too! What will she think ? Women go into hysterics over every little thing."

"Every little thing !" echoed Guy, slightly astonished.

"Helen won't though," he added, quietly, "she is too sensible. Besides, you will be back in a week."

" Yes, that is true," with a sigh.

"Why, man, you sigh as if coming back were the bore instead of going!" and Guy laughed as he selected a Havana. "But we have an hour yet, let's smoke."

Fielding took a light from his friend and said, "Guy, you are the least curious person I ever knew. Why don't you ask me some question about this sudden marriage? By Jove, I really wish you would! It would help me."

"Well, then, in two words, why did you marry? You, a contented bachelor, living in Europe like a prince and enjoying the smiles of every beauty in the capital; why, indeed, did you pick up your traps, rush home and in less than a month after arriving, marry this young woman whom you had never seen? I never was so thunderstruck in my life as I was when, on getting across, your laconic telegram was handed me. 'Come and see me married,' it said! Two months ago you were in Paris."

"Very true," replied Fielding quietly. "It is a short story. My uncle Ralfe, for whom I was named, was an eccentric old gentleman. He married a wife whom he sincerely loved. She died very soon after their marriage. He was faithful to her memory. I was his only nephew. He adopted me when I was twelve years old. Helen was his wife's only niece. Some years after, he adopted her also. He sent me to college, then to Europe, as you know, to study medicine. He educated Helen in a Convent school until she was eighteen, when he took her home to live with him. Meantime he had amassed a great fortune. He built this villa and his residence in New York, and had fairly begun to live and enjoy himself, when he was suddenly taken ill with what proved to be a fatal disease. When his will was opened after the funeral, it contained simply two clauses and one condition. If the condition was not fulfilled, the whole estate was to pass to charitable institutions." Ralfe paused and sighed. He then went on slowly. "The property was to be equally divided between his niece Helen Gray and his nephew Ralfe Fielding, on condition that they should marry before the young lady should attain her twenty-first birthday. Meantime each was to enjoy the income of their respective shares. The estate was in the best possible condition. There was not a debt of twenty dollars. It was excellently invested. There was just one year and seven months in which we were allowed our freedom. To-morrow Miss Gray — I mean my wife — will be twenty-one."

Guy puffed a long line of smoke from his lips, and ejaculated, "Hum!"

"Of course," continued Ralfe, "it would have been absurd to have given up a million apiece! She felt that as well as I. At least, her lawyers so informed mine. I sometimes think those old fellows patched up the match between them," with a half laugh; "but, at any rate, I was unable to decide, and in the only communication I ever had from her I was given to understand that, in answer to my question, she had nothing to say, save that perhaps it would be best to settle it in a personal interview; so I packed up and came. We began awkwardly enough, but as you say, Guy (though I don't see how you found it out in a few hours), she was very sensible, and after a month's courtship — that's the proper word, isn't it? — we — well, here we are, married, thoroughly married by rule, law and bond, clergyman and ring!"

"A finely settled business arrangement. Quite Parisian!" murmured Guy in a slow, sarcastic drawl. "Not a vestige of love about it."

"Love!" exclaimed Fielding, "don't talk to me of love. That's all past with me forever."

"Is it possible Sybil Visonti made so deep an impression upon you as that?" cried Guy in a sympathetic tone. "Did you indeed love that strange, magnetic woman? What charm did she throw over you? I thought I was hard hit, but I almost ceased to think of her three days after I left her."

"And I have thought of nothing else!" exclaimed Ralfe, passionately. "I see her before me, I dream of her, I still love her."

"Hush! don't speak so loud — what if Helen — but she was not, she can never be worthy of your manly love, Ralfe," said Guy, as Ralfe drew the heavy curtains closer. "She treated you with shameful silence. Forget her!"

"I cannot."

"But your wife! Helen!" cried Guy, getting up a little faster than was his wont. "She! Is all love past with her? or all beginning? What is her feeling in this matter? Have you questioned her heart? Or is she as cold as you are, and as mercenary, by Heaven!"

"Hold on. I don't think either of us were very mercenary. We both did our best to get out of it by bestowing our millions upon each other. But the lawyers said 'No,' and — well! it is as you say, a sort of French marriage; but it is said those sometimes turn out very well indeed." And Ralfe came and put his arm on Guy's shoulder. "Look here, Guy," said he, "Helen is as you said, sensible. I told her that she must take me as I am. I said I would always be kind, true, tender to her. I conveyed the best possible friendship. I treated her as a gentleman should. I respect her; I may say

I honor her. She has acted the part of a most delicate and refined lady in the whole matter. But I really don't think she expects me to love her. Why should she?"

"Does she love you?"

"Love me?" repeated Ralfe in a startled tone. "Why, I never thought of such a thing. Love me? Why, no; of course not. Why should she?"

"Well, she might, you know, old fellow. You are not such a bad specimen of manhood, and she was in a Convent up to eighteen. For God's sake, Ralfe," said Guy very much in earnest now, "I hope she does not love you. If she does, Heaven help her!"

"Don't be foolish," smiled Ralfe, incredulously. "The young lady is this moment in her room, planning some new fichu or filagree with her maid. But truly we must let her know that I must leave. We must send for her. Please ring the bell."

The gentlemen waited some little time before Mrs. Fielding made her appearance. She came in with a laughing remark about her delay. Guy thought he had never seen a more beautiful woman. Her delicately carved features were of a marble-like paleness to be sure, but on her cheeks bright red spots burned warmly. Her eyes sparkled with some hidden excitement. Dark as night, large and glowing, they seemed to flood her countenance with a radiance of beauty. Her long, sweeping dress of some delicate tissue, with a thousand dainty puffs and laces, displaying the gleaming white throat and the snowy arms, made her appear so queenly, so statuesque, that even Ralfe, whose artistic sense was most exquisitely sensitive, could find no flaw in her. She turned to him with a smile.

"You wished my presence?"

"Yes," he said in an embarrassed tone. "I have just received this telegram," placing it gently in her hand.

"I feel it impossible to neglect such a desire in one so near our uncle. Indeed," he added deprecatingly, "I see no way but to go."

She read it slowly. Her hand trembled a little. Guy noticed it; Ralfe did not.

"Of course you must go," she finally replied. "I think there is no possible choice in such a matter. And what can I do for you?" cheerfully. "How can I help you away?"

"Oh!" exclaimed Ralph, very much relieved, "Wilson will do everything for me. In fact, I have given him his orders. I am sorry to have disturbed you," he added kindly, and then, with the least hint of forcing himself, he continued, "I regret exceedingly this inappropriate event; but I shall only be gone a week at farthest. Make yourself happy, and do not for an instant think of me. Miss Lulu will remain with you, and Guy says, if his society will make up for mine" (with a smiling grimace), "he shall be only too happy to stay until my return."

"He is very welcome," said his wife, cordially. "No doubt we shall manage to amuse ourselves. By the way, I expect two good saddle horses down from the farm to-morrow (I believe I did not mention it to you, Ralfe), and Miss Lulu and Mr. Thorne can have a canter."

She had not seated herself, and at this moment Wilson appeared with bags and traps, standing respectfully in the hallway.

"The carriage will be around directly, sir," said he.

"Then I will not wait, but bid you adieu now," quietly said Mrs. Fielding. "A pleasant journey! And you, Mr. Thorne, I shall see you in the morning." And with a gracious bow and charming smile she slowly moved up-stairs.

"Well!" exclaimed Guy under his breath, "I don't

think there is much to worry about there. Her heart is safe enough."

"What did I tell you, Guy!" remarked Ralfe as she disappeared. But he had followed that graceful figure with a wistful eye, and while he was bowled along through the darkness, he thought of her more than he had ever supposed he could.

CHAPTER II.

AN UNUSUAL PROPOSITION.

"And yet, and yet," —

A week had passed and Ralfe had returned. Dinner was over and the two guests had started away on their evening gallop. "Do you care to drive, Helen?" inquired Ralfe as she watched them ride gayly off. "I really feel a little weary with to-day's travel, and if you don't mind," —

"No indeed! and besides, I really wish to have a little chat with you. I believe we have not yet been alone for a moment since" — she hesitated, and then went on softly, "since our wedding-day." Ralfe gathered himself together with what grace a man may who expects to be thoroughly bored.

"Certainly," he acquiesced, gently, "I shall be charmed."

"What can be in his mind," thought Helen, noticing with a quick eye every change in his countenance.

"You know," said she in an off-hand sort of way, so new that it rather startled Ralfe, "You know that any pretence of love between you and me would be mere folly, and so, since you have been gone, I have been thinking of a plan." She stopped to let him take in her full meaning. Ralfe swung around on his seat. She was sitting on the stone steps of the veranda. Great stone columns and balustrades covered with ivy and honeysuckle were her background; the setting sun flooded the whole scene, and sent a soft, roseate glow over her pure, fair face. Her favorite costume of soft white, rippling with laces, became her perfect figure as does a drapery about some old-time statue. She was the picture of quiet, harmonious loveliness. Ralfe was shocked. Could a beautiful woman like this talk in such a practical way? He longed to hear her utter something less harsh. He only said, " Indeed ? "

"Yes," she went on swiftly. "Of course I understand that all sentiment would be a farce; the only thing to do is to banish the very idea of it. So, if you please, let us be jolly good friends, comrades, hail fellows well met. Surely we can get along nicely in that way. We need not be at all intimate. When we like, we can talk, and when we don't like, we certainly can avoid each other! As for troubling ourselves about each other at all, I cannot see the need. Thanks to your kindness, I am to have my own income, and as old Judge Davis advised, we had each better keep our own accounts. Then we shall not be annoyed as husbands and wives generally are, by questions of money. You can have your choice of the establishments, and we can live together or apart, just as we please, — only we must not give Mrs. Grundy a chance to gossip."

Her manner was quite unlike anything he had ever seen in her before, but Ralfe was too much a man of the world to show his surprise. Indeed, he told Guy afterwards that he had never felt so relieved in his life.

He said promptly, " My friend, Helen, then ! " and shook hands pleasantly. " I only object to making a choice of establishments. Let us occupy either as we please, and go up to the farm when it suits us. As you say, we will give Mrs. Grundy no chance to talk; at the same time we may each feel perfectly free so far as honor and courtesy and mutual respect permit." He said this last with a rather grand air.

"You take for granted I respect you, comrade!" she laughed.

"Do you not?" he asked almost sternly.

"I do respect you, I may say I honor you, sir," she answered with a haughty grace, and swept into the house.

As Ralfe remained in the twilight, pondering his wife's last words, they seemed strangely familiar, yet he could not tell why. He was of an analytical mind and given to silent consideration of even the most trifling events. Educated with the utmost care, and always free from petty annoyances concerning money, he had developed into a leisurely thinking and leisurely acting man. Intellectually he was serenity itself. Emotionally he was somewhat impulsive. He generally abandoned himself to an easy repose verging on indolence, but which was full of a pent-up energy which only needed occasion to exert itself with surprising power. He carried with him an air of reserve which was softened by a graciousness which won, while it did not permit the least familiarity. His countenance was what might be designated as fine rather than handsome. Dark hair brushed back from the high forehead, eyes grave and quiet, but filled with a subtle sweetness of expression which sometimes flashed into rarest humor.

His mouth alone betrayed the sensitive, poetic, easily wounded and easily aroused temper of its owner. Under the dark, silky mustache, this delicate and beautifully cut member trembled and smiled in defiance of Ralfe's will. It was well at times that it was nearly concealed.

Mr. Fielding's manner was one of thoughtful courtesy. With rare delicacy he never trespassed nor intruded, never forgot proprieties, never intentionally annoyed. To women he was deferential; to men, cordial.

He aimed to enjoy life as much as possible so long as he wronged no one and deprived no one of equal pleasure.

His ideas were based upon a certain personal morality rather than upon the customs of society. As Guy had lovingly remarked, he was "not such a bad specimen of manhood, you know."

He was thinking now of a woman quite opposite in style and character to this lovely wife of his, — "wife in name," he sighed to himself. His memory called up Sybil Visonti as a vision. What a woman! How that dark, fascinating face, with its eyes of velvet flame, passionate, humid, glowing, flashing, all in a single quarter hour, the lips that breathed a peculiar music in every tone, the arms that seemed to always long to embrace, the strangely moving hands which made such subtly expressive gestures, adding an undulating and rhythmic grace to every tender word, rushed upon his sight, and even in imagination almost blinded him. He shuddered as he stood in the warm June air. A chill, a sudden deathly feeling, swept over him. "What was her wonderful power?" he murmured. "Why was I left without an answer?" He went down into the garden, and paced a long time, thinking, thinking. He laughed a little scornfully at last. "What a fool a man can make of himself! She went without a word to answer my passionate declaration. Yet how she looked at me that last night when I put her into the carriage! Her touch was like fire — a caress of fire! I must not think of her. I will not! and yet, — and yet," —

"I say!" broke in Guy's voice on his reverie, "come in here, Ralfe, we want you."

"Yes," cried Lulu Morris, coming down the path, "come, Mr. Fielding, we have a project. Don't you love projects? I do. I think projects are the nicest things in the world, especially when we don't know what they are, and none of us do but Helen. It is she who has gotten it up. Isn't she nice?"

Lulu was a real little ray of sunshine. Breezy, jolly

little Lu! Her merry laugh and rattling talk would make the dullest party gay. She "loved" everything, from strawberries to flirtations; and every living thing, from kittens and babies up to the sternest old grandfather in the world, loved Lu.

"Helen is a darling," she went on, as they mounted the steps. "I never saw a pony go so in my life as hers did to-night, didn't it, Mr. Thorne? Isn't Helen a darling to let me ride every single night?"

Ralfe looked at Helen and smiled amiably.

"All pretty women are darlings; but Helen — she is a comrade," and he gave a short laugh.

"A what?" said Lu, astonished.

"I am a comrade. And I mean to make a loyal one, too. See how I have begun. Ralfe will be pleased to acknowledge my immediate fulfilling of duty, I am sure. See this list of people whom I have invited to amuse him!"

"Is that your project?" he asked, in a disappointed tone, while Guy looked pleased, and Lulu went into raptures.

"Yes; do you not like it? I was sure you would like to fill this great house with people, so I have invited the ladies, and thought you and Mr. Thorne might select half a dozen agreeable gentlemen."

Ralfe was again smiling. "Ah, so kind. I shall be delighted. Guy," he added, indolently, "whom shall we have?"

"But you don't know what ladies are coming!" exclaimed Lu. "You must match them with suitable partners, you know."

"Well, whom are we to welcome, Helen?"

"I wanted Jo Millard, because she is so witty, so fertile in invention, and such a fine hand at arranging all sorts of entertainments; then she is 'dying' to come to

the sea, and I know the poor child needs a change.
Then I have asked Cecile Gray, my cousin, a dear, good
girl with a history, — a little quiet, but plays divinely,
— and Sybil Visonti."

"The Visonti!" "Sybil Visonti!" cried both gentlemen in a breath.

"What surprises you so?" said Helen, turning from
one to the other. "Do you know her?"

"Of course we do," drawled Guy in his most indolent
manner, coming to the rescue of Ralfe. "We have both
flirted our heads off with her in Paris, and I don't know
many fellows who haven't."

Ralfe flushed a dark red. His lip quivered beneath
its silken shield. He was silently angry with Guy, at
the same time that he thanked him for announcing in
this cool manner what must inevitably be known if Miss
Visonti arrived.

"I think you wrong her, Guy," he was about to say,
when Helen remarked with considerable spirit, "You do
Sybil Visonti wrong! I cannot believe that she flirts
with every man she meets. She has too much discrimination. I admit that she enjoys flirting, but her taste
is irreproachable. She is thoroughly accomplished, and
one of the best bred women I have ever met. Even as
a young girl in the Convent, she was our model for grace
of manner."

"And of morals also?" murmured Guy; but the
query was covered by Ralfe's "Oh! That is where you
knew her. Have you seen her since she left school?"

"No; I have not seen her for several years. She is
considerably older than I. We correspond regularly,
however. She writes letters which are as fascinating as
her conversation, and I value them in a literary way
more than those of any acquaintance I have."

Ralfe had almost uttered, "Did she ever mention

me ? " when he remembered Helen had asked, in a surprised tone, if he knew her, which convinced him that Sybil had not been disloyal, had not paraded his love before the eyes of a schoolgirl "intimate." A feeling of renewed faith and gratitude swept over him at the thought.

"There is one thing I may frankly say of Miss Visonti," said Guy, pleasantly. "She never says an unkind or evil thing of any one. If she cannot find some beautiful quality to praise, she says nothing at all. But she seldom discusses others anyway. I never saw a person whose whole conversation circled out like the spokes of a wheel so, as hers does."

"And what is the hub ? " asked Lu, earnestly.

"Herself," said Guy.

"I think we have discussed her long enough," calmly remarked Helen. "That she is a magnificent woman, no one can deny. Her beauty, talent, birth, and wealth are all in her favor. I shall be happy to have her here."

"So shall I," cried Ralfe, for the instant forgetting policy or believing policy unnecessary. "This place shall be made a paradise to welcome her."

As he thus exclaimed, his wife rose and, seemingly without motive, sank on an ottoman near his feet. A shaft of moonlight irradiated her countenance. She raised her eyes to the sky, and seemed absorbed in thought. Her head, with its golden crown of hair, her exquisite features, all saddened by a wistful droop of the mouth, yet unutterably lovely, appealed to him even in the midst of his speech. He gazed at her at first critically, and then, by some singular attraction, almost tenderly.

"So unlike," he thought; and then again, but in so different a sense, "and yet, and yet " —

As before, Guy's voice broke in: "What men shall we have, Ralfe?"

"Oh, I don't know. Who are back from Europe? Is Charlie Vane at home yet? They say he made one of the finest copies of 'The Ascension' that an American ever painted."

"Yes; he came over in the same steamer with me. And Sardia. Do you know Sardia?"

"I should think so," laughed Ralfe. "I was becalmed with him ten days in his yacht, on the Mediterranean, and he and I were the first men who stood on the Pyramids that year we did the Nile. Is he over? But we cannot get him. He is always engaged ten deep."

"I think we can," put in Guy, positively. "He told me hardly any one knew he was coming. We can try, anyway."

"Oh, do, do!" cried Lu. "I think Sardia is a splendid name! He has a steam yacht and has done the Pyramids! What a splendid conversationalist he must be! I like travelled men so much. They amuse me without making me amuse them."

"Ha, ha!" laughed Guy. "Wouldn't Sardia smile at that! Think of setting the elegant, the irresistible Sardia, the 'grand seignior' to 'amusing' a little chick like you!"

"*You* do it," said Lu; "you put yourself out to do it," and she pouted like a little child.

Helen awoke from her reverie, and laughed in so musical, so bewitching a way that they all joined in together. "Little goose!" she said with the sweetest accent, "of course he does! I shall be glad to meet Sardia again," she added. "I remember he spent a few days with my uncle some years ago. I thought him then a kind of prince. He always brought me a bunch of violets."

CHAPTER III.

CONFIDENCES.

"A child of our grandmother Eve, a female ; or, for thy more
sweet understanding, a woman."

Love's Labor's Lost.

SEVERAL weeks had passed by. The gay watering-place
was in the height of the season. The drive was brilliant
every afternoon with every possible style of turnout,
not the least admired of which was Mrs. Fielding's quiet
landau. A singular curiosity had attached itself in the
minds of "the best people" to the marriage of this
young couple. Something of the story which Ralfe had
told Guy had found its way into the current of daily
chatter, and had become exaggerated until it made Mr.
and Mrs. Fielding "the rage." Their "cottage," which
was in fact a villa of almost enormous dimensions, was
the scene of all possible gayeties and the most unique
and agreeable affairs. Filled with guests who had been
selected with the utmost tact and comprehension ; surrounded by grounds so extensive and so beautifully
arranged that even the English visitors could do nothing
but praise ; the sea, ever glorious, in full view and all
the attractions of a fashionable watering-place close at
hand, together with a host and hostess whose first greeting put every one at ease and whose overflowing and
thoughtful hospitality made every moment more enchant-
ing, the place seemed indeed a Paradise. All gave themselves up to unalloyed enjoyment, and, as Lu demurely

remarked in a sudden silence one evening, "We are all positively seething in flirtation, aren't we?" There seemed an exception to the rule. Ralfe certainly could not be accused of the slightest tendency to while away the summer hours in idle dalliance. His horses, his various little trips, the clubs, the hotels, and some mysterious writing which he regularly pursued in the library every day, seemed to occupy his whole attention. A model host, he still held himself aloof from the least attempt to amuse himself with the ladies. He was quite as courteous to one as to the other. "An awfully impartial creature," said Lulu, discontentedly.

"But the Visonti has not arrived," answered Guy in a confidential tone to this little observation. "We shall then see what we shall see!"

"Was he dreadfully 'hard hit,' as you men say?" curiously questioned Lu.

"I don't know, dear," for things had gone on quite fast between these two and they were sometimes very quietly, 'dear' and 'darling' to each other. "I don't know, but I rather think he was worse than the rest of us. *I* adored her, you know."

"Oh, Guy!" reproachfully. Then with a soft little twinkle, "But you adore *me now*, don't you, Guy?"

"Yes, awfully! who could help it?"

"Is she so fascinating?"

"Yes, dear, she is a fascinating woman. I know, pet, when I say that, no idea of jealousy will ever enter your lovely head. You are my heart, — but yes, a fascinating, dangerous, subtle woman. Her whole aim in life is to have her own will. The end is what she means to gain, no matter how. She will twist, turn, tease, hang, act a thousand different moods from farce to tragedy to accomplish the least object on which she has set her mind. If she cannot move by persuasion, she will make a mar-

tyr of herself, weep, mourn and then smile, turn herself
into a saint, and so wrap herself in an atmosphere of
'sweetness and light,' that you are led to bend the
knee in adoration.   She manages to throw a glamour over
her lightest action, and beware, Lu!   She wins women
as easily as she does men.   I have seen her table loaded
with gifts from women.   She possesses a strange undefinable power to which all must, more or less, yield."

"Helen loves her," said Lu.

"Yes, even our beautiful Helen seems to have the
same thrall over her; but still, Lu dear, at times when
we have mentioned her coming, I have seen a singular
expression flit over her countenance as if she had some
secret dislike even to her name."

"She turns pale sometimes when I ask her about
Miss Visonti.   I wonder if she fears her?"

"Why should she?" asked Guy in a surprised
tone."

"If Helen were in love with Ralfe, she might indeed
be afraid, not," — he added hastily, "that the Visonti
can compare with Helen as being a true, beautiful,
noble woman, but she has arts that no innocent woman
can know; subtle, entrancing ways which only come
from a combination of experience and unscrupulousness."

"How utterly different to Helen!   She is so good
as well as so intellectual!"

"She is a woman who can express fine thought finely.
Her soul is of a more delicate cast than many."

"She always makes me think of that peculiar flower
we find in the dim old woods, the Indian Pipe.   The
perfume is spicy, the texture exquisite, the color pure,
spotless white."

"The Visonti is the deadly night-shade, or the scarlet
poppy!   I never think of her without remembering what

Charlie Vane said of her the first time he saw her. You know how clairvoyant, how keen-sighted Charlie is! How he seems to pierce one through and through, and read one's very soul!"

"Yes," said Lu; and then irrelevantly, "I think him the most of a saint I ever saw."

"So do I," echoed Guy, heartily. "Well, I asked him one evening after his first presentation to the Visonti, 'What is she, anyway, Charlie? Can you make her out?'—'She is a vampire!' he answered. 'She eats one up body and soul.' And he meant it!"

"How do you know Helen is not in love with Ralfe?" suddenly queried Lu, with an air of just hitting upon a hidden truth.

"Would she invite that woman here and persist in praising her? Would she throw those two together, as they must be in this house, if she cared one iota for Ralfe's love?"

"Of course she does not know Ralfe really cares for her! I don't believe she knew Ralfe was acquainted with Miss Visonti when she proposed to invite her. Besides, she has not seen her for years, and may not know she is a dangerous flirt. She defended her with great spirit the other night. You need not be so positive. You men think you see everything, but you are blind as bats, as bats, I say. I don't know why they should not love each other, they are a glorious couple."

"Yes, but they don't. Love goes where it is sent."

"You were sent with it to *me*, were you not, Guy?" she said, innocently. "Did you wish to come?"

"I found you waiting," he laughed, provokingly; "waiting and ready."

"I confess," meekly, "and now love is going where it is sent again," solemnly.

"Where ?   Where ? " cried Guy eagerly, as her bewitching little face turned down the garden walk.

"To be amused by Sardia," she sang saucily, and off she went, leaving Guy to finish his cigar, with just the least touch of jealousy in his heart, for Lu was a coquette and never let him feel too secure.

CHAPTER IV.

COMRADES.

> " By the pricking of my thumbs,
> Something wicked this way comes."
>
> *Macbeth.*

THE advent of the Visonti was quite in character. Ralfe and Helen, as it chanced, were sitting alone. They did not expect their guest until six o'clock. It was about four in the afternoon. The house was deserted by their guests. The ladies were driving, the gentlemen were variously engaged. Ralfe had seated himself in the library, and was reading some of his own manuscript. The room was dark, cool, and inviting. Roses clambered about the old-fashioned, diamond-paned windows, and nodded their perfumed heads at the big bowl of blossoms in the great fireplace ; the sun, softened by a glow of color in a window high up in the wall, threw a circle of rich hues on the mossy floor. Books, books, books, how many, how rare, how intelligently arranged they were! and peeping out from curtains whose rich color and texture made a fitting background were bronzes, marbles, and an easel on which rested the only picture in the room — a portrait of Helen. Ralfe looked up from his paper to meet the eyes of both portrait and original. " Stand still ! " said he, in a tone too courteous to be imperious. He gazed at one face and then the other with a critical expression. " Huntley did well," he said at last in a satisfied way, then again glanced interestedly at his sheet. Helen stepped aside a little, and smiling gravely, with a half-timid air approached him.

"May I come in, comrade?"

The least shadow, almost undefinable, crept across his face for an instant, then he rose with his usual indolent grace, and taking her hand, led her as he might have done an honored visitor to the easiest chair, brought a foot-stool, and to her surprise gently lifted one foot and then the other on to this pretty resting-place. A perfumed fan lay on his desk. He handed it to her, and then, leaning over her chair, asked pleasantly, —

"Are you answered?"

"How graceful you are!" in a monotone. "I could half believe you were foreign. Does living in Europe impart this delicacy of manner?"

"I admit that Americans are not so particular about trifles as foreigners, especially Italian and French gentlemen; but I hardly think true courtesy is due to association or race. It is proverbial that America is the country in which a lady may travel alone from Maine to San Francisco and only meet with perfect deference all the way."

"I did not express myself well," said Helen, humbly. "I meant a certain grace, almost homage, which I find in the manner of Europeans, and Americans who have long been resident in foreign lands."

"Sardia is an excellent specimen of that class of men. I believe ladies consider him to be irresistible."

"He is my idea of Bayard, without fear and without reproach," murmured Helen, dreamily. She sank back in her chair, and behind the great fan which she swung with languid grace to and fro Ralfe could see a slow, bright flush steal over her face and a deep, warm light into her eyes. For an instant he felt almost hatred of Sardia. He thought in a flash, "She is my wife, and she loves Sardia!"

"Sardia is a very good fellow," he assented in his usual calm way. "By the way, you are engaged to ride with him this evening, and after that a look in at the hop at the Arnolds' — who is to take care of Miss Visonti ? "

"Why, you, of course!" starting up in surprise. "Are you going to preserve the supreme indifference of your manner even to her ? I thought nothing would please you better than to renew that pretty Parisian affair Guy mentioned. Will it not ? "

This every-day way of putting his great love for Sybil Visonti seemed to Ralfe almost an insult. "That pretty Parisian affair!" How impossible it seemed that any one should dare so to touch upon his passion. Yet what could he say ? Could he own that the "affair" was so important to him that his very soul seemed rent when his bouquet and his declaration of love were returned, the latter rudely torn open ? Could he appeal to Helen's sympathy or display anger at her innocently gay phrase ? He took refuge in his favorite sentence when thoroughly perplexed or annoyed.

"I shall be charmed."

"I do not wish to intrude upon you," went on Helen in a moment, "and I do not expect confidences. But are we not comrades ? Should we not try to be interested in each other ? " She paused and looked at him in so sweet, so entreating a way that he could but feel her winsomeness and be touched by her beauty.

"What can she wish me to tell her ? " thought he. "Does she really think I shall give her a history of what she calls 'that pretty affair ?' — I need not try to be interested in you. I am so, always," he remarked, quietly evading her.

"But will you not tell me ? " she persisted; "may I not know," —

"About Miss Visonti?   Why, there is little to tell.
I "—

"Oh, Ralfe! do you think me so rude, so unwomanly
as that?" cried she, rising and bending towards him with
blushes chasing over her beautiful cheeks and flushing
even the snowy throat.   "I do not wish to know anything of Sybil Visonti.   I am not in the least curious as
to your past; it is the present," she murmured, her voice
growing mellow and sweet; "it is something nobler and
higher, I believe, than a passing flirtation.   It is your
work, Ralfe.   This."

She laid her hand on the pile of manuscript which he
had been correcting.   She touched it reverently, and
looked at him with an expression of pride and interest.

"They are poems," said Ralfe, briefly.   "I have always
written more or less.   I am collecting and arranging them
with an idea that some time I may publish them."

"I am so proud."

"Are you, really?" he asked eagerly.   "Are you glad
I am not always a mere idler?   Do you take interest in
such things?   I have never yet found a woman with
whom I could sit down and really converse on poetry.
They all admire it, they all quote it, they all 'do' a little
of it themselves; but none criticize it in a masterly way.
No one tears what I do to pieces!"

"Is that your idea of a good critic?"   Helen laughed,
and catching up the first sheet, she playfully tore it
straight across.

"Why, Helen!" cried he, catching her hand and looking at her in amazement, "what a strange thing for you
to do!"

"Oh, there's mischief in me," she laughed defiantly,
and then demurely handing him the pieces said, "It was
blank, you see."

Ralfe looked pleased.   His wife had never been so gay

or so free with him before. He liked this little show of
fun, without questioning the feeling.

"Read one, will you?" she pleaded.

"Yes," said he, with a new and agreeable sense of
companionship, "I will with pleasure."

Helen resumed her seat, and turned to him a face so
full of pleased expectation that he felt a strange intellectual exhilaration. To a man of his temperament appreciation is the sweetest thing in life. Without it the
whole being droops and fades; with it the germs of
beautiful deeds spring into leaf, flower, and fruitage with
wonderful celerity. He took up a sheet lying apart from
the rest, and had just opened his lips to announce the
title, glancing at his beautiful auditor with a new delight,
when suddenly, without a sound, a tall, dark figure stood
before them and startled both, as if she had been a mes-
senger from L'Inferno. For an instant no one spoke, and
the figure remained motionless as a statue, when her
low, clear, peculiar voice uttered, "I interrupt. I am so
sorry."

"Sybil! Miss Visonti," cried host and hostess in a
breath.

"I startled you! Ah! I am used to it. I came a
train earlier. I am weary," and sinking into the proffered chair, she drew Helen down beside her, and covered
her with swift, passionate caresses.

Ralfe shuddered in spite of himself. He felt a sick-
ening sensation when he saw Helen return those kisses,
yet, in an instant he was jealous of her right. The mere
hand touch of the Visonti had given him a thrill which
ran like electricity through his veins.

CHAPTER V.

THE PRINCESS.

> "But who is this?   What thing of sea or land ?
>   Female of sex it seems,
>   That so bedeck'd, ornate, and gay
>   Comes this way sailing,
>   Like a stately ship
>   Of Tarsus, bound for th' isles
>   Of Javan or Gadire,
>   With all her bravery on!"
>
> *Samson Agonistes.*

In quite a different part of the town was situated an unpretentious little cottage, surrounded by a neat, old-fashioned garden, and only modernized on the outside by a very wide piazza and some bright awnings, which shaded every window, making the house appear like a cluster of striped petunias, or hollyhocks, growing out of a green embankment. Here one morning Sardia found himself in the cosey drawing-room of his friend Madame Menshikoff. It was a singular room indeed, and was a startling transition from the simple American gate and macadamized pathway, which led to the entrance of the cottage. The doors were hung with draperies of the finest India shawls, and the walls were faced with the richest stamped leather. Low couches were built along the sides of the room, and were puffed into the easiest possible curves of deep crimson plush, while occasional pillows of Indian embroidery on velvet were carelessly piled together or thrown in a heap on the floor. Rugs of the whole skins of leopards and the tiger, with the heads and jaws formidably life-like, were stretched in every available spot over the foreign carpet, while wonderful Japanese jugs and Chinese bowls, unutterably horrible monstrosities in ceramics, and æsthetically ugly bronzes gave one a sense of being in a curio's sacred *salon*. An alligator was hung over an archway, and on Madame's table stood a small stuffed baboon, dressed in a tall hat, a "dicky," and a ministerial white tie. Gods in gold, in wood, in ivory; busts in marble, small figures in wrought silver, rare cabinets and tiny paintings; every possible implement for smoking, some curious weapons, and a large silver urn hissing over a spirit-lamp made up the paraphernalia of this odd apartment.

The morning sunshine streamed through a very small window, evidently made of late in the eastern wall. It was circular in shape, rimmed on the inside with an asp carved in cedar, which was swallowing its own tail; and it was filled with a plate of glass as thick and clear as those in the staterooms of an ocean steamer. All other windows being darkened, this single round ray made a curious illumination, especially when it glanced upon a huge ball of crystal, which Madame Menshikoff was indolently rolling about the floor. A very small dark dwarf was placing the ball over and over again within reach of her foot, so that she might kick it about without rising from the luxurious divan on which she was reclining. Dressed in some strange, gorgeous costume of Eastern manufacture, with a small gold-hilted poniard in his twisted sash, he looked like a tireless little imp. Sardia had assumed a position of utmost ease, and was smoking a Turkish water-pipe with a grace which indicated long usage.

"Satan!" exclaimed Madame in a deep, musical basso and with an unmistakably foreign accent. "Cease! Get my cigarettes." The little fellow whose name indeed seemed appropriate presented a bowl of fine tobacco, rice paper, and wax matches. Madame took them and frowned. "Go," said she. An eastern salaam at the doorway was unheeded by both Sardia and the Princess.

"Do you never allow him to speak?" asked he, lazily.

"Ptsh! his tongue is slit."

"Indeed!" still lazily. "Did you do it?"

"Had it not been done I should not have chosen him. It is inconvenient to have slaves who speak."

"Slaves! Hush, Madame. This is America. Slaves? Why, no, of course not! An adopted son only!"

Madame laughed.

"Not so bad, Sardia," said she, "not so bad. Come! talk! Whom do you know here? Who am I to know? What amusement do you provide for me? Any fine women? Men, faugh! What women, eh?"

"Perhaps I intend you to amuse them."

"Oh! I? Yes-s-s. I shall amuse them. But I study, I study, I study them, my great lord." And she puffed round and oval rings from her mouth.

"How long do you remain in this country now, Princess?"

"Ah, let me see! Two, three, four months and four days and four hours! That ends my probation. I am then a citizen of America. No more passports, no more recalls to St. Petersburg, no more persecution, political or religious! I am then no longer cosmopolitan! I answer no more in French, in Italian, in Hungarian. I swear no more in Russian. Ah, my native fine Russia, my hated, wide, horrible Russia, then I shall be no longer a Russian, I shall be an American, so!"

And with a tempestuous grace she rose and flung her arms wide in defiance. She was dressed in a loose, flowing costume of black, lined with vivid scarlet. It resembled the Grecian *himation*, and was exquisitely expressive of her angry mood. Her arms gleamed through a silk gauze network which covered them to the wrist and fitted like a glove. Her feet were in loose Eastern sandals.

"Do you forfeit your title, Princess?" inquired her guest, watching her gestures with a softly amused smile.

"Speak not of it. I renounce it. La, let's smoke." And suddenly dropping upon her couch, she hid her face with a gray cloud. When it emerged it was serenity itself.

Observing this Sardia said quietly, "There are two women. I will bring them to you, and I would like you to go to them."

"I never go," said Madame briefly.

"I know, my royal mistress. But perhaps you will feel inclined, who knows?"

"Well?" impatiently.

"They are quite opposite in style. One is American, the other Italian. The American is a blonde, the Italian"—

"Yes, yes, dark as Erebus of course. Well?"

"They are"—he hesitated a moment and then said in a low, significant tone, "rivals."

"A married man?"

"Always suspicious, Madame," Sardia laughed indulgently. "Yes, you are right. The Italian loves the husband of the American, and the American"—

"Loves you?"

"No," said he gravely, growing a shade paler, "she loves her husband."

"Ah, I see. It is plain. You wish the Italian to succeed. You wish her to win the husband away. You wish a clear field.   *You* are a rival ! You will win the blonde American, ah, yes, my fine, my fine lord."

"Madame, you mistake," said Sardia slowly, rising and standing before her and looking down with a rare, deep smile. "You mistake. I desire the wife to win. I desire the Italian to be beaten. I wish the American to be happy." His voice grew exquisitely sad and tender.

"Come here. Show me your eyes. There ! Sit down again. You love this American, and you love her so well that you will abnegate yourself and help her to win whom she loves. Sardia, you are noble, true ! I desire to adore your spirit." And she bowed until she touched the hem of his garment. Tears were in her light blue eyes when she raised her head, and her large expressive mouth was slightly trembling.

"O friend, O companion !" she cried. "Come back to India ! Come to India with me, and find repose ! Come away from this cold, new, crude land where every one pushes and hurries, where money is the soul and show the heart ! where the cities are poisonous, putrid with the immoral exhalation of so large a crowd of mixed people. Come where there is no mental malaria and the astral body is free; where the soul may meditate until it becomes one with and absorbed in Nirvâna ! O India, land of my love and my adoption ! win this great heart to be one with thy greatness !"

She clasped her hands, and turned fervently to the east.

Silence unbroken prevailed for a moment, then, "The time is not yet," said Sardia, in a low tone. "Is there no greater mission than seeking the repose of one's own soul ? May I not in this very place find a higher work ? Let me make this good, sweet woman happy. Perhaps then I will go."

Madame again became serene.

"Bring both," said she. "Bring a party. I will give them Russian tea and Indian religion, judiciously mixed. Oh! I will shock them, and I will study them! I will chill them with a whiff of Siberia, and melt them with the sun of Bombay! I shall laugh in my — what do you say ? — laugh in my slipper!"

Sardia ha-ha'd out loud.

"It is 'in one's sleeve,'" he said. "Ah, Madame, you know English remarkably well, but not the phrases yet! You are correct, — bookish, in fact. There is hardly a scholar in the country who can equal your elegance of speech — when you choose." He smiled pleasantly.

"Yes, yes, I know," she answered impatiently; "but your accent. I cannot get it. Yet I know phrases! I know many good phrases. Listen. 'You are a brick.' 'You are boss.' 'You are a bully boy.' There!"

Sardia actually roared.

"For heaven's sake, Madame, where did you pick up that slang ? It is too ridiculous."

"I studied, sir. I study everything. Thus do we advance towards perfection. I heard the Americans themselves in the street. Do not tell me that I do not know phrases. I know I can say 'Damn.'"

She was perfectly grave and very much in earnest. Sardia laughed and laughed.

"You are incorrigible, Madame! But the morning is going, and I am to take a sea-bath. You will not bathe ? It is not so very cold! And when shall I bring some people to amuse you ? When shall it be ?"

"Ah, any time, any evening. I have a few friends here. My pupil is here! I have my little levee as I did in New York. There will always be tea and cigarettes and always talk, talk." She called "Satan!" and began to search with intense impatience among papers, bric-à-brac, books, ash-holders, pens, pencils, and a thousand trifles on her table. "Oh, I am dying, dying! My last rice paper is gone. Satan! Imp! Evil one! Come, come! I am dying. I have no cigarette! I am dead!"

Sardia left her in this whirl of heart-rending emotion, merely saying to the dwarf in Hindostanee, "Bring the death-robe, Sirrah!"

CHAPTER VI.

THE BATTLE BEGINS.

"Imagination bodies forth
The forms of things unknown."
Midsummer Night's Dream.

DINNER at "Spray View," as Helen had named the villa, was particularly gay that evening. The weather which had been intolerably warm had yielded to a brisk sea-breeze, and every one seemed exhilarated in consequence. Sardia was thrilled to the soul with the beauty of Helen as she stood for a moment at the end of the table before taking her seat. The rich glitter of crystal, silver, flowers, and mellow light about her; the background of deep plum hangings and the delicate costumes of her guests but added to that unspeakable grace and loveliness which was as if an angel soul had blossomed into human form. As he glanced from her to her husband, who was moodily seeking the Visonti with jealous eyes, he felt a sudden indignation burn in his heart with such ardor that for a moment he would have been pleased to cry out "Fool!" and strike his host and friend with a blow of punishment and awakening. He seated Sybil, however, with his accustomed graceful suavity, and engrossed her in a conversation which won her keenest attention. "The world is gradually approaching realism," he was saying, "but so slowly and by such transitional stages that people do not realize it. A great many things that once would shock polite society are now allowed, not as in the Court of Charles II., from a spirit of sensualism and of bad morals, but from an appreciation of false shame and a nearness to Nature's naked truths."

"What are bad morals ?" asked the Visonti in a low, curiously confidential tone, lifting a glass of Sauterne in a slow undulating curve to her lips. "What are bad morals ?" she repeated, while her dark eyes sought his own with a significant meaning.

"Abnormalism," said he pointedly. "Depravity for its own sake; methodical sensualism; in women, the gratification of vanity through lying illusions; in men, the subjection of his infinite powers to the winning the bliss of a moment, or the bending them to the service of an ignoble ambition."

"The bliss of a single moment may be worth a lifetime!" she murmured, and drooped the long silken lashes over her marvellous eyes. "I do not believe in keeping one earthly law," she added, looking straight before her, with a hard, determined line growing about her voluptuous mouth.

"There are divine laws," Sardia returned coldly.

"How do you know ?" defiantly.

"If you do not," he answered quietly, "let me take you, sometime, to a certain quarter of New York, where you will see the results of breaking them. I can show you such sights as will make you admit that the physical laws are divine; divine in their inevitable, inexorable, eternal punishments, if nothing more. And I fancy the moral and the intellectual laws are based on the physical."

Sybil slightly shuddered. She glanced about the elegant apartment; saw the smiling, happy guests, heard the soft intoning of their varied conversation. She sank more comfortably into her chair, sipped her wine luxuriously, and turning softly to Sardia, murmured, "Society demands convention. It pays!"

He turned away from her for a moment to hide the infinite disgust which he felt. Why should he argue with her? Why should he try to lift this woman from her self-desired laxness? "Did you ever experience for a second," he finally said, "the serene, sublime glow, the adornment, the refinement, the enchantment of fancy, which for just one moment endowed in your mind some being with perfection?"

"Yes, yes," she replied breathlessly, her bosom heaving with a sudden ecstasy of reminiscence.

"And did you not feel pure, good, exalted?"

A soft, womanly look transformed her face into a finer beauty.

"True," she said simply.

"Shall you so endow any human being again?" He looked at her with eyes filled with a certain earnest pity.

"Never!" she exclaimed scornfully.

"So it is, you see. There are divine laws. The delicacy, the purity, the honor, the glory of divine perfections which you believed in, were stripped away. By not believing in keeping one earthly law, the law of your soul was cheated! In one transient emotion all vanished, and what remains but satiated appetite and palled senses?"

"Hatred," said she. "A grand, general hatred. A hate of myself, of you, of all the world!"

"And you ask me what are bad morals!" with a cynical smile. "Would it not be wise to ask yourself?"

"What do you know of me?" asked Sybil suddenly, with a new suspicion darkening her face. "How do you judge that life palls on me? Are we not strangers? Did you ever see me before we met here?"

"World-weary women may preserve their loveliness

intact, their grace unaltered, their fascinations unchanged for years, but they cannot conceal the inevitable consequences of experience. Miss Visonti, a little child might read you."

She turned a yellow, ashy gray. Every vestige of color left her lips. Her very eyes seemed to fade into horrified paleness. Under the table one hand clinched itself so tightly that a tiny drop of blood stood in the palm when she took up the tapering stem of her glass.

"Allow me," said he, courteously presenting a napkin. "You have wounded yourself."

With a world of hatred in her low, expressive voice, she answered, —

"The edge of the glass is broken."

"But it still holds excellent wine," said he lightly.

At this moment, Lu, whose cheeks were like roses and whose eyes were like stars, broke out impatiently with an annoyed exclamation. She had hurried down at the last moment to be surprised by finding Charlie Vane waiting to escort her to her chair. The chat seemed to be a little less general than usual. Guy was in earnest conversation with Helen. In his frank, open way he felt an affectionate interest in all her projects and ideas, and she often found him a help and encouragement in many of the perplexities natural to her position. Beside him was seated a gentleman whom she had never before seen. Presented as Signor Zante, his venerable appearance and distinguished air of somewhat old-school politeness instantly won her confidence. But as she noted this complete absorption in each other that seemed to prevail around the table, she exclaimed, breaking into one of her own sweet rollicking ripples, —

"A real country picnic! Everybody in pairs! or, a Noah's ark, two by two!"

There was a general start at this sally, and Guy, with a

comprehensive glance at the gentlemen and a sudden memory for Shakespeare, quoted, —

" ' Masters, spread yourselves ! ' "

" Yes, tell us some way to amuse ourselves. O dear!" she moaned, with a long, comical sigh. " I'm tired of doing things over and over; let's get up something new. I have waltzed, boated, driven, ridden horseback, listened to those tiresome lectures at the Casino, eaten caramels, read novels, and flirted until I am absolutely worn out for something to do. Sir Sardia, can't you suggest something besides sailing, lawn tennis, and archery ? Billiards and pool are antique, and I don't suppose it would do to gamble, would it ? " dubiously. " I caught my maid with seven lottery tickets in her apron pocket this morning, so it would be ' low-tone ' to suggest those. What *shall* we do this evening, Helen ? Say, Mr. Fielding — somebody, tell us what to do ! "

" I suggest hashish," said Charlie Vane.

Every one looked surprised. " Why, Charlie," exclaimed Guy, " do you know anything about it ? Did you ever eat any ? "

Charlie looked annoyed. " Why should I not know about it as well as any one ? " said he.

" Well, do you ? " cried Lulu, greatly excited. " Tell us about it ! Is it like what is described in ' Monte Christo ? ' Oh, let's have a hashish party ! Wouldn't it be glorious ! "

" While I was in Paris half a dozen of us students made up a party to test the effects of this drug. Three were to take it, and three were to take care of them. I was one of those who took it, and I assure you I have never regretted it."

" What was it like ? Can you remember your sensations ? Was it horrible or delicious ? " was chorused eagerly.

"Ah, there I am at fault," said Charlie disconsolately. "It is a confused jumble of delights, fears, surprises, agonies, and ecstasies, in my mind."

"I have eaten it not once, but many times," interposed Signor Zante. "I presume Mr. Vane would remember more distinctly the second time." He spoke with a strong accent, but with perfect understanding of the language.

"Will you not describe it?" said Helen, turning to her new guest with a singular graciousness of manner.

"Madame honors me," he said, rising from his chair, and bowing with reverential homage.

As he continued standing for an instant, Ralfe also rose and said inquiringly, "Are we finished? Shall we go with the ladies, or shall we all remain here?"

Every one rose with alacrity. "Quite finished." "To the drawing-room, by all means," they assented.

Helen ordered the coffee to be served in the smoking-room, and, putting her arm about Lu, said, "Gentlemen, you shall not be deprived of your cigars. We will be Bohemians, and join you in the smoking-room." It was a luxuriously furnished apartment, with a large skylight of tinted glass in the ceiling. This was open, and the numerous windows, reaching to the floor, gave it almost the semblance of an arbor. Soft couches and lounging chairs were scattered about, and these were soon occupied by the interested group who listened to the quaint accented syllables of Signor Zante.

"If you know how to use it, it is not dangerous and leaves no bad effect. The first idea you have is that you are dying. No one could convince you of the contrary. This passes away, and you then begin to have the most remarkable consciousness of the duality of your being. Indeed, I think there may be given to a person no more striking or convincing proof of the immortality of the soul than a trial with hashish. You know you have a body, but you do not feel that you are in it. You are conscious of all your acts in the body, but yourself appears to be disinthralled, separate, and individual. All things look at great distances. It is as if you were looking through the large end of an opera-glass. If it is night, and you look above and see the moon, you feel that you have watched the grand procession of the ages go by while she passes through a tiny cloud. Everything seems infinitely stretched out. Sounds seem years in arriving. You can see words come solidly from the mouths of persons speaking. They float towards you like a ribbon waving and waving for years before you catch the sound, and yet you get it and answer it in the ordinary length of time, and none could perceive that anything was the matter with you."

"How remarkable! How wonderful! Dumas describes everything as assuming beautiful forms and colors," remarked some one.

"Yes, the skies appear living sapphires; grass, emeralds; every glitter of sunlight, diamonds. All things become superb, endowed with new colors, magnificence of texture and loveliness of contour, or they are grotesque and comical, or as horrifying as it is possible to conceive. Whatever it may be, it is wonderfully exaggerated. Indeed," he added, smiling a little amusedly, "when I have listened to some of the tales of fishermen and sportsmen in this country, I have often made up my mind that they were told under the influence."

Every one laughed at this little hit, while Guy lazily murmured, "He knows our weak points, Ralfe." For Ralfe had gravely declared that morning that when fishing down in Maine, he had drawn in one hundred and two mackerel in thirty minutes, over which he had been very much chaffed.

"If you really seat yourself in an omnibus," continued Signor Zante, "you believe you are flying at a most fearful rate of speed."

"Impossible! That is really too much!" laughed Lu.

"You fancy you are tearing through dense crowds of elegant equipages," serenely pursued the signor, "drivers and footmen in embroidered liveries, jewelled harnesses, velvet robes, prancing steeds, rare women — everything that a vivid imagination can conjure up, always taking the real object in view for a basis on which to build. There is nothing that fairyland can boast which this drug will not produce for your entertainment; and the best of it all is that you can almost invariably distinctly remember the experience afterwards and enjoy it over and over again."

"How much do you take? What is it like?" asked Lulu, excitedly. "Can we get it this side of New York, do you suppose?" appealing to Ralfe, who had listened to this narration with considerable interest.

"I fear not," said he; "but we can try. It is a dark greenish paste, and comes prepared in porcelain boxes, I think."

"I have some," said Sardia quietly. "Who wishes to try it?"

"Sybil will, won't you?" cried Lulu, at the same time aching to be invited herself.

Ralfe bent over Sybil for the first time that evening, and said in a low, passionate whisper, "Will you oblige me?"

She returned the glance with one which burned like a smouldering fire. Something subtly magnetic seemed to draw him to her, heart to heart. It was fortunate that the chatter of the others hid the intense longing of his voice, as he almost caressed her with the word "Darling!" She was lying back in a long movable chair, and was the picture of sinuous, flowing, voluptuous abandon. The only counteracting element of the effect was her dress, which was of sombre black lace and satin ; her fine arms and bust only lightly covered with the meshes of woven jet, which gleamed and sparkled from the tip of her satin boot to the crown of her ebon locks. She was about to answer, "Yes!" in a voice as meaningful as his own, when Helen touched Ralfe on the shoulder, saying, "Are you willing I should try it ? "

Her fair sweet face looked at him with a certain deferential trust, a confidence which stung his conscience as nothing else at that moment could have done. He answered her with more gentleness than usual, " Why, Helen, does it depend on me ? Am I willing ? Surely, you will do as you please." A shadow rested on her face as she turned away. He followed her and said, "I assure you there is nothing harmful in it. You will probably only be a little exhilarated."

"But, if I should," — she hesitated, looking into his face with the first look of dependence upon him that she had ever shown. It touched his manly sense of protection to the quick.

"Fear nothing," said he; "I will guard you." And as they entered the group who were gathered about Sardia, who had brought from his room a box of little pellets covered with capsules, he forgot for a moment the beautiful woman, who, still reclining in an attitude of luxurious ease, was biting her scarlet lips with rage.

CHAPTER VII.

WHICH WROTE IT ?

"I have an exposition of sleep come upon me."
Midsummer Night's Dream.

SARDIA approached the Visonti with his most gracious air. It was impossible to resist that sweet imperiousness of manner, which he assumed when he chose. The irrevocable will behind the fastidious indolence; the unswerving purpose, hidden by the careless cynicism; the supreme patience which lay beneath the elegant exterior of his courtly presence, could make themselves felt and obeyed by the simple raising of his golden eyebrows, the velvet pressure of his white, relentless hand.

The contrast between the reclining woman and the man who bent smilingly over her was almost startling. She, dark, dark even to the shading of the little hands, the curves of the neck, the rounded contours of the ears and well-shaped nostrils; dark with a clear, rich, tropic darkness, through which the thick blood of a Southern climate ran riotously; the visible exponent of emotion in all its passionate luxuriance, in all its deadly unscrupulousness; — he fair, calm, and stately, the tawny mane covering his massive head in heavy matted curls, cropped ruthlessly short; the steel-blue eyes cool, unfaltering, unabashed, indicative of a reposeful intellectuality. a rigid self-discipline, and a rare severity of honor.

His voice was very softly distinct as he said, "Miss

Visonti will take this. Allow me." And as the scarlet lips opened to receive it, he dropped the little pellet into her mouth. "Pleasant dreams!" said he. Then handing one to Ralfe, he said laughingly, "Here is a pearl of price for the modern Helen." And left her husband to do the pretty duty which he would have given a year of his life to have performed.

"And mine!" cried Lulu. "Am I not to have one? Are not the gentlemen to take any?"

"Please don't," whispered Guy anxiously. "You are so excitable, pet, and — please don't, for my sake!" pleadingly.

"I want to!" she said, stamping her tiny foot like a spoiled child.

"But you will not know how the others act if you do," he said slyly. "I should think you had rather watch them, the first time."

"Why, I should, come to think of it," she answered good-humoredly. "I really think it would be better fun."

"It would be useless for me to take it," said Signor Zante, on Ralfe's invitation, "I have taken it so much." And the others seemed for various reasons equally disinclined.

"Are we to remain breathless with suspense, and sing hymns and the 'Sweet by and by,' as they do at spiritual seances?" whispered Lulu in an awed manner, as a silence for a moment fell on the little company. Her eyes were as round as saucers, and her pretty baby-mouth tremulous with mock-dread. Every one laughed and chaffed her until she sought refuge behind Helen's shoulder.

"There will be no effect for some time," said Signor Zante. "It will be wisest to pay no attention to the ladies." And with a smile he turned to his hostess and began to leisurely converse.

"You said you were a pupil," said she; "but I did not catch the idea of what art. Shall I intrude if I inquire? Sir Sardia has frequently mentioned your name in connection with the Princess Menshikoff. What a remarkable writer she is! Can it be true that she is so young?"

"Madame must pardon me," he replied with a smile; "but she seems to ask so many little questions! She is from New England, I fancy."

"Yes, indeed," returned Helen with genuine amusement. "I am a Yankee born and bred! That is the secret of the questioning."

"Certainly, I shall name you the art with pleasure. It is the divine art of reaching Nirvâna. I am a pupil of the Princess Menshikoff in the principles of the Buddhistic religion. I seek to become an adept. I must smile, however, when you ask if my master be young. She is more than seventy years old. Why, Madame, I am sixty myself."

"But Sardia says she is vivacious, youthful, gay, impulsive! He describes her as a woman of thirty or thirty-five," exclaimed Helen in astonishment.

"She certainly appears no older than that," said Signor Zante; "yet I believe her statement nevertheless. But you must see her!"

"Is she in this country?" asked Helen in surprise. "Sir Sardia has not mentioned it."

"No, I presume not. For the present she desired repose. But, yes; she is here in this very place, although she has been established but a few days. She will spend the season if she is not too much besieged!" and he smiled as if in reminiscence.

Helen began to look about her in a singular manner. Her beautiful eyes looked more radiant, her lips took on a soft entranced smile. Her body assumed a pose so eager, yet so subdued in its eagerness that she seemed like a bird on the spray, just balancing itself for flight. "What delicious music," she murmured; "you hear it of course?"

"Yes, Madame," assented Signor Zante, who understood her delusion.

"Why, it is your voice!" she exclaimed delightedly. "And now all the voices; they are seraphic. What a chorus! How divine the organ tones, how exquisitely mellow the horns!"

She seemed wrapped in an ecstasy of sound, her whole being suffused with a flood of music.

Ralfe, who had been anxiously awaiting some signs of the potent drug in Miss Visonti, now turned to his wife and remained motionless with genuine admiration. "Sappho listening to the sea," he murmured to himself. The others suddenly realizing that Helen was affected, looked at her with love, wonder and delight. Sardia felt so deep, so terrible an agony in his heart that he became suddenly faint and leaned against the window. "Never to be mine, never to be mine," his mind kept idly going round and round. "Dear, true angel-woman, and never to be mine!" He roused himself by an intense effort of will, thinking, "I must be brave." "And Miss Visonti?" he asked, directing the attention of all but Ralfe to the other "patient."

She was evidently sound asleep. Her sleep grew deeper even as they looked. Her countenance assumed a new expression. All the glow, the enthusiasm, the glamour with which she enchanted her adorers faded out. A cold, hard, malicious sneer tightened the upper lip; the under lip hung loosely down and rolled outward with so animal a look that Lulu in innocent disgust turned away with a shudder. She sought Helen, and Ralfe followed the others who gazed at the Visonti with varying emotions.

"What is it?" he asked anxiously, regardless of the tenderness of the accent in which he said it. Stepping close to the chair he looked squarely in the face the woman who enchained him. "My God!" he said.

Guy broke the embarrassing silence with his hearty laugh. "Well," he cried, "it is pleasant dreams indeed with her, Sardia! How differently hashish affects people! What a pity it did not awaken her to the height of improvisation! Don't you remember, Ralfe, that evening in Paris when she improvised so beautifully? She has the true Italian talent," turning to the others who were occupied in watching first one and then the other, and commenting on the possibilities of the thus vivified imagination; "I may call such a song as she sang a production of genius! Don't you remember it, Ralfe? How did it go?"

Ralfe said slowly, "Of course I remember it. I could never forget so exquisite a thing. She sat at the piano and laughingly declared that she was an *improvvisatrice*. We urged her to favor us, and after some demur, with a very little thought she sang this: —

> "Oh, life is such a little part
> To the great love within my heart;
> For free as air my spirit seems,
> If she but visit me in dreams.
> Time rules not and old Death is weak,
> When I can hear my dear one speak;" —

"Yes, yes," interrupted Helen, coming forward and joining him. "'And blue and deep as are the skies.' Yes, I wrote it when I was in the Convent. Come, I will sing it to you. I have my old book yet." With a step as light as air and a smile as one inspired, she led the way into the drawing-room, and with very little trouble, hunting among her music-books, she found a little volume of manuscript music. Hurriedly running

over the pages she exclaimed like a pleased child, "Here
it is!" and immediately striking a few rich chords,
sang in a clear resonant contralto : —

> "Oh, life is such a little part
> To the great love within my heart;
> For free as air my spirit seems,
> If she but visit me in dreams !
> Time rules not and old Death is weak,
> When I can hear my dear one speak;
> And blue and deep as are the skies
> They cannot match my darling's eyes;
> Laughter and tears are little worth ; —
> Or blows the wind from south or north,
> Or goeth friend, or cometh foe,
> When my own true Love loves me so.
>
> Then sorrow welcome! joy pass by!
> For these no care nor thought have I !
> When in the garden walks my maid
> I know not if 'tis sun or shade.
> And if she turns and leans to me ; —
> Or if her rosebud mouth I see,
> Or if her little hand I press,
> Or feel the motion of her dress,
> Or looking deep into her soul
> My image makes of joy the whole, —
> To highest Heaven I would not go,
> When thus my true Love loves me so !"

No one had dreamed of the depth and sweetness of
Helen's nature until she had finished her song. There
was a hush of genuine emotion pervading every heart.
Her whole beautiful soul with its capacity for love
seemed opened to their view. They seemed to themselves to be trespassing upon some sacred thing, too
delicate and pure for such exposure.

"It appears that Miss Visonti did *not* improvise in
Paris," remarked Sardia in a dry, cynical voice; "it was
your wife, Ralfe, who was her inspiration."

Ralfe's natural dignity and reserve now stood him in good stead. He resorted to his favorite phrase, "I am charmed."

Helen had dropped her head on the music-rack of the piano and her eyes had assumed a far-away expression as if she were weary. Signor Zante suggested that she would soon be asleep and perhaps it would be wise for her to retire. Ralfe approached her and said gently, "Will you sleep now? Let me take you to your room."

She aroused herself, smiled at him brightly, but looked at Sardia and said, "No, I prefer he should take me," pointing to him in a pretty, pettish manner. "His face is brighter than yours. It is golden. It has an aureola about it," and going to him, she confidingly took his arm.

All laughed at Ralph's discomfiture. Signor Zante lightly touched Sardia's curls. "A lucky dog to have this nimbus," said he.

They started into the broad hall and up the stairs, all following and watching Helen curiously, with still a certain awe upon them. The light pressure of her form as she slightly leaned against him made Sardia tremble. Her door which was at the head of the stair-case was opened by a maid. He gave Helen into her charge saying, "Your mistress is not quite well, and needs especial care." Giving some brief directions he turned to go, when Helen caught his hands in her own, and glanced at him with a look of admiration.

"How beautiful you are!" she said in a soft whisper.

"Good-night," he answered gently, as he released his hands. But as he went slowly down-stairs, he was very pale. Arriving in the smoking-room he found every one in consternation. Sybil Visonti was gone.

CHAPTER VIII.

AN ENEMY.

"She comes unlooked for."
Pope's Temple of Fame.

As the guests had passed into the drawing-room, one had inadvertently hit Miss Visonti a soft blow on the cheek with the drapery of her sleeve. It awakened Sybil, who remained perfectly quiet and indeed, for a few moments, only half-conscious, while a strange, dull pain throbbed through her temples. She roused herself, however, as the laughing voices came floating to her from beyond. She sat up. All was still in the little smoking-room, silent and deserted. The lights which had been turned down, mingled with the brilliant moon-rays streaming in the broad, low windows; a soft haze of smoke from the cigars hovered near the ceiling — all the place was familiar, yet all seemed strange. "What a dream !" she whispered with a little shudder.

At this moment a noiseless servant appeared with the tray of coffee, and the tiny musical tinkle of the china and silver called her back to reality.

"Give me some," she ordered, somewhat eagerly. "Give it black with no sugar."

"Milk ?" said the well-trained domestic with a slight shade of surprise in his respectful voice.

"Milk ? No ! Am I a child ?"

"You are no babe, miss," acquiesced the man in his

mind, but his outward gravity was unruffled. He was about to retire when Miss Visonti turned to him, with an imperious air, holding out her cup.

"Put a tablespoon of cognac in this," said she.

James silently departed and returned with a decanter sparkling like a jewel. She took it in one dark, dimpled hand and poured into the little cup, half full of coffee, until it touched the brim.

"Go, now," said she with a smile of condescension.

"Here's a rum quean," muttered James to himself as he sought his own region.

The first chords of the piano struck on her ear, but she did not heed them. Picking up a foamy white shawl of floss, which some one had dropped, she flung it over her shoulders and stepped into the garden. "Ralfe will follow and find me. Moonlight and the sea, these are excellent adjuncts. I wish I could always play my little drama in the midst of such well-devised scenery. That was not hashish Sardia gave to me. Sardia! I could see him in that water yonder and laugh to hear him shriek. He should drown for all me! Who is he? What is he? What does he know? Ah, he meant I should sleep while his adored Helen should for once be brilliant. To me he gives a sleeping-powder, to her hashish. Well, he shall pay. The moral fool! telling me of 'nature's punishments!' It will not be long before I am missed. Ralfe will follow me, and I shall tell him why he was — Good Heavens!"

She had left the garden which sloped to the sea and entered a path which ran along the edge of the rocky cliff, and her exclamation was one of sudden fright. What seemed to be a large monkey had suddenly scrambled up the rocks and stood like a very little demon in her pathway. His dress was scarlet and gold, his little fez with its tossing tassel, his dark hands and darker visage, and a singularly uncouth noise or cry which came from the lower part of the throat, were enough to startle even the Visonti, difficult as it was to shake her steady nerves.

"Satan!" exclaimed a voice from the shadow of a rock which hid the speaker, but who now emerged. "Imp! Why do you frighten the lady out of her senses? Go to the carriage!" stamping her foot. "Madame," she said, advancing as swiftly as her unwieldy body permitted, "madame, I am foreign, and that little dwarf there is my servant. I dropped my fan and sent him down over the rocks for it. I beg pardon for his startling you. He is an execrable object!" She laughed and advanced quite near, and then suddenly grasped Miss Visonti's hand as in a vise. "Ah," said she, "it is as I thought!" in a clear, bell-like tone. "It is as I thought! It is *you.*"

"Princess!" gasped Sybil.

"Be silent!" she thundered. "You never thought to see me again. America is far away from Venice. You wonder how I am here. You will yet learn that I can be anywhere I choose whenever I choose. You think I don't know your design in coming back to your old friends. Let us see. Here is your design, my charming saint. Let me read that cultivated mind of yours!" and standing directly in front of Sybil whose whole face was illuminated with the moonlight, she said scornfully, "You bear the name of Visonti and wear a beauty of your own; but your heart is cold, your mind cruel, and your soul stained with a thousand blots; your aura at this moment is black with a set, malicious purpose. Money, luxury, ease — these you must and will have, and to gain them you are here trying to win the love of the husband of the pretty American blonde. La! It sounds like a little primer lesson of English into French. You will steal him and his money away, you think. You mean to work the ruin of a happy family for the sake of gaining a future for the little — *bambino*."

Sybil interrupted with a cry. She clasped her hands entreatingly. ' " Madame, madame ! " she breathed, pleadingly.

" Ah, ptsh ! never mind. I know it all."

" Madame," said the Visonti, mortal anguish and fear for once making her truthful, " you do know everything. How many times I have cursed your fatal power ! But do not, do not ! What have I done to you ? What are my secrets to you ? How have I injured you that you must interfere with me so ? Is it womanly, fair, kind, to take advantage of such knowledge as you may have gained ? "

" Is it womanly, fair, kind, to deliberately break another woman's heart, and that woman your intimate friend for years and your hostess now, while you plot your wicked plots against her happiness ? "

" Is that any reason why you should play the part of God, and try to regulate the lives of strangers ? " asked the Visonti, growing bolder as they parried.

" You are not so much a stranger to me as you are to yourself," said the Princess, irrelevantly.

" I do not understand," said the Visonti coldly, glancing over the sea and half turning away.

" Who are you ? " in a most significant tone.

Sybil faced about. " Of that there can be no doubt," said she proudly. " I am the only Miss Visonti in the world." She said the name Visonti with all the fine imperial pride of one who knew it to be old, great, and stainless.

" Let the young American woman and her husband alone," said the Princess Menshikoff in a voice like the cutting of a Damascus blade. " There is no Miss Visonti !" and left her.

Sybil looked after the thick-set, ungraceful form which slowly approached the open roadway with a dignity of mien from which not even much flesh could detract, and thought of those last words, which, as it were, ignored her and put her out of existence with one stroke, in a maze of fury and wonder. She heard the call for "Satan," the orders to the coachman, and the driving away of the carriage with a strange, creeping sense of physical fear.

"So *she* is here," she thought, "and doubtless will have her revenge. Who and what is she? What may she not do? Yet she has hitherto been silent. No Miss Visonti? She is full of mysteries; but what could be more correct? In what kind of a net am I being caught? What possible interest can she have in Helen? I have never heard her name mentioned in America. Why is she here?"

She sank down on a rock and looked out over the limitless ocean, with its broad glitter of silver rippling to her very feet. The soft splash of the waves gave her a new sense of quiet. She laid her hot cheek against the cool, rough side of a rock, and then laid her throbbing wrists against it while she drooped her head on her arms. Plash, splash, ripple, recede, advance, came the ever-sobbing monotone and the distant roar, speaking eternally the same deep, wonderful message.

"Better not to think," she murmured, shudderingly. "Better to live it out from day to day and then sink into the ocean of oblivion. Hate or love, failure or success, what does it matter? Oh, how weary I am! how sad I am!"

The soft sound of mellow horns and stringed instruments swiftly seemed to infold her. Over the rumbling base of the sea the most exquisite melody rose above and around her. A large yacht came speeding along

like a beautiful vision. The musicians were on board,
and soon rich male voices were singing that delicious
barcarolle : —

> "The stars in heaven are glowing,
> The moon her bright face showing,
> But ah ! my tears are flowing,
> My heart is sad and lone !
> My heart is sad and lone !"

"Yes," she murmured, "my heart is sad and lone.
My soul is sad and lone.   I feel as if I were the one forgotten thing of all the universe.   Home forgotten, love
forgotten, God forgotten," and she adds "name forgotten."
She shook with a sudden passion of tears.   The
voices in the yacht grew fainter : —

> "Come, then, ah, come thou my own love, come !"

She rose and stretched her arms out towards the flying
vessel with a gesture of despair.   "Yes, you beautiful
white-winged thing !" she cried.   "I would I could go
with you away anywhere, anywhere into eternal space,
darkness, annihilation !"
"Oh, horrors !   What an awful wish !" laughed Lulu's
innocent and happy voice.   "We didn't know but you
had eloped or something.   I ran ahead of the others, for
I was certain you would be down here.   Isn't it a perfectly splendid night ?   We couldn't find you, you know,
in the house, and they took Helen off to bed.   We all
came out in the garden to search for you.   Here they
come.   Guy, Guy !   I've found her, wishing herself in
perdition !" and she laughed a merry peal.   But she
stole her arm in that of Sybil's, and gave it a little
squeeze.   In spite of her instinctive distrust, she felt a
strange attraction towards this beautiful, dark woman,
and now was tenderly moved by those tears in the voice
which had so longed to get "away."

CHAPTER IX.

THE SPIDER SPINS.

"And out of good still to find means of evil."
Paradise Lost.

LULU continued affectionately clasping Miss Visonti's arm until they all reached the house, and after some light chat, when the company dispersed for the night, accepted an invitation to stay a short time in Sybil's chamber before retiring. Nothing had been said of the little revelation which had so unconsciously been made by Helen, of the Visonti's powers of deception. All were too well bred to pain a guest of the same house, and therefore only a general description was given of the "Hashish party," with some discussion as to why the drug had simply put the Visonti to sleep. She betrayed no hint of her belief as to the real cause, save by a sudden glance at Sardia, which might have killed him could it have turned into a dagger, so full of keen, sharp, suspicious hatred it was. But his calm face indicated no consciousness of the thrust. Ralfe had not followed the party into the garden nor did he appear again. He had retired into the library and swung the door nearly shut after him. They could see a portion of his figure seated at his desk, as they went up-stairs. Serenely unconscious then of anything in her disfavor, Sybil welcomed Lu to an easy-chair in her richly furnished bedroom and proceeded to make her guest "perfectly at home." That she was an artist cannot be gainsaid.

Not a person in the world was too insignificant for her
to regard with some slight thoughtfulness. Each human
being represented to her a tool, a lover, or an enemy.
She intended to make the whole world serve her. Whatever goodness she possessed only tended to make her
more dangerous, since it cast aside by some unlooked-for
act, the suspicion which her subtlety had aroused. Cultured she certainly was, and to an accurate taste in art and
literature she added an acute appreciation of nature and
a sufficient idea of science to fascinate men of all grades
and interest even envious women. With these she possessed that infinite grace of movement, that caressing
manner, that honey sweet voice, which is perilously
entrancing to even the soberest minds. Intellectually
and physically the exponent of a fine civilization, she
was morally a barbarian. While smiling a seraph smile
she was perfectly cold at heart, and as calmly plotful as
Machiavelli.

"You will not mind my removing this heavy dress?"
she now queried of pretty rosebud Lu, who was looking
at her with a soft, captivated gaze.

Something in her tone produced an odd effect upon
Lulu. Her cheeks drew to themselves an even brighter
color. A certain unnatural light came into her eyes.
She seemed to anticipate something, she knew not what.

"I shall be glad," she said breathlessly.

Miss Visonti's face became a study. What was that
subtle triumph, that gratified vanity, that sense of power,
which made her even more alluring? Like a fallen
angel who smiles at the possibility of enticing an innocent mortal to his own low estate, Sybil for an instant
showed a gleam of fiendish satisfaction. "They shall
all be like me if I can make them so," she thought, "I
will teach this silly child a few ideas." She slowly
drew off one garment and then another, talking the

while in a low, vibrant tone which seemed to thrill her listener like a draught of wine.

"How can you be so graceful?" asked Lulu presently, as Sybil draped about her a light, large shawl, of *crêpe du chine* which clung to the voluptuous figure as if in love with it and seemed to caress with its soft folds the person it but half concealed.

"Ah, that is taught in Paris, and I was long a pupil of the greatest master of expression in the world! Alas, that America should never have so exquisite an art taught to every one who has an appreciation of beauty!"

"Why, we have schools in which pupils are prepared for the stage!" exclaimed Lu in surprise. "Didn't you know it?"

"Yes, but how!" impatiently. "They are taught the mere rudiments. Can they do this?" And suddenly with a grace which seemed marvellous, she raised her arm and described an undulating curve.

It was silent music. There was something in that delicious curve which touched Lulu's sensuous nature to the core. Her imagination ran riot, and seemed to see it in a thousand different forms, colors, and materials.

"Ah, you see! even ungainly and disagreeable objects in themselves will become beautiful and harmonious when that curve runs through them : they become satisfactory to mind and soul. How much more lovely then would a lovely woman become if she could know the delicacies of gesture!" And she bent over Lulu with a dazzling smile. "Why, with that curve in my possession to use as I will," she went on, "with the grace that undulating line can give my body, I will yet become rich, famous, beloved! I make every whit of my body serve me for my pleasure," she added significantly.

"There must be some rules by which one could learn," said Lulu thoughtfully.

"Certainly. They are the law of rhythm and the law of opposites. The law of rhythm is the making of gesture at the exact instant and to the exact time of the words. •As the language grows more impassioned, the delivery quicker, the movement of the body, the sway of the limbs, the play of the features, the rapidity of the changes must be in harmony, or that magnetic power which springs from an appreciation of beauty in the audience is lost. The law of opposition is that when one hand moves to the right the other should move to the left. 'Keep your balance' is one of the maxims."

"Oh, do something more!" said Lu curiously.

Sybil stood perfectly erect, the drapery of fleecy silk carelessly wound about her. Slowly, with a sinuous, gentle movement, she made Lulu aware that she was happy in a quiet, pensive way; then she became mirthful, then joyous, then radiantly glad, and finally passionately blissful; growing thoughtful, doubtful, suspicious, jealous, angry, and, at last, raving mad, in a series of gestures and expressions of the face which so flowed into each other, yet kept their individuality, that the whole seemed like an acted poem; its feeling, rhyme, music, rhythm, cadence, and harmony being made literally visible in this magnificent woman's person.

"It is wonderful," breathed Lu in astonished admiration. "No wonder you can make any one love you whom you please."

"And do you love me, little one?" approaching so swiftly that the shawl became entangled about her feet.

Lulu turned her head away and did not answer.

"When I let my draperies go," Sybil remarked coolly, gathering up the tissue and knotting it about her waist, without noticing Lulu's averted head, "I always think of that charming poem of 'Hero and

Leander,' so admirably put into verse by Arnold. Do you remember the bridal scene ? You know the line :—

" ' With that soft leave he loosed her virgin zone!' "

She had hoped to awaken another response than Lulu's " Yes, I read it with my mother. I remember how beautifully she spoke of it and how delicately. She said, ' You will understand, dear, how this utterly transcendent whiteness of passion exceeds all the lotus buds, champak, and melting music of the " Song of Songs," ravishing though they be. The scene is Greek, just like a statue. It is strong, clean and classic. My child, when you are older, you will know it is a beautiful thing to feel that some time, some where, nature culminates in purity when left alone.' "

The Visonti had failed. She had only fired the intellect. The imagination remained untouched.

"Your mother speaks freely with you," she said dryly.

" She desires me to know enough of human nature to be good from principle, not from ignorance. ' Untempted innocence is possible guilt ' is one of her sayings, and then " added Lu, with a tender accent creeping into her voice, " it is so beautiful to learn life from a mother instead of from schoolgirls ! "

" Innocence does not set well on a woman of thirty. It will not pass for virtue!" exclaimed Sybil, as she stood before the mirror and surveyed herself with complacent admiration. "But come, child, stand by me and see what difference there is besides age between you and me."

Lulu with a bound sprang to her side. They stood for a moment gazing straight at each other's faces in the reflection, when the Visonti suddenly clasped the young girl close, in a magnetic embrace. Her bare, rounded arms and full, throbbing throat softly caressed Lulu, who, with an enraptured expression and a filmy haze in her eyes, still kept her charmed gaze on the other's face.

"What is the difference between us, darling?" murmured Sybil, with soft, clinging kisses on the high, white forehead, and hot, flushed cheeks; "only this, *chérie!* that thou art light and I am dark; thou art North and I am South; thou art unawakened and I am all awake! Beautiful innocent, how thy lovely youth appeals to me!"

Lulu felt herself losing all power of reasoning. Her heart seemed ceasing to beat, her eyes were suffused. She felt herself about to press a kiss on Sybil Visonti's lips, when suddenly she seemed to hear Guy's voice warning her. "Beware!" it rang out; "she wins women as easily as she does men. I have seen her table loaded with gifts from women. She possesses a strange, undefinable power to which all must, more or less, yield."

"I yield no more!" she thought, catching a long breath, and stepping quickly away.

"I can't endure women's kisses," she burst out bravely, and with all the vehemence of an offended child. "Miss Visonti, I will not be so kissed!"

Lurid lightning leaped for a second into those dark eyes; but she answered tenderly, "You were so beautiful, dear, I could not help it! I am such a passionate admirer of beauty, and your sweet face is so fair. Will you not forgive me?"

Lulu dropped her defiant mood instantly. "How bad I am!" she thought. "I have wronged her completely. I am worse than she is!" And with an air of penitence which was positively touching, she lifted up those warm, red lips which a moment before she had angrily withdrawn, and suffered the Visonti to take her fill of their fragrant loveliness.

"How potent is flattery!" sneered Sybil to herself,

completely misjudging her. "Do you smoke?" she asked suddenly, as she tied the satin ribbons of a creamy wrapper about her. "I have some excellent cigarettes here and a little wine. It is a cordial, rather, — do you know it, Benedictine?" She held up a short fat-paunched bottle, prominently marked D. O. M., with a cross and sealed with leaden strips.

The matter-of-course way in which she set about making her little guest comfortable made Lulu feel very simple indeed; for she not only did not smoke, but she had never seen a lady smoke, and as for Benedictine, she had never even heard of it. But what young girl desires to appear "green," especially before a graceful woman of the world, who would lightly ridicule the slightest touch of false shame! Nevertheless, Lulu herself did not wholly lack diplomacy.

"I will not smoke," said she nonchalantly; "but I will drink your health."

Sybil gave her a delicate wine-glass filled with the delicious liqueur.

"Oh, violets! heliotrope! roses! spices! the whole garden of Paradise!" exclaimed Lulu rapturously, as she held the glass to her pretty little nose. "I never knew a wine could be a perfume too!"

"Drink, sweet!"

She did so. "Honied flame!" she cried.

"It has been made by the Benedictine monks ever since 1510, and they say the receipt remains unchanged. A friend of mine wrote a sonnet in its praise. I wonder if I could remember it," —

"Please try," sipping like a bee at a flower.

> "Delicious nectar! by the monks of old
>   Made precious, mingled with their prayers and sighs;
> Or, if perchance some lamb within the fold
>   Found just approval in their critic eyes,

> Drank with a wild, delirious throb of joy
> To beauty, youth, and passion held at bay, —
> Or, if permitted, — he, the wingèd boy
> Clipped i' the wings, never to flee away!
> How in this later age, thine amber flame
> We hold on high, and pledge with equal praise
> Fair loveliness and pleasure, quite the same
> As beardless priests in darker, saintlier days!
> Thou Benedictine! Lift thy golden bloom!
> Spread violets and summer through the room."

Lulu listened with a pleased but puzzled air. "'The wingèd boy — Cupid? clipped i' the wings, never to flee away?'" she repeated questioningly.

"They kept their nuns very close," said Sybil significantly.

Lulu jumped up and set her little glass down with a crash. "This is wicked," she said, with an angry frown. "I do not like it!"

Sybil laughed a low, languorous, seductive laugh. "How good it is to renew myself in you," she murmured.

Lulu walked to the door, and unceremoniously tossed a good-night over her shoulder. "Charlie Vane was right: she is a vampire," she thought, somewhat irrelevantly.

"I suppose this is what Sardia would call bad morals," murmured the Visonti to herself, as she laughed a little sneer after the indignant Lulu. "I hate young girls!"

CHAPTER X.

ALL ABOUT A LETTER.

" I'll example you with thievery."
Timon of Athens.

THE very excellent and methodical waiter James, who was the model of butleristic virtues, for once had forgotten a duty. As he had replaced the glittering decanter of French brandy in the sideboard, he had suddenly become aware of a singular and searching pain in the abdominal cavity. That this pain should arrive at so appropriate a season, was a coincidence which somewhat astonished the good James, but he hailed the fact as an indication of a very intelligent stomach, and so proceeded to reward it accordingly. Having reduced the pain to a state of serenity, he then treated it for the sake of its good-humor, and finally, while holding the beautiful bottle between his critical eye and the light, he discovered that it was not tinged with the slightest shade of brown. Not a drop remained. Now some hours afterwards, having retired to his bed, he suddenly sat up. Something was disturbing his well-governed conscience. He endeavored to remember whether the plate had been carefully stowed away and locked in the velvet-lined safes; yes, that was all right. Perhaps he had forgotten to lock the hall window? Oh, no, not at all! Well, what had been left unordered? Would anything be lacking for to-morrow's breakfast? What day was it? Saturday! Ah, that was it. It was Saturday night and the great clock had not been wound.

Now twice within "a quarter" he had forgotten this simple duty. Now again he would be taken to task in the morning, and be the recipient of a frown from his master — that master whom he would give up his life (but not his brandy) to please! For was not the clock an old heirloom, and was not the regular winding of it positively necessary for its internal welfare? So it had been impressed upon him. James laughed to himself, and slowly stuck a rather large foot and fat calf out of bed. " Cognac is positively necessary for *my* internal welfare," said he.

The house was all dark and quiet as he proceeded in loosely hung habiliments and soft list slippers, to make his way slowly down into the lower hall. When there, and standing by the ancient time-piece, he discovered that the library was still lighted and the door half open. Mr. Fielding was pacing rapidly up and down the room. He seemed disturbed and frequently gnawed his upper lip, — a habit of his when in deep thought.

Now large clocks with brass works make considerable noise when being wound, and James was sure if he attempted to do it his master would hear him. That would be most unpleasant. His personal vanity would not permit a rencontre in so light a dishabille; indeed, he feared he might meet with genuine disapproval of many other things about himself at such an hour. What should he do? As he hesitated, Mr. Fielding approached his desk and took up a letter. He removed it from the envelope, began to read it and exclaimed, " Dated at Paris, March 16! How few months since this was written, — and now!" He threw it down and began to pace the floor again.

Just then, something above him attracted James's attention. Had he been of Irish descent he would have probably cried out with superstitious fear; but he was

"Hinglish" to the backbone, and so slunk into the deeper shadow by the side of the tall clock and waited. Slowly a vision of snowy white stole down the stairs. It was a woman in a long trailing garment which made not a sound on the thick pile of the carpet, but fell silently step by step after her quiet feet. With held breath James tried to discern in the darkness who it could be. "It's the mistress, certain," thought he, "and when she goes into the library, maybe she will shut the door, and then I can wind up the old ticker in a hurry." But when she had approached the door he suppressed a start of surprise. "If it isn't that rum quean!"

At that moment Mr. Fielding again sat down at his desk and took up the letter. He opened it out before him as if to read it thoroughly. Sybil Visonti silently stole in behind him. It was her intention to put her hands over his eyes and then with a soft kiss and word to awaken him to who so blinded him. She approached with arms outstretched for the purpose, when her eyes suddenly caught the date of the letter, and with a start, she withdrew her hands and stood perfectly still. With one more keen look at the sheet, she began to slowly retreat. Long practice alone in the difficult art of carrying a train could have given her such grace and ease in the departure backwards out of that large library. But she did it so noiselessly that Ralfe read on, as unconscious of her presence as if he had been under the influence of an opiate. She gained the hall and stood in the shadow, watching him.

If she held her breath, how much more so did James! He felt his heart knock against his ribs, and could have sworn at himself until morning to think his "wind" would make the least noise in escaping.

Having carefully read the letter through, Ralfe replaced it in the envelope, tossed it into the desk, carelessly turned the key without taking it away, and stepped to the window.

Not a sigh stirred the leaves. The moon at the zenith was gloriously white and full. The silence of one o'clock lay over the scene. He pushed aside the curtain and stepped out. In a moment his steps could be heard going in the direction of the sea. In a flash, Sybil sprang into the library, turned the key of the desk, caught up the letter, returned the key and came out into the hall, slipping the paper into her pocket. She then quietly went up to her room, shut the door softly, and locked it.

James stood for a moment quite dumbfounded. Then with a sardonic chuckle, he said, —

"I might as well take my little advantage too!" and began to wind the clock. Ascending the stairs, he passed Sybil's door still drolly chuckling, and finally got into bed saying, "Ay, but she's the rummest quean I ever see! First, she drinks brandy, then she gets lost, and arter that she creeps down at midnight and hooks the master's papers. That's high life, that is! Rum kind o' life too, just like a book. Jinks, but she's a game 'un! None o' my business though. Jeemes, if you knows yourself, don't you tell no tales below stairs!" And he settled himself with a profound sense of his own wisdom.

.   .   .   .   .   .

Ralfe had spent a very unusual two hours. He was not given to taking himself to task, and seldom troubled himself to criticise his own state of feeling; but the events of the evening had seemed to throw his thoughts into inextricable confusion, which he vainly endeavored to disentangle. Until now he had never permitted himself to compare Miss Visonti with his wife. He was so firmly convinced of his deathless passion for Sybil that the very thought of comparing her with any other woman was obnoxious to him. The imagination of feeling, the poetry of emotion which filled his sensitive spirit with delight, made the very name of his loved one a sacred thing. To her he had given the first bright, unsullied ardor of his life. And beautiful was the awakening of a soul so responsive. It had vaguely occurred to him at times that he made his own paradise as he went along, for he had that gift of the gods, acuteness of perception, and the power to take advantage of it. All that was sensuous in nature he took to his heart and felt. The perfumes from the garden and the orchard brought him keen delights. The flush of roses that burned along the hedgerow lingered in his memory long after he had entered the dust and heat of the city. The brave, free carol of the bobolink, who piped and trilled to him in summer dawns, awakened in his receptive fancy those indescribable emotions which lend enchantment to the livelong day. The mountains seemed to lift him to their heights. The ocean bore his soul upon its bosom. God's stars he saw and loved as something near : close to the unseen, he was still in thorough sympathy with the seen. The keenest wit, the subtlest philosophy, the most gracious charms of poetry and symmetry were all but ministers to serve or give him absolute contentment. Fantastic, sportive, pathetic, half spiritual, his moods grew out of the experiences of the hour. The tenderness of his nature lent to the simplest phrase or commonest greeting all the eloquence of a caress.

The gay whirl of European dissipation had enlightened him as to the blunt realisms of life, quickened his intellect, deepened his character, confirmed his habits, settled his morals, but never once had touched his heart. Not until his eyes had rested on the dark face destined to enchant him had he felt one quicker throb of the pulse which arose from anything stronger than ordinary causes. The mental and physical excitement which rounded character and person, in no wise trespassing upon the soul, left it as virginal and responsive as that of a child. Discriminating the perception and fine the art which could discover that hidden treasure, and could assume the semblance of a being worthy to receive its pure yet fervid glow!

But now, with the mystery of the returned declaration undisclosed; the strange secret which had haunted him ever since the first hint of it had inadvertently faltered from Sybil's lips, and yet which he had accepted without question, with a faith and love that could not brook a thought of evil; with the superb woman under his own roof, who had magically given the very air a new zest, while some adverse fate had as yet given him no opportunity to see her for a single moment alone, — he felt himself growing desperate, his senses became even more enthralled, while his instinct coldly warned him of — he knew not what.

Yet with a singular curiosity he analyzed his own condition. Inevitably with this came the remembrance of the new legal barrier which he had voluntarily placed between himself and his idol. He cursed his folly in a thousand eloquent terms. The thought of his bondage was agonizing. For if she did not love him, why was Sybil here? But then, his promise to be true to Helen. What was it to be true? To what extent might he morally go? If Helen loved him, there could be no question. But if she did not? If she, too, in her secret heart, longed to shatter the ties of convenience as he believed he did? Surely, Helen loved Sir Sardia. Had she not preferred him this very evening, and when quite irresponsible? Was not her choice the natural expression of her heart? He involuntarily thought of her beauty. Her pure, sweet face turned so trustingly to Sardia suddenly came before him with a sensation of pain. He all at once felt angry, hot and disgusted. He would like to thrust his friend out of his path like a dog. His blood rose in fire to his temples at the thought of Helen, his wife Helen, lavishing her devotion on another, and perhaps to her future grief and chagrin, giving forth an unreturned affection. He would defend his comrade. Comrade! The word struck coldly and bitterly on his ear. How far away it made her seem, how remote from any possible love for him!

How deeply blue her eyes had looked when she appealed to him, yes, to him, not to Sardia, for protection and encouragement! He felt a glow of chivalrous tenderness replace his vague jealousy. Helen was a darling woman. How exquisitely she had sung! Now he remembered he had never heard her sing alone before. She had joined her voice with the others when sailing, or when they had gathered about the piano, but he could not remember that he had requested her to sing particularly for him. His conscience troubled him.

"I have not been so polite to her as to an ordinary guest. What must she think of me! I have accepted her proposition of being a mere comrade with a vengeance! No wonder she turns to one who watches her lightest word, who is never for an instant forgetful of what is due a beautiful woman and his hostess. But the song!

> "'Oh, life is such a little part
> To the great love'—

And she wrote it when a mere schoolgirl. By Jove! in Paris I called it a work of genius—then I thought it an improvisation, and Sybil's—and now, it shows a deal

of talent. So my little wife is a poet. A pair of poets!
How keenly appreciative she seemed of my work that
day! How sweet she looked when I was about to read
to her, and that — I must be mad! I almost said 'that
woman!' How she looked in her sleep! What a
strange, horrible expression! Guy was a brick. Dear,
courteous old boy! He would excuse the Devil. But
the proof of her deliberate deception — theft!" Thus
he suddenly characterized it. "It was not even literary
plagiarism, it was simple theft. Yet all women make
use of these little arts. She could not have dreamed it
would ever injure Helen — 'all is fair in love and war,'"
he argued.

Reading the letter so coldly returned to him his sense
of doubt and wrong culminated, by a slow mental process,
in a feeling of bitterness with all the world, and finally
left him, as it were stranded, neither on sea nor on land.
His quiet walk down the garden to the water ended
abruptly with the thought, "I will see Sybil alone, as
soon as possible. She shall explain, and I know. I know
I shall find her the very incarnation of goodness and
truth."

He turned and approached his dwelling. How stately
it looked in the brilliant light. The graceful balco-
nies, the grouped windows, the open arcade, the statue
and vase-bordered terraces, all indicated the gay and
sunny social temperature of a summer residence. How
sensitively alive he was to æsthetic surroundings he had
displayed in the picture-gallery, adorned with some wonderful selections which he had cautiously made during
his Continental stay. Then the well-planned library,
the conservatory, all showed the direction of his artistic
tastes. His dignified love of leisure and repose had
found expression in the cool and spacious verandas
which he had added immediately on his arrival. He

had brought home with him a cultivated perception of truthful beauty and, so far as he could, he had improved a villa, already the exponent of a refined architectural discernment.

He now gazed affectionately at this home, which had so soon become a vivid interest to him, and noted immediately that through the broad, rustic lattice, diamond-paned and draped with honeysuckle, which faced the sea, came a soft, golden glow. The white shade was drawn, and to his surprise, Ralfe saw upon it a perfect silhouette. "Why, that is Sybil's room. Can she be up at this hour?" he thought, as he eagerly traced the graceful outline. Very soon the shadow moved and showed Sybil slightly leaning forward. In a moment he discovered what she was doing. She was reading a letter.

CHAPTER XI.

THE VISONTI SOLITAIRE.

" Speak to me as to thy thinkings,
   As thou dost ruminate ; and give thy worst of thoughts
The worst of words."

Othello.

WHEN Sybil had lain herself upon her soft bed, with a pretty amber cigarette-holder between her teeth, and the smoke drifting idly out of the diamond-paned casement, which she had opened, she slowly went over in her own mind the events which had brought about the stealing of Ralfe's letter. She bluntly called it stealing in her own mind, with the singular frankness to themselves which sometimes belongs to people who are anything but candid to others. The edge of her moral sense was so turned and roughened that her thoughts of others, of events, of things in general, took on a brusque practicality while, in contradistinction, she was so keenly alive to her own beauties, so absolutely vain and sure of her physical charms, that her mind became an unconscious homage to her body, and the very sentences of her brain, self-flattery. She smiled now, as she thought of the exploit, with the satisfaction of one who has accomplished a shrewd manœuvre.

" It is singular to me what can have become of father's money," the train of her thoughts began. "What a glum old couple they were — mother and father ! They were rich, or they always appeared so, and now what a shabby income I have from the property. What is two thousand dollars a year for *me?* Why, I can remember that I spent that at sixteen. They were indulgent old folks. Strange, what an odd make-up I am! Now I don't believe I ever felt towards my mother and father as other girls do. I liked them, but they were so dull, so melancholy always. I don't remember that father ever kissed me six times in his life. The older I grew, the more chronically shocked he got. I was a madcap. And mother — mother was a sweet old woman, but some way I didn't feel as if I could mourn much about her. I *am* hard-hearted, except when I love, and then I am cruel. I did love them when I was a child, but I never could see that I was a bit like either of them. I hated their grandeur and courtly etiquette. I preferred to play with the boys in the street. The dark closet and bread and water made me polite — and a liar.

"I suppose they ate up nearly all their fortune in their fine living, leaving me some paltry remnants. They no doubt supposed I should marry. Well, the miserable little sum comes regularly, thank Heaven! What an untroubled, careless life I led until I left school! But I was not so stupid as Lu, innocent little fool! Yet, what did I know of life? Why, I was the 'model scholar,' the pattern of propriety, ha, ha!" and she shook with bitter laughter at her own reflections. "That is how Helen knew me. She supposed I was a model scholar now, the pink of convention, no doubt, or she would not have invited me. If she had dreamed I knew Paris from palace to hovel! What a tame, proper, milk-and-water creature she is! She hasn't spirit enough to say her soul is her own. I have little to fear from her. But she's generous, which is convenient. Just give her a hint, and she gives you the spoil. She is beautiful, in her way. But she has no art, no style, and such natural grace is so horribly commonplace nowadays. Then she is so dull. I suppose she is religious, although she never says anything about it. How the men respect her! They never say one word before her that an angel might not hear. But men don't *love* these doses of cold water. Oh, these conventional, calm, selfish hypocrites of women, so good, so churchy good, — they take, *as wives*, with some men. They softly steal into the masculine confidence on their merits. Merits! I hate the word. It makes me think of the rewards of merit she would slip into my hand and make me carry home from school, when I had lost every one of mine by my downright mischief. So she was marked down, and I got the prizes. That shows she was a fool, even as a child. She said she loved me, pooh! I suppose she has revelled in an inner consciousness of her ' goodness ' ever since. She is just that kind. She leads an irreproachable life because it pays her in secret self-complacency. It is all selfishness, come to the bottom of it.

"And as for Ralfe — well, as he is worth a couple of hundred thousand for each letter of his name, I think I will pursue what I have begun. She will not be so likely to hand over that prize to me. But it is worth a struggle. She will have her own money, and that adorer of hers — Sardia — can console her for her loss. Ah, this dear, accommodating country of mine! where a slight incompatibility of temper, a well-worked-up flirtation, a simple charge of abuse, backed by a still simpler little tribute of friendly feeling to the judge in the way of Government bonds, for instance, can brush away like a cobweb those holy, pure, sacred legal bonds that make up marriage.

"Marriage, bah! Who would be tied to it for any consideration but cash? Julian didn't want marriage, and I didn't want Julian, after the first fools' paradise. I fear his fatherly influence would be anything but advantageous to my — Good Heavens! why cannot I keep my thoughts in order? I could once. Ah, it is just as well, my handsome, enraged Julian, that you turned up at so apropos a moment, and sent back this letter for me, torn and open; that you vowed I belonged to you body and soul; that you were my master, and no other man should dare to intrude upon your rights! It was just as well, my cruel, haughty Julian, that you prevented me from making an honorable marriage then, without the million. But can you stop me now? Can you prevent it now?"

A slow, triumphant smile swept over her face.

"And yet the dear old boy was the only man worth having. He tossed me a thousand francs or ten sous with equal nonchalance. He was a savage creature. I loved him for it. His temper was like a great whirl-wind. I felt swept away in it. How his eyes flashed, and then, how he caressed me! But poverty — the horrid changeful life — life in a trunk! Now here, now there, sometimes high, sometimes low, the gambling and the men about town — faugh! I endured it long enough! Respectability henceforth, Visonti. Respectability, and — luxury! I hardly know which was the best luck to-night, to get the letter or to have surprised Ralfe with a soft kiss on his forehead as I intended. But the interview shall come, and perhaps under still better circumstances. He was reading the letter, so was thinking of me, and finished his dreaming in the garden, no doubt. He trembles lest I do not love him; he marvels why I am here; he is getting even more wild than ever before. It is just as well to play him a little. He is gamey enough to make pleasant sport. He loves me, and I love nobody but myself and my — my cigarette's out! I will *not* break my own rules."

She remained quiet for a long time, looking straight before her without seeing anything, her mind became so thoroughly absorbed in the next thought that presented itself — the Princess Menshikoff. A thousand speculations, plots, plans, evasions, diplomacies to outwit and baffle her evident enmity, crowded that busy brain. But at last, with a characteristic reckless courage, she exclaimed to herself, "There is time enough when she strikes!" For out of her past came up memories of many situations when a sudden inspiration had carried her as safely along as if she had planned it all for years; and now she determinedly dismissed her anxieties with an "I'll risk it!" and glancing around the room, "Ah!" she yawned, "this is a good bed," and slipping her hand under the pillow to be sure the letter was safe, she kicked the downy covering more comfortably over her little feet, and stretched out her limbs in the very epicurism of indolent and sensuous pleasure. Soon she slept. Soft, silver rays crept in to steal steadily up the lithe, graceful brown arm; to touch the rich lace and creamy ribbons at the throat; to glisten on the glossy black hair; to light up the strangely expressive countenance. But they seemed to shudder and go out as they fell upon the mouth — the dropping under lip, rolled out and heavy, the wicked dark shadows of it as it slightly parted. A cloud had hidden the moon.

CHAPTER XII.

A WOMAN'S HAND.

"While overhead the moon sits arbitress."
Milton.

How that same moon which now for an instant hid
her face in the clouds, had followed, followed, followed
Sybil around the world! How many places had been
full of serene moonlight, when her heart was mad with
gay revels, dark with despair, or defiant of fate! How
it had looked upon her when she came from stately ball-
rooms, wrapped in her ermines, and ready to step into a
carriage like a jewel-box! How it had stared at her
coldly and sarcastically when she had flitted along the
uneven alleys of the foreign city where she had hidden
name and shame! How it had laughed and jeered at her
as she had stood on the deck of the great steamer, homeward bound, after years of a life filled to overflowing
with incidents which finally had brought her to this last
and greatest venture! How it shone now upon the
graves of those old people, who, buried in a land foreign
to them, rested beneath a proud Italian marble, carved
with the record of their nobility, their goodness, and
their family fame! Strange representative of a stately
name! She sometimes felt an alien and plebeian protest steal into her veins, against the necessity for continuing in her person the conditions of her race. "I
sometimes wish I had come of common stock," she had
once petulantly exclaimed to Julian, whom nothing ever
shocked; "I wish I had not been hampered with this

name, so old and grand! It limits me so! Don't you see? I feel as if in bondage to my own cognomen, or to those fine ancestors of mine whom I solely stand for. I bear about with me something besides myself. I am saddled with the virtues of ancient ladies and the honor of old heroes! If my doings are found out, I not only ruin myself, but blot forever the escutcheon of the Visontis. We must be a thousand times more careful than as if I were nobody. And what advantage is it after all? Perhaps it is my American education, perhaps my natural depravity, but I can't see any good in an old name, excepting the money, worldly esteem and position, which accompany it."

"You are not proud, then, of the character which your forefathers must have possessed to have gained their honors?" answered Julian, with a peculiar smile.

"Character? No. All I am proud of or care for is what accrues to my benefit at this moment. That is what the old fellows were made for!" and she smiled with pleasure at her own irreverence, for she fully believed it. Her parents had indeed been wealthy and liberal. They were aristocratic, reserved, well-bred. Of pure and ancient lineage, they had, like many titled Italians, found themselves the last of a race whose fortunes had dwindled, until now, only a dim and dreary palace in Venice, stripped of its fair belongings, and of necessity rented from basement to roof to a miscellaneous collection of foreigners, remained. They dropped their titles and came to America. Here was a new field, and here they prospered. One dream possessed them, a dream never to be realized, — the restoration of the old palace, and the resuming of somewhat of the splendor of ancient days.

Once when she was a child, Sybil had crossed the ocean and journeyed with them to their beloved Venice.

Once had she tarried for a brief period in the home of the Visontis. Never had she seen her parents so sad as when there. Never had they seemed so mysterious. But she was a child, and the impression faded. Then, just at the end of her Convent life, they had died, almost together, and she had been left at nineteen without a living relative. Made mistress of a small income by the executors of her father's property, chaperoned by a fashionable widow, she had gone abroad, and her beauty, wit, accomplishments and name had won for her the admiration and homage her insatiable and ever-present vanity craved. Then came the meeting with Julian Savelli! Escaping from the gentle espionage of her chaperone one day in the Louvre, and ever ready for the least adventure which savored of the forbidden, she had seen him gazing at her with undisguised admiration, and had flirted slyly with her pretty fan, then had dropped it, and blushed a little as she accepted it from his hand — and with it a lifelong bondage to bitter memories!

Oh, the wild escapades the moonlight saw when Mrs. Mellen, an invalid at all times, really fell ill at her hotel and could no longer take charge of her young friend! The meetings, the dinners, the trips to the country, the rides and walks in the great squares and parks, the dainty little suppers, a thousand times more enjoyed because no one knew or dreamed of them. For, who and what was Julian? An American by birth, he said, — but oh! the passion and fire and fury of the Italian blood which he confessed burned in his veins! Julian, whose life was the life of a gambler, a sport, a roué, whose stories of adventurous existence in this gay, mad Paris made her quiver with delight, — he could show her "life!" He could teach her the "go," the "vim" of the only existence worth a — short word! He refused to be introduced to her "set." He scorned the conventionalities of the American colony; he despised the bondage of etiquette.   He was Bohemian, and he snapped his long white-fingers at rules.   His morals were as broad as — the world; his idea of principle — to enjoy himself!

Well he taught the easily won girl the code of his existence.   She eagerly breathed in the sophistries of his philosophy.   The sudden exigencies of his changeable life seemed to be her element.   To elude, to watch, to risk, to plan, to scheme, and to trust luck, — these were the lessons her acquaintance with Julian taught her, and she entered into the amusements he favored with unguarded enthusiasm.   The moon followed this surreptitious intercourse with a watchful eye, and soon love, that beautiful and sacred word, became on their lips a significant sound.

Then came the sudden death of Mrs. Mellen.   Sybil excused herself from returning to America with the remains of her chaperone, — she had begun to study for the stage.   None to contradict her, none to interfere with her, with a certain amount to draw upon every three months, — life in Paris became life with Julian. But soon the moon looked down upon deceit, jealousy, reproaches, quarrels, coldness, and at last desertion. Julian had ceased to find her quite and completely absorbed in himself.   She had profited by the breadth and looseness of the limits he had preached, and he found her applying them to herself, not to any extent, but enough to first madden and then disgust him.   Even a divided smile did not please this much-divided lover. Besides, there were consequences, and he believed in assuming no responsibilities.   He was engaged in a little scheme in London, and to London he went; first-class and smiling.

She was left alone in great fear and trouble.   She knew what it was to tremble at night and to weep in the morning. She felt the uncompromising and stern atmosphere which surrounds the guilty press on her heart and crush out hope. The food that to her had been as luscious as honey, had shortly become as bitter as gall, and she ate it in sorrow and silence, hiding beneath a gay smile the horror and affright of her racked soul.

She had long ago deserted her fashionable associates, on pretence of absolute seclusion for the sake of " her art." She had given up all, everything, for this handsome, impetuous, terrible, yet fascinating man. And now, where should she go? Where could she hide? To whom could she appeal? Back to America? Never. There she was still the true, modest, well-bred girl who had left them. Stay in Paris? Impossible. Soon one step in the street, and she might be detected. Ah, the old Visonti palace! She knew of no one whom she should fear to meet there, for she would never go out by day, and at night the gondola would protect her from observation. She packed with feverish haste, travelled without a pause. Soon she was established in a little apartment next the sky, — alone, unknown, uncared for by any living soul.

Many a night the great mellow moon of Italy rose and glowed through the high stone casement, as she sat thinking, planning her future, — many a time it found her with head bowed on the dark, dimpled hands, in an agony of tears. Many a time it saw her with pale face and frightened eyes, almost ready to appeal to the first woman she met for direction, for comfort; and then the determined checking of desire, and the undaunted will which bore her one day more through her silent trial. But the waiting and the silence brought to her no repentance. She drew no lesson from her position save that of caution and concealment. She only hated fate and the world and Julian, and then longed for Julian with all her weary, misguided mind.

At last one night, when the great silver orb seemed to pursue her with relentless light, she came up the wide and winding stair of the Visonti palace heavily and as if in a dream. The evening sail on the lagoon had been an intoxication. The poetry and charm of the lovely city had seemed to fill her spirit with rapturous peace. Drifting slowly on the placid waters, over which mellow music floated like an invisible mist and melted into delicious silence; where lights in many colors were caught and reflected as trembling jewels; listening to the tones of the distant bells striking the hour, she had yielded to the spell and half-forgotten, for once, herself. But now as she climbed the stairs she began to pant for breath. Her heart seemed ceasing to beat. Her head was on fire. She called faintly, and then fell. When she awoke to consciousness she found herself lying upon a gorgeous bed in a lofty chamber, surrounded with chattering women. Sybil had never ascertained, had indeed never asked, who occupied any of the apartments. She only knew that the establishment of a titled lady occupied the first floor. She had avoided seeing or meeting any one, and had maintained a scrupulous seclusion. But now opening her eyes, she saw for a moment a face she was destined never to forget. She closed them again in utter weariness. She was gently treated, and the women seemed kind. She could ask nothing more. Her mind was dull. Her brain seemed dormant. She believed she was dying.

Later she found herself in her own apartment. A French nurse was attending to her wants, and occasionally she received messages through her, of fruits, flowers, and pretty gifts from the generous lady who had pitied her helplessness, befriended her in her hour of direst need, and allowed her the attention of her own servant with all the goodness of a mother.

But soon came a more formal announcement. Her benefactress would, with her permission, call upon her. "Ah," Sybil instantly thought, "and if she calls, she will question me. I must answer her, I must tell my story!" She sent word that in a few days she should feel strong enough to receive the kindest lady in all the world, then set about avoiding such a meeting. Her nurse had betrayed an intense homesickness. She was French, provincial and longed for her native village. But she was bound to her mistress by ties of gratitude, and was in some respects indispensable to her. Sybil easily worked upon her feelings, and persuaded her that to go away silently, without a word, would be the easiest way to reach her longed-for home. She bribed her to accompany her to France, and promised to retain her in her service on her arrival. Succeeding, it was an easy matter to carry out her plan, and Sybil returned the care, the goodness, the unquestioning benevolence of the lady, who was the Princess Menshikoff, with flight. Weak, but resolute, with the assistance of the efficient maid she had thus so conveniently secured, in the moonlight, which now seemed to mock and threaten her, she stole away from the old Visonti palace, leaving no trace behind.

"Self-preservation is the first law of nature," she coolly said to herself, as she glanced back at the fast-receding lights of the "Bride of the Sea." "Now for the lies of society, the shams of decorum, and the boredom of our set. I shall appear with a quiet companion. I can find one in two hours in dear Paris! She will tell people how persistently I have been studying under an Italian master. She will say how proper, how self-contained, how earnest in pursuit of art, has been my existence. I will go on with Delsarte, and if I do not find an

eligible party I will go on the stage in earnest.   Money,
money! I must and will have it.   The world owes it to
me, and shall pay it.   Am I not beautiful?   Have I not
wit and grace and culture?   For what was I born, excepting to rule, to revel in all the enjoyments of earth?   Let
the ugly and ill-educated plod!   Let the sallow-checked,
heavy-eyed, low-born, stupid sewing woman work her
fingers to the bone!   I am a Visonti.   Yonder is the
palace of my ancestors!" smothering a sardonic grimace
and a stinging laugh at her own equivocal relation to it.

"With the blood of the Romans in my veins I should
be a queen.   What else is there to live for?   Luxury and
power, beautiful dresses, gay parties, my carriage, my
bouquets, — with these, I can forget, — forget and bury
my past in a sea of pleasure."   She sat motionless for a
while, watching the flying landscape as the train rolled
onward; then with a fierce light in her eyes, glancing at
the maid whose face was buried in a bundle of lace and
down, she murmured, "If this should ever be known,
every woman's hand would be against me.   Until then,
my hand shall be against every woman!"

CHAPTER XIII.

PRINCESS MENSHIKOFF'S RECEPTION.

"Dost sometimes counsel take — and sometimes tea."
The Rape of the Lock.

" Enjoy your dear wit and gay rhetoric."
Comus.

IN a few days after the hashish party, a note from Signor Zante announced in rather lordly fashion, that the Princess Menshikoff would " receive " the following evening, and sent a general invitation to Mr. and Mrs. Fielding and their guests. " You know the eccentricities of madame the princess," he wrote, in an apologetic vein, " she never goes out of her own house excepting to drive, and her drives are almost invariably in the evening or at night, when she 'can breathe free in all space,' as she calls it. But to her undoubted genius perhaps you will accord the honor of your presence, since she is sought by the distinguished of all lands."

Every one was very happy to accept this invitation, since the great Russian writer had become a constant topic of conversation in society circles. Her rank, her literary reputation, her singular religious theories, promulgated with a fearlessness and frankness verging on what was " horrible " and " shocking " to Puritanic principles, but none the less fascinating for that, combined with her extreme exclusiveness and the superb yet odd appointments of her establishment, made her the mysterious delight of whispered wonder and the acme of excitement to those satiated worldlings who had ex-

hausted all ordinary amusements. The party at "Spray
View" felt an agreeable interest in the possibilities of
the evening, and they had formed an impression from the
"pupil" of the princess, which exacted deferential
respect. The grave and courteous dignity of the "stu-
dent of ancient Buddhism" carried with it a profound
sense of his moral excellence, while the quiet modesty
of his bearing imposed on them no check to their accustomed pleasures.

Sybil, however, announced most decidedly that she
should not go. She sneeringly alluded to the "rages"
and "crazes" which carry away Americans with the least
novelty, and assumed an air of indifference to the many
speculations and imaginings as to how they would be
entertained. Sardia, who had absented himself all the
morning, came in while the discussion, as to how they
should dress, was going on among the ladies. Helen
appealed to him.

"The princess being an old friend of Sir Sardia, he
must know positively what would be appropriate to
attend one of her receptions. Does she require full
dress in her august presence? or in deference to her
nationality, shall we assume the Russian costume?"
She playfully laughed.

"Oh," said he, "dress precisely as you please! She
will never know if you are in gold cloth or common print.
For herself, her costume is invariably the same excepting
in choice of material, — the flowing sleeve, loose gown,
sandals, and mitts, with sometimes a silk or velvet cap, or
even Turkish fez, whenever she happens to think of it!
There is not the least formality. You go and leave
when you please, and examine all her curious things
without the slightest conventionality. 'My guest can
take no liberty in my house,' is one of her mottoes; and
I assure you, ladies, her mind and her heart are as open,

as free, and as generous, as the liberty she loves. We will all drop in as we find it convenient. The only thing she desires is, that every one shall talk, and that there shall be no formal introductions. 'My guests are equal,' and 'My guests are brothers,' I have often heard her say. Oh, yes! I must remind you that if a Russian offers you a cigarette it is the most insulting breach of etiquette if you refuse it, so by all means take a puff or two, out of respect to the custom. Miss Sybil, you will not object?" smiling at her pleasantly.

"I do not smoke, — but then, I am not going," she answered carelessly.

Lulu looked dumbfounded.

"Do you *never* smoke?" she whispered significantly.

"Mind your own *p*'s and *q*'s you little Pinafore!" she replied, but flushed enough to betray herself.

"Oh, yes, you will go, I think," remarked Sardia in a musing way, as he watched without comprehending this little by-play. Then he repeated, looking her straight in the eyes, " You will go I am sure."

And strange to say, when night came, she had languidly concluded that after all there might be some amusement to be gained in talking to this titled stranger. Her superciliousness and lack of interest were charming to Ralfe, whose ideal of womanly grace was repose. He did not realize that the true quality he admired was repose of spirit, from which spring the abiding harmonies and beauties of human nature. The semblance of it in manner, to his infatuated judgment, was sufficient.

On arriving at the cottage the party were astonished at the absence of lights streaming from the windows. The house was quiet and dark, only a glimmer here and there indicating occupancy. But Sardia assured them that they would find the princess at home; and pressing an electric bell, the door opened as it were of its own accord, and they were ushered into a smaller compartment which, in all but atmosphere, breathed of a polar winter. Soft white bearskins, couches, and hangings of richest white tapestries and plush, made it a seeming snow bower, while the clear glow of an amber light shed a subdued radiance over the whole. A woman dressed in the costume of a Russian peasant assisted them with their light wraps, while Sardia put the gentlemen in charge of Signor Zante's man, who happened to be present. Laughter and the thrumming of some stringed instrument came from the drawing-room, and when they entered, a few guests, some of whom were known to them, rose or turned and gave a general greeting.

The princess was enveloped in a robe of rich yellow satin, which was lined with black brocaded silk, embroidered deeply with rare Persian colors along the edges, and held by a cord and immense tassels of knotted silks studded with precious stones. Nothing could impress one with more simplicity, yet the wonderful quality of the fabric was worthy of the wearer. Her small expressive hands with their untiring gestures were ornamented with but one stone, — a sapphire of immense size and beauty, carved intaglio with the asp, crown, and tau of her crest.

By her side was a little table on which stood a massive samovar, of a rough gray ware bound and lined with beaten gold, under which the blue flame of a spirit-lamp danced and flickered. The fragrant steam of the tea mingled itself with the little puffs of Turkish tobacco which issued from her mouth as she deftly arranged glasses clear as air, but tinted all shades and colors, and dishes of little cakes unlike anything they had ever seen.

"Yes, yes!" she exclaimed, as if continuing a conversation interrupted by their entrance. "To me the sexes are utterly indifferent. Spirit is spirit, whether it be in man or woman, bird or donkey. I like people for what they are in soul, not because they wear a coat or a robe;" continuing to busily prepare the tea. "You Americans, no doubt, will want a little sweet. Here is the honey; but only one drop, one drop!" warningly. "My dear madame," turning graciously to Helen, "will you drink with me? This tea will exhilarate us. We can talk. Ah, you like it!" as pleased as a child.

"But you could not always have liked people irrespective of sex, could you?" questioned Ralfe, who had taken up the idea. "Do you love no one?"

"I love, — I, a woman of seventy, love!" energetically.

"But in your youth."

"This is my youth. Some of my ancestors lived, hale and hearty, to be one hundred and thirty years old. It is in the historical records of our family. But, no; I always hated men. No; I never loved in my life. I could not. I am incapable of partiality. I know nothing about it. To love implies personal preference;" and she puffed a vigorous rebuttal from her tightened lips.

"Yet you married," said Sardia.

"Married! Yes; and how? At sixteen. Against my will; forced to it by scoldings, threatenings, and persuasions. Married to an old man, — old enough to be my grandfather; a vile creature — faugh! because he had money. But I paid them back. I protected myself. I crept under my grandmother's couch as soon as we came back from the church. I found a keen stiletto, and declared if they came near me I would kill myself. I shall never forget my old nurse and my grandmother kneeling and praying in their satin wedding-dresses on the floor beside me, while I curled myself up in one corner under the couch like a kitten. But I would not come out. Hunger drove me out in a day or two, but they saw I was desperate. They let me alone three weeks, and then, after being utterly worn out by their entreaties, I was persuaded to go to the old prince's palace. Did I not lead him a life ? My savage scorn, my insults, my horror of him, he called 'pretty childish petulance.' I taught him I was a tigress. I struck him, and one day, goaded to fury, I caught up a large silver candelabra and flung it at him, knocking him down. I hoped I had killed him. I rushed out, hailed a sledge, and rode as far as the gates, and then procured a horse and galloped across country to my grandfather's house. I demanded protection. I got it. That ended it."

In her vehement and dramatic gestures, and the forcefulness and earnestness of this story, she seemed to live it all over again. Yet at the end she laughed. They all laughed too.

Guy drawled in his slow, diverted way, —

"I supposed you would say the prince demanded protection. What became of him ? "

"I don't know. He was dead long ago. The worms have him, thank Christu ! " with a sigh of relief.

The tea was certainly animating. In all corners of the apartment could be heard bright and earnest conversation. Many were foreign, or could speak several languages, so one standing silent would be surprised at the conglomeration of sounds. Beginning a sentence in French, the princess would frequently finish it in Russian or English or Italian, as she turned to Signor Zante, Helen, or Sybil, whose Italian was as beautifully correct as that of those who speak the unadulterated music of Dante.

If the Princess Menshikoff had ever known Sybil before this evening, neither gave the least sign. And although a wary and attentive look frequently crossed the latter's face, which was singularly pale and mysteriously attractive to Ralfe, her manner was tinctured with a certain pride which rendered her even more fascinating. The unconscious courtesy, which seemed to be the only possible atmosphere of this "Bohemian" house, was extended to her, with neither more nor less attention than that given to the others.

Ralfe still referred to the topic which first interested him. He turned to Signor Zante and remarked, —

"Our hostess in denying love for mankind seems to advocate a pessimistic philosophy which tends to have a depressing effect on me. Naturally the philosophy of persons and things, offered by so distinguished a thinker, must echo more or less loudly in any mind. 'Facts are facts,' I know, but they may be interpreted rightly or misinterpreted. So far as I am concerned, I believe it to be just as absurd to have no faith at all in humanity as to have absolute faith in it. Nature has given us the power of discrimination, and a philosophy which is all pessimistic is as vicious and insufficient as one that is all optimism."

"No doubt," replied the signor gravely, "by the contemplation of evil, we insist on the assimilation of our minds with the bad aspects of life to the exclusion of the elements that might be agreeable to our finer and more beneficent traits. But the princess spoke in the personal, not the general sense, I am sure."

Attracting her attention he said, "Madame, you have given the impression to Mr. Fielding that you have a pessimistic view of humanity, because you cannot love. But I do not discover in you that morbidity which prevents that nice discrimination between right and wrong, which has been singular to you;" and he smiled.

"I pessimistic!" she exclaimed, gravely. "Not so

much! not so much! He who has a cold, raw, merciless theory of life is not possessed of a wholesome, elevated, and strong mind."

"And who bitterly believes there is no sweetness in existence, cannot possess sweet and beautiful attributes of character," added Ralfe. "There is no affinity existing between him and the better part. He is a dead and decayed portion of the great, complicated system of the universe, and he and not the system will be cast off by inexorable law."

Helen had been listening to this conversation with cheeks flushing and paling with excitement. "My dear sir," she addressed Ralfe formally, "it does not do to speak of any individual from one side only. If a man is cold and hopeless, if he doubts the goodness of human nature, if he speaks bitterly of the selfishness of his kind, if he seems raw and merciless and predicts an extinction of a race he seems to hate, ask him what made him so. Find out what trials he has been through. See if his childhood was sad, gloomy, and restrained. Inquire if his young manhood was harsh, unfriended, and disappointing; then go back to his parents and see what black blood of hereditary vices they poured into his innocent and helpless veins. Then you may say that he shall be cast off, and the universe of matter and being shall go on, if you think just, and perhaps he will be cast off; but again, perhaps he will be taken into the pitiful bosom of the Supreme Power, and covered and sheltered by the almighty hollow of God's merciful hand."

They looked at her in surprise, for her deep eyes were moist with unshed tears. Sardia gave her a sympathetic glance. "Maybe she knows some one whom she is secretly defending," he thought.

The princess nodded approvingly towards her. "Let

us not cherish pessimism," she said; "and yet let us remember that the world is made up of two words, 'bitter, sweet.' I cannot quite agree with Mr. Fielding that a character like that which he describes is incapable of assimilating fine and beautiful things, or that it is necessarily devoid of original excellences. He need not be wholly deaf, dumb, and dead to the glories of those laws which work so steadily. Truly, I cannot consign him to oblivion and annihilation with that cool assumption that one or the other 'must go,' as they say in your California of the Chinese!" and she smiled pleasantly towards Ralfe, who, although half defeated, smiled back.

"It seems to me," said Helen more quietly, looking with grateful eyes at madame, "that even dead matter (if it be dead) has in it elements of mercy as well as laws of inexorable justice; else why does Nature grow roses out of a dung-heap and wear away her adamantine rocks with her softly flowing streams? Surely, from the very ground we can draw lessons of material beneficence! For it casts off nothing, but takes us in our corruption, and hides us away with a loving tenderness, only at last to transform our fœtidness into the delicate fragrance of the violets which cover our graves."

"It seems to me," remarked Sardia, quietly, "that the difference between the philosophical creeds of Mr. and Mrs. Fielding is that hers turns constantly around the individual as the centre of a broad circle, whereas he sees the individual as a point on the circumference."

"It is well to be in a country where women may be allowed an opinion at all," remarked the princess, lightly, "and truly you are so independent — such queens of your houses here — so sure of deference! Even the young girls seem to rule their own lives."

One of the guests whose eyes twinkled with amusement replied, "Yes, I happen to know a true story of an

American girl, — the incident occurring quite recently. Now mind you, we are speaking strictly of the individual. There is no general application. A friend of mine who happens to be the most eligible catch in one of the great Western cities, and who persists in remaining a bachelor, although for at least twelve years he has been besieged with matronly and girlish attention, not feeling in excellent health went to the Hot Springs in the season. There he saw a beautiful young girl, fresh as a rose, exquisitely dressed and surrounded with lovers. She was so young, sweet, and childlike, seemingly without a worldly idea, that his seared heart stirred within him, and he felt a strange longing to read her innocent heart. He was soon introduced and hesitatingly requested her to take a little stroll with him. She took out her tiny watch, studied the time a moment, and said, ' Well, I'm engaged at four and engaged at six, but I could give you an hour at five.' The delighted mamma smiled approval, and so it was settled.

"When the time came they went a little way from the hotel, and sat down under a tree. He flung himself at her feet and began to talk. But she did not seem to respond. He tried art, amusements, the opera, the springs, and even flirtation, in vain, until he finally said, in his softest tones, kissing the tips of her pretty glove with considerable enthusiasm, 'Tell me all about your own sweet self,' thinking that, being a woman, that topic at least would interest her. She looked him very pleasantly in the eyes, then, dropping her lashes, said, ' I'm sure I don't know what I can tell you about myself. There isn't much to tell — but ' — cheerfully and earnestly, ' I can give you *the very best of references.*' — ' My dear child,' said the eligible gently, as soon as he could catch his breath, ' your youth and beauty are quite sufficient references for what I may require of you,' and escorted her back to her six-o'clock engagement. He afterwards remarked dryly that she could easily have invented a new idea which would save considerable trouble. A young lady should have printed on her card, besides her name, the name of her banker, her family physician, and any distinguished ancestor whom she chose, with the name of her pastor, so that a man could see at a glance what sort of a wife she would make and whether she would do."

It was impossible not to be merry over this "o'er true tale," and the princess, who had been "studying" everybody and every word, laughed outright. To say she laughed, was the same as to say "Laughter was present," for of all clear, mirthful, rollicking laughter, hers was the essence. She seemed, indeed, the *Genius* of the mood she displayed at all times, so intense was her vitality. She now exclaimed, "Ah, you Americans! How spick and span you are!"

"'Spick and span!'" cried every one, amused; "why, what can she mean?"

"Why, queer, droll, brand-new, fresh, fire-new, original," said she. "I hunted all those words up this very day, and 'spick and span' means each. All your sayings are so 'bright,'" she went on enthusiastically, "but sometimes you drop your letters in a curious way. Now the other day I noticed an example. I saw a woman in the street hop to one side at least six feet. She cried out very loudly, 'Sakes alive!' I looked to see why she called so, and found she had almost stepped on a little green snake. It was alive, to be sure. But tell me, why did she drop that letter? Was it her agitation? Why did she not say, 'Snakes alive'?"

This serious appeal set every one in a roar. She frowned nervously, and then gave it up with a sigh, murmuring, "I am too tedious to learn the oddities of your idioms."

"You are far from being dull, madame, I assure you," said Ralfe courteously, coming to her rescue. "We laugh because you are unconsciously so witty."

At this moment some one called attention to a little painting which hung almost hidden by a curtain, and Lulu, who had been watching the princess with the lovable curiosity of a child, glided up to her, and taking up her delicate old hand, said softly, "Madame, may I not look at your pretty ring? I see it is engraved with the same crest which encircles yonder window."

"Certainly my dear," taking it off. "It is a sapphire given me in India, and the great lord who presented it assured me it was the genuine tear of Brahma."

"The tear of Brahma!" repeated the girl, not comprehending.

"Yes; there is an Indian legend that Brahma, the Creator, once committed a sin, that he might know the torments of remorse and thus be able to sympathize with mortals. But the moment he had committed it he began repeating the Mantràs, or prayers of purification, and in his grief, dropped on earth a tear, the *hottest* that ever fell from an eye; and from it was formed the first sapphire."

"And this stone is that tear!" holding it up in superstitious awe.

"My child," said madame, "I fear great lords in India are capable of exaggerations as well as other people."

Lulu looked disappointed. "I might have known," she said innocently. "But what a poetic legend! Is there any peculiar property in the stone?"

"The Buddhists assert that the sapphire produces peace of mind, equanimity, and chases all evil thoughts by establishing a healthy circulation in man. So does an electric battery, with its well-directed fluid, say our electricians. The sapphire, say the Buddhists, will open barred doors and dwellings for the spirit of man; it produces a desire for prayer, and brings with it more peace than any other gem; but he who would wear it must lead a pure and holy life."

The evening passed without any other event than the agreeable chatter promised over the tea. When the ladies took leave, the princess followed them into the snowy reception-room, and to Helen's entreaties, gave a half-affirmative reply that she would some time visit "Spray View," at least in the evening, but insisted that no other company should be invited to meet her.

"You know I am an old woman, darling, so old, ugly, and fleshy that I find it impossible to carry my great elephant's body about. I find it best to stay in my own little den and growl at all the world;" but her large, good-natured face was full of warm feeling as she tightly clasped Helen's hand.

At that late hour the moon was just rising, and they all preferred to walk. The carriages were sent on, and the group of ladies and gentlemen wandered along at their leisure.

"Guy," whispered Lulu to her escort, "I have decided about the ring."

"Have you, darling? I am glad. May I get it for you right away?"

She hung on his arm a trifle heavier and looked down.

"Can I have *just* what I want?" said she.

"Any thing in the world!" replied Guy, with all the open-handedness of a lover.

"Then I want a sapphire. The princess says they bring holy thoughts and peace."

"How sweet she is!" thought Guy, "dear little innocent, full of holy thoughts and holy deeds. How I love you, *love* you !" he murmured. "Yes, you shall have a sapphire, but it can never match your eyes."

"I don't think this has been such a wonderful evening after all," exclaimed Lulu, disappointedly. "I expected the princess would talk such grand things that we should all sit still and listen. But she did not say a word to me that I could not understand. She spoke as simply as anybody."

Guy smiled at her artlessness. "Of course she did. Have you not often noticed that when we have grand anticipations of any thing, the reality seldom approaches them ?"

"But I have grand anticipations about *you !*" she exclaimed, darting aside and looking him doubtfully in the face.

Guy caught her back to the path. "Lulu, you are the most tantalizing little witch, you turn a man's words topsy-tur " — The next was lost in a confused murmur.

The others strolled along almost in silence. Helen and Sardia were the last to reach the house, and they lingered for a moment on the great stairway to say some latest words. In parting she gave him her hand with a strong, frank pressure, and looked at him with so sweet a glance of respect and admiration that he could not control himself, and, trembling, breathed rather than said, "Helen !"

CHAPTER XIV.

A THOROUGHBRED.

"The accident of an accident."

Lord Thurlow.

On the following morning all the gentlemen made themselves ready to spend the day on board Sardia's yacht. They laughingly declared that women would be in the way, and that they were to have a genuine "stag party," uninterrupted by so much as a glimpse of a petticoat. Signor Zante had accepted an invitation to join them, and as they all bowled along in the various carriages down to the wharf, many turned to gaze enviously or admiringly at the equipages and the men.

"We shall not get up steam to-day," Sardia had said, "it is fine sailing weather!"

Guy, whose tastes ran somewhat to horses, had sent for a pair of gay "steppers" from a plantation he owned down in the heart of old Kentucky, and as he flung the reins to the groom, stood watching them trot up the street with a connoisseur's critical glance.

"Fine creatures," said Charlie Vane. "What a glorious animal a horse is! If they only had a mind where would man stand in creation?"

"A mind," said Guy, in evident surprise, as they followed the others. "Some of them know a great deal more than the men who own them. Why, my 'Lady Lucy' could tell me a thousand things I don't know, if she could only speak. She is just intellect, and nothing else. A power of reasoning and remembering which gives her a 'great advantage over others of less character."

"Character in a horse," said Charlie, incredulously.

"I tell you," cried Guy, in some excitement, "that character is the right word to apply in her case, or in the case of a good many splendid creatures I've known about. Take 'Harry Bassett,' for instance, one of the best thoroughbreds I ever saw run. Upon the track, when his rivals were plunging and rearing with excitement and impatience, his calm sense of power and perfect confidence in himself made him unusually quiet and dignified in demeanor. He seemed to look upon victory as a matter of course; and the fine manner in which he would draw away from his competitors, with no urging save a light word of command, proved how fully he had his body under control, and what a thorough comprehension of the situation he possessed. His adaptability to situations was like the tact of a well-bred person. Nothing disturbed him or made him uneasy. Like a man of the world, who has been tossed by circumstances from the busy din of ever-noisy cities to the breathless solitudes of the eternal hills, from an Arab camp to a Paris salon, he accepted all positions with the utmost nonchalance; and in travelling at full speed by rail, in crossing ferries from point to point, in changing from stable to stable, in the midst of the deafening roar of a crowd of half-maddened spectators, or left to run alone in a quiet country pasture, he was fearless, steady, and self-possessed, notwithstanding his nervous temperament and inbred energy and fire."

The gentlemen had gradually grouped together as Guy talked vehemently on, and as they entered the little row-boat, manned by the sailors of the yacht, in their dark flannel suits and scarlet stars embroidered on ribbons and collars, Signor Zante remarked slowly, —

"I fancy you are talking of a racer, although I did not catch the beginning of the conversation. To tell the truth, I am not at all posted on the subject of thoroughbreds, and I beg to know what *is* a thoroughbred? I know they speak of dogs, horses, and cattle in the same way."

"I believe the word may equally apply to human beings," said Sardia.

"Yes; you are right!" Guy assented, glowing with enthusiasm; "the world over, a thoroughbred is a thorough-*blood*. A creature made, physically, intellectually, or morally, of the finest fibre; a God-natured being worthy of association with the highest."

"I can never forget the morning when I first asked that question," pleasantly observed Ralfe, pulling out his cigar-case. "We had driven up the boulevard and over the bridge, out into that country space beyond New York, where Jerome Park, the great racing-track with its rolling greenery and breezy lanes, its sunny stables and Mayflower-scented woods, gave to our senses, after a winter housing between stone and brick walls, a new taste of paradise. Standing by one of the stables, with its yellow straw and its grinning darky boys, its many protruding heads of fillies and stallions thrust from open doorways, and its sweet, fresh smell of hay, I said to the owner, 'Colonel, what is a thoroughbred?'

"'Hi, Jim, thar! Trot out Harry Bassett! Bring 'im round even thar,' said he, and pointed without another word to his favorite. By Jove, gentlemen, there was no need! It was a picture which I was forced to contemplate in silence. A word, a sound, seemed for a moment to torture me, so harmonious was the spell of that vision. I hardly dare attempt to tell you what he was like, but in color he was a golden chestnut. As he stood in the sunshine, I involuntarily glanced around to find his reflection, so surely did his burnished coat seem to give forth a lustre of its own. His mane and tail were shaded from a darker hue to a fair tint on the edges, and there wasn't the slightest wave or curl, but each like glancing silk hung neatly " —

" A powerful proof in themselves of his stainless breeding," put in Guy.

" The lightness of his head and neck, with their inimitable pencilling, was only equalled by the chest, which wide and deep, held a great heart whose perfect action must have been one of his finest points. His back, ribs and hind quarters made for weight, spring, and power; the elbows and lower arms; strong broad knees and pasterns of medium length and great strength; the feet excellently proportioned to the limbs, — all spoke of muscles like steel, veins through which the richest blood was flowing, and bones like polished ivory beneath the radiant skin. The head, whose pride of carriage was only equalled by the gracefulness of its every motion, was surmounted by ears which seemed to be the last fine touch from the hand of Dame Nature before she sent her darling into the world. The eyes, in which the ardor, determination, and mettle of all his wonderful ancestry appeared concentrated, glowed with that scarlet light which seemed struck from the fire and energy of his own courageous spirit. When gazing on that remarkable creature, I recognized the possibility of perfection, and, turning to the colonel, I murmured, ' I am answered. A thoroughbred is the climax of all good influences.' "

" Your definition, if applied to human beings, must narrow the circle to a very limited number," thoughtfully observed Signor Zante, as they finally had boarded the yacht and were softly gliding out into the stream. " To be thorough-*blood* is difficult in a new nation, and especially in one made up of such odd admixtures as we find in America. 'Good influences' is a wide term also, and means, first of all, leisure and wealth. While a people are necessarily engaged in the pursuit of bread, clothing, and shelter, or the immediate comforts beyond that, they have little time to devote to that culture which rounds character and polishes manners."

"I do not know that I shall make myself understood," answered Ralfe, "but I consider the engineer who, rough, uneducated save in the make-up of his engine and the rules of the road, sees before him certain death, but firmly stands at his post and puts on the brakes, forgetful of all but duty and the precious trust he holds, is a thorough-bred. The woman who nurses patients with yellow-fever; the man whose moral courage rejects the most subtle temptation; the woman whose self-respect and virtuous pride keeps her stainless, and a queen amidst the horrors of poverty, vulgarity, and abuse, — these, and a thousand others who retain unaltered the noble elements of character inherited, or given as an especial grace to them, are thorough-bred and thorough-blood, if born in a gutter and dying in neglect. They are the pure and sweet of spirit who shall see God."

Sardia had hearkened to the conversation in almost absolute silence. He had quietly given his orders to the captain, who had listened as silently as the Sphinx, but who instantly carried out to the letter the wishes of his employer.

Apparently indifferent, and occasionally moving away, their host for the day seemed to take no interest in a chat not especially including himself, but he missed not a word of Ralfe's earnest discourse, and while idly watching the smoke which lightly drifted from his cigar, thought wistfully, "He is worthy of even Helen. No wonder she loves him, for she need not idealize him. His reality is better than the highest imaginings of some women. Yet I believe all women idealize in spite of themselves! And if he returned her love he would not fall short. But the Visonti! Blind, unreasonable fellow that he is, with all his fine perceptions. He is in the net of his own poetic illusions, and drawn by her magnetism to a fancied transport of love. But if he ever finds her out! I can conceive a terrible reaction. His patience and loyalty are almost unbounded, but if they go" — and he made a magnificent gesture of repudiation.

Lines were now brought out, and the captain respectfully assured them that they would soon run over an excellent fishing-ground. The breeze was so gentle that trolling was possible, the yacht moving along at an easy speed over a placid sea. Lunch was announced in the midst of their sport, which continued good, and as no one admitted hunger it was not until an hour later that they finally gathered about the table. So exquisite was this dainty meal, from Julien soup, clear as drops of topaz, to the dessert of fruits *glacé*, fairy conceptions in cakes and ices, and wines glowing with the sunshine bottled long ago in far-away vineyards, that Charlie Vane sighed a long breath of artistic satisfaction, and said most prosaically, —

"I am just *not* hungry."

" That is the way I intended you should leave lunch," laughed Sardia; "but I assure you at dinner you shall be 'filled to overflowing, pressed down, and running over,' if I dare to badly quote from a good book."

They were soon stretched out on easy sea-chairs or in hammocks swung under the gay awning, and the "puff-puff" of their cigars was mingled with all sorts of talk.

"By the way," said Guy, again referring to the topic of horses, "why can't we all take a run and attend the

races? We can invite the ladies and have a jolly time.
What do you say, Ralfe? Would Helen go?”

“I haven’t the slightest idea,” he answered, smiling
indifferently, “but for my own part nothing would suit
me better. The last race I saw was the *Derby*, and
I lost seventy-five pounds just as e—easy.”

As they chatted a stiff breeze sprang up and soon
ruffled the waters, so that the seething brine sang as
they flew along; white caps tipped every rolling peak
with froth, and the smaller craft began to put in towards
home, rocking and dancing as if with delight. All at
once Vane cried out, “Look, look at that little bird!
It is a land-bird, I am sure. See how weary he is!
What a melancholy cheep! Why, let’s catch him!” for
the tiny creature, driven by a sudden gust, almost
touched the sail.

Ralfe sprang forward, pulling his cap off his head, and
had almost captured the fluttering fugitive when a lurch
of the vessel sent him off his balance, and in a second
he had plunged overboard, and far down into the chilly
waters.

All sprang to the side, and for an instant were dumbfounded. He had disappeared so suddenly it had seemed
impossible.

“Good God, Ralfe is overboard!” shouted Guy, tug-
ging at his clothing, while Sardia was already divesting
himself of shoes and coat while giving orders in a voice
that sounded like a trumpet. In a moment he had
espied Ralfe’s head, and with an agile spring, was over
the stern and lustily swimming towards him. But the
head had disappeared again, and soon they saw him give
a dive and go under. It seemed an eternity to the
friends before both reappeared, Sardia supporting his
companion on his arm but laboring considerably. The
jolly-boat had been swung off, and in a few moments

was pulling towards them. But the yacht had flown a long distance before the "Heave to!" of the captain had been obeyed, so that the two men were very far behind.

"Ralfe is no swimmer, even in smooth water," said Guy, in that hushed tone which betokened his horrible apprehension, as with white faces they leaned anxiously watching the exciting chase of the brawny sailors. "He doesn't seem to be helping himself at all. If they were not loaded with clothing, — but Sardia is a regular fish, and as strong as an ox. By Jove! look at that. He has actually gotten Ralfe half out of water. But what is the matter with the poor fellow ? He hangs as limp — Charlie, Charlie, it cannot be he is drowned ?" And they grasped each other with wild eyes and breathless lips in an agony of suspense. But it was not long before they saw both their friends dragged into the boat, and soon they were assisting Sardia to carry Ralfe, who was unconscious and ghastly as if dead, to the cabin. He was immediately undressed and placed on a broad lounge, while every one performed some necessary office for his recovery.

"He is not drowned," Sardia said, confidently. "He said 'Old boy!' a second before he closed his eyes. I am sure we can bring him around in a few moments!" And while some of the men vigorously rubbed and chafed his skin, their host forced a small glass of brandy between his teeth and applied his smelling-salts to the delicate nostrils. But their efforts proved useless for so long that they all became very much alarmed. They used all the prescribed methods for reviving a drowned person, but he remained cold, white and motionless, without any sign of life. "He is not drowned!" persisted Sardia, as they for an instant ceased their efforts and stood with horror and despair written upon their faces. "Perhaps it is his heart," suggested Signor Zante; "let us pound it thoroughly, and endeavor once again, with all our might, to get up a circulation. Make a strong mustard plaster," he ordered.

After these directions had been carried out, their joy was unbounded to see Ralfe's eyes slowly open and a faint sigh escape his lips. Guy and Sardia wrung each other's hands in silence, while tears ran down Charlie Vane's cheeks.

"May the Eternal Spirit be praised!" solemnly ejaculated Signor Zante, doffing his hat, which he had forgotten, and wiping the perspiration from his forehead. "He will live!" He stood gazing at the fine pale face for a few moments, and then turning away with considerable emotion half murmured, "I am glad. 'His life was gentle, and the elements so mixed in him, that Nature might stand up and say to all the world, This was a man!'" Then smiled at the familiar quotation.

Sardia suggested that they should now remove Ralfe to a berth, and after making him comfortable, they all left him to his host, lest any excitement should prove injurious. On going up to the deck they felt a new glory in the sunshine and a fresher enjoyment of the afternoon breeze, which now steadily sent them onward towards the town. Not one but felt something precious had been saved to them. Ralfe's nature was so winning, yet so quietly strong, that he gained the true friendship of all who knew him. Suddenly Guy burst into a laugh. He had seen Sardia's valet. "Oh!" he cried; "I hadn't thought of it, but Sardia is as wet as a merman now. His clothes are dripping with salt water. Go down and attend to your master, Jaques. What are you thinking of?"

After a little Sardia appeared, fresh and vigorous. His eyes were almost black, and his cheeks ruddy with the exercise and excitement of the hour. "He is asleep, and will be all right by the time we get home. What do you think were the first words he uttered ? "

"Can't tell."

"Don't know, of course."

"Thanked you, I supposed."

"Why, not at all," said Sardia, laughing. "He finished the sentence he broke off in the water. ' Old boy, did you catch the bird ? ' said he, just like a child."

"I wish we had caught it after all this row," Charlie Vane said, regretfully. "There's Ralfe's cap ; shouldn't wonder if 'twas under that."

He stooped and picked up the cap, and sure enough, by some chance, the bird had fallen under it. They were all surprised, and grouped themselves about the tiny brown thing, looking down upon it in silence. For it was lying on its back, its pretty wings stretched out, its graceful head put under in a pitiful way. The little swallow was dead.

CHAPTER XV.

UNREQUITED LOVE.

" Alone ! — that worn-out word,
  So idly spoken, and so coldly heard ;
  Yet all that poets sing and grief hath known
  Of hopes laid waste, knells in that word — Alone ! "
Bulwer Lytton.

" And vain ! yes, vain !
For me too is it, having so much striven
  To see this fine snare take thee, and thy soul
Which should have climbed to mine, and shared my heaven,
  Spent on a lower loveliness, whose whole
  Passion of love were but a parody
  Of that kept here for thee."
Edwin Arnold.

" How still the night ! How dark the sky !
  How lonely on my bed I lie, —
  O God, how near Thy love should be,
  To comfort me, to comfort me ! "

RALFE murmured these words which he had written long ago with a strangely pathetic accent. He was lying in his great chamber, as he supposed, quite alone. He had slowly awakened from a state of unconsciousness which he little knew had lasted many days. Very gradually and quietly the last scene he could remember stole over his mind. He had been lying in the berth of Sardia's yacht; and now the pretty clock by his side rung its muffled church chime of two solemn strokes, and his room, lit only by the rosy gleaming of an open fire, together with the melancholy sigh of the wind and the dashing of the rain against the windows, made it seem to him as if he had slept a Rip Van Winkle slumber far into the winter. Doubting his own personality, yet dreamily aware that something unusual must have happened to him, his heart grew cold and uneasy, with that vague horror and undefinable dread which is apt to come in the night with unaccustomed weakness. He fancied he was in the midst of some mysterious calamity, and with an aspiration like a cry, he breathed, —

> "O God, how near Thy love should be,
> To comfort me, to comfort me !'"

Before he had finished, Helen, like a living Love, stood beside him, smiling down into his eyes with a look so thankful, so glad and so tender, that it seemed to his half-aroused imagination that she was an angel sent instantly in answer to his prayer.

"Oh," she said, with a fragrant sigh, "you are here again!"

Her voice was so full of good cheer, strength, health, that he felt as if struck by a fresh breeze.

"Where have I been?" he asked, smiling rather feebly, and taking the warm, fair hand that smoothed his pillow.

"In dreamland. In No-man's-land, leading an enchanted life. You have not condescended to notice me for more than a week."

"Have I been sick?" he questioned practically, still retaining her hand.

"A little, and horribly out of your head. You have raved of birds, from the sparrow to the eagle, from the ostrich to the 'common domestic fowl.' It was as good as a lesson in natural history to sit by and listen to you."

"And have you sat by and watched me?" he asked earnestly, but with difficulty, his throat seemed so strangely thick and his lips so very dry. “Why did you not leave that to Wilson ? Have I had a score of doctors and all that sort of thing ? ”

“ Wilson has certainly done his accustomed duties, and you have had three physicians attending you,” said Helen, quietly. “ I beg you will allow me to give you this,” and she offered him a tiny glass.

He swallowed the medicine without a protest, then again took her hand and said even more earnestly, “ But it is long past midnight. Have you watched me and taken care of me all this long time ? ” He looked straight into her eyes with a most embarrassing eagerness.

She turned her own aside for a second, and then look-ing at him calmly, answered, “ Yes, I have watched with you and taken care of you all the time.”

“ What did you do it for ? ” he said, bluntly.

“ Because I am your wife,” she replied, growing visibly pale.

He flung her hand aside, then caught it up again and kissed it.

“ It was your duty,” he murmured, with a little scorn-ful laugh. “ But I sincerely thank you for it. I did not know that comrades took so much trouble for each other. I shall know what to do when you are ill. I shall not forget it.”

Helen grew even a shade paler. He noticed her singu-lar expression and added languidly, for it seemed impos-sible to talk, his voice was so husky, “ How tired you must be ! Do go to bed. You certainly can leave me now. I am quite conscious, and will take my medicines as you direct if I am not asleep. I begin to feel very well.”

“ Do you prefer it ? ” she asked gently, turning away with a hesitating step. “ I thought I heard you say something about being lonely.”

"No, I confess I do not prefer it," he answered emphatically, half starting up. "It is very selfish, I know, but some way I feel as if I could not be left by myself. I wish you would sit by the fire until I am asleep again. I am lonesome. I am very lonesome indeed."

He sank back and suddenly turning closed his eyes and remained silent. Helen returned to her seat by the fire. The chill of a great gale made the soft glow most agreeable. Thoughtfully she looked at the flickering blaze that a sudden gust of wind would start amidst the coals, and as the hour wore on, after a brief and solemn thanksgiving for this precious life and reason restored after unconsciously approaching a most appalling death, a thanksgiving which lighted her beautiful face with a touch of the heaven her soul for a moment entered, — she took counsel with her secret heart, and found therein a dull but positive pain, which, crush as she would, and hide from herself, as she had striven to do all these long weeks, now asserted itself with inexpressible power. "Out from behind your screen! Come out and speak the truth. It is useless to protest. I know all and expose it," she seemed to call to her soul; and to meet her white, sober face, seemed to rise the spirit of her own hidden love, which up to this moment she had ever put aside, rejected, or ignored.

While watching beside her husband that day, she had read "Antony and Cleopatra." Now the wonderful story swept over her with exceptional significance. Their supreme loves ending in a supreme tragedy uplifted, sustained, inspired her.

Almost at the very moment when she was forced to admit that she was possessed by a new passion full of an infinite sorrow, yet tinctured with as deep and new a joy, the vivid picture of those lovers arose in her mind and seemed to mingle itself with the rapture, yet the anguish, of her feeling. "Be life what it may," she slowly thought, "and it seems that nothing awaits mine but a monotony, — there is to be found in past loves, past agonies, a something which aids the soul to bear. With the remembrance that one is not alone, but all humanity have each and every one had in their time some touch of this sorrow and suffering, the spirit becomes brave and can be silent." For she did not endeavor to conceal from herself what was so palpable, that Ralfe had no thought, no emotion, no desire, which did not lay itself yearningly at the feet of Sybil Visonti.

By the keen consciousness of her growing passion, without the necessity of a word or look from them to convince her, she had become aware that Ralfe's devotion was no fancy, no trifling ardor of a moment. He was under a sway imperious and sustained. It was a force that moved his whole being with a magnetic spell which as yet had been undisputed by any counter attraction, and had but gained by long poetic dreams concentrated on one object. For, neither glory nor work nor invention could satisfy his vehement nature. Love alone could gratify him. for beside his senses and heart, it alone could content the brain. All his powers, imagination among the rest, could find in it only, their true inclination, their best employment. She saw, through the simple courtesies of his daily life, the dominating idea that more and more absorbed it. He appeared to her like one over whom an enchantment had been thrown, whose fascination drew him on and conquered all resistance.

"Can this be love?" she reasoned. "Is this mighty and majestic emotion which so exalts me, what they also feel towards each other? Or is it but a terrible passion, which like a flood drowns all repugnance and all delicacy, all preconceived opinions, and all received principles! Can it be that for her sake he could forever keep silence as I shall do for his, or would she, to grant him a life of happiness, put aside her own? For oh, to make him happy, I will imperil my own great joy! What does it matter if he drink the wine and I the lees? He will never know how I have endeavored to conform my very intellect to his preferences; how in my hidden heart and brain I preserve and ever shall preserve the worshipping attitude which his dear spirit has rendered sweetest! He will never dream while he sees me daily in his presence, that I carry with me that unalterable affection which would save him the slightest anxiety by the giving up of the most perfect pleasure, — which will yield itself, fly, run, rejoice to yield itself for his slightest advantage without one hope of recognition! I can do it. I will do it. For he has almost told me his secret. He almost makes me his confidante. He thinks me his 'comrade!' His true 'comrade' I will be! Into his life shall be poured the brightest sunshine, be it what he longs for or some still far sweeter joy!"

For she had heard his waking words plainly enough, and the aspiration, the murmured cry for comfort, touched her sympathy to the quick. "How he loves her, and how hopeless he thinks his position! Tied to me by a bondage which he never would have assumed had he believed there was the least hope of winning her, he lies upon his lonely bed and calls on God to comfort him! If she sat here what transport would light his face! If she had said 'I am your wife,' he would have clasped her to his heart in a bliss too deep for words! Oh, my Father! Help me to do what is right! If it be Thy will, let me sacrifice myself to the uttermost! If they love each other, how much better do I love him! If he suffers, how much more do I feel unavailing anguish! For he may yet be happy, but I, — I! Vain and brief is all human consolation! Dear Comforter, come to me, for I too am very lonely."

She bowed her head on her hands and the great tears fell one by one through her fingers. She forgot, for an instant, and gave one quivering sob. Alas, what a Master one should be, who would express what that sob meant, — who could translate into words that one great human emotion, the one essence of being, the one incentive to higher life, the one incomprehensible enthusiasm, which having taken possession of the soul, wields over it an unerring and inevitable rule, reducing it to utter misery or raising it to proudest heights! How inspired should he be to utter in words that secret ecstasy, that silent pang, that hoping, longing, fearing, despairing sensation, which makes the body a furnace or an iceberg; the heart a trembling, panting thing, or strong and brave as a lion; the mind a confused and ungoverned power, or a calm, clear, delicate perception; the honor at odds with itself or transcendent over matter; the whole being transformed, "changed in the twinkling of an eye," to something sweeter, more desperate; finer, more uncalculating; nobler, more reckless; truer, more confiding, fiercer, yet more weak!

Poets in the universal language of genius try to teach what loving means. Philosophers weigh human feelings in the scales of their scientific researches, and attribute it to race, color, climate, habit, food, and education. Painters with rainbow pallets depict some phase of its unlimited career; priests point us to the one great Love as model and pattern of it all; Nature breathes it in her sighing winds, her flowers, her beasts, her hills, her streams; but still the unsatisfied soul cries out, "Love is uninterpretable! Love hath no translation! It hath but one medium, — personal contact! It hath but one language, — the touch of lips, the clasping of hands, the glances of fond eyes, the glowing of pressed cheeks, the glory and beauty and radiance of the countenance, the grace and freedom of the gesture when man and woman meet, heart kissing heart, soul melted in soul, to make a wedding of two lives, a unit of a duality!"

Day, gray and dusky, began to creep into the room before Helen raised her head. Her spirit had calmed itself with earnest prayer. With her constant habit of turning ever Godward, she had sought His judgment, sympathy, comprehension, tenderness and love, as a trusting child creeps to the yearning mother heart and lays its innocent soul bare in utter confidence. Rising with a quiet look, she stood for some time watching Ralfe, whose fine features in the sullen light seemed placid as marble, then softly stole out of the door and sending his valet to take her place went to her own still chamber.

But as she went, Ralfe, who had not slumbered for a moment, gazed after her with so profound a pity that he almost called her back to him, but did not, thinking, "How sad she is, yet who would have dreamed it! She, too, is lonely. She, too, loves. She chafes at her bondage, and longs with secret grief to give her pure self to another! Ah, if we were not alone! If we knew that those we love seek us with equal longing, the very fact that we beat our wings against our prison bars would have something indescribably beautiful and comforting in it, for then the circle of our desires were rounded. and wishes would fly from one to the other with a divine communication! Alone? We are never quite that after all!" for some verses of his poem which had haunted him since he had awakened, again ran in his mind:

> " Thou dost not leave us quite alone!
> We sorrow that we may atone, —
> We suffer that our aims may yet
> On Thee be set, on Thee be set!

> Thy love doth try us like fine gold.
> To Thee we cling, to Thee we hold, —
> Faith keeps us close, dear Lord, to Thee!
> Our Father Thou, Thy children we."

Wilson at this moment appeared, his face shining with delight.

"Oh, sir," said he, a suspicious moisture glistening in his eyes, "how glad I am to see you alive once more!"

Ralfe laughed.

" Have I been dead ?"

"Nigh to it, sir, nigh to it! If it had not been for the mistress, you would have been gone, I'm a-thinkin'."

"No doubt you also deserve much credit," said Ralfe very kindly. " Tell me, Wilson, how long have I been sick ? "

" About ten days."

" Are all the guests here still ?"

" All but Miss Visonti, sir."

"When did she go ? " asked Mr. Fielding sharply.

" As soon as she found out what was the matter with you," said the man, honestly putting it exactly as he thought. He began to mend the fire with considerable energy.

"Why, what has been the matter with me?" cried his master as loud as he could for his throat, which so mysteriously troubled him, and half started out of bed.

"Well, besides the fever, it was awful catchin'," said Wilson turning squarely around. " You have about up an' died with diphtheria."

CHAPTER XVI.

LONGING.

"**Th'** idea of her life shall sweetly creep
 Into his study of imagination, —
 Into the eye and prospect of his soul."
       Much Ado About Nothing.

As the days passed, and Ralfe slowly began to feel the incoming tide of health sweep over his waiting being, he somewhat chafed at his confinement to his rooms, although they were so ample and luxurious. His face had a wistful look as in the fresh mornings he idly sat at the open window and saw parties of guests ride up and go away, or the few who still remained in the house, join them in their various little trips. But he could not fail to notice how seldom Helen was to be seen among them; or if she stood in the garden and waved them a gay adieu, she soon disappeared within the house, to gently tap at his door and request him to desire something. Seldom she came empty-handed. A choice flower, a bunch of grapes, a new picture, a book, — always her pretty white hands were full, and her serene countenance touched with a pleasant smile. If she came not, he missed her, and while he would say nothing when she finally appeared, he felt a very keen desire to upbraid her.

"Why didn't you come before?" he asked her rather sharply one day. He was sorry he had uttered it in an instant. His tone sounded harsh to him. He was ashamed.

But she only answered indifferently, — "Oh, I was busy," and that indifference cut him to the quick. "Excuse me," he said grimly.

She came quite near to him then, and holding a sheet of paper in her hand, blushed a little, looked at him shyly, and finally took his hand. "Ralfe," said she, her big eyes blue with enthusiasm, "don't laugh, will you ?"

"At what ?"

"Me."

"You !" in surprise.

"Yes, me. You won't ? Truly ? Then I will tell you. I have written a sonnet, — and for you." She drooped those golden lashes lower and lower until she seated herself, a complete personification of guilt.

"Let's hear it !" Ralfe said, heartily. "A sonnet ! and for me ! My little — comrade ! What a poet you must be !" and all the genial, gracious, tender beauty of his soul flashed over her like a gentle benediction. She drew a contented sigh, and holding the paper very nicely between her face and his, was about to read, when she suddenly dropped it. "Oh ! I forgot. Don't you remember, you never read me the poem that you began that day Miss Visonti came ? You had just opened your lips to read it, when she stole into the doorway I was so disappointed. Will you read it to me now ?

"I wish you would not mention that," said Ralfe testily.

"Why ?" she asked, innocently.

"I was disappointed too," he answered. A soft flush crept like a ray of light over the sweet countenance before him. A look of joy hidden beneath a little confused laugh, transfigured the eyes and lips. Ralfe felt a sudden tremor of happiness. He leaned forward and shook one of her ribbons into a tiny breeze. "Helen, go on !" he said. So, with a gentle dispossession of him of the ribbon, in which she lightly touched his hand, she read softly, —

LONGING.

Grant but this one rare thing, O God, to me:
This single, rich, sweet gift, oh! make it mine.
Since all the glories of the earth are Thine,
So small a thing were never missed by Thee.
I grow so tired with ever gazing far
Across the weary distance to my need ;
Stretch out thy hand, dear Lord, and break the bar,
Letting my soul for once be wholly freed!
Then, having gained and held it to my breast
In all its granted wealth, my being, thrilled
With gratitude for hopes divinely filled,
And all the love of one so deeply blest,
Shall feel the strength to take it all, and know,
Why I have prayed and hungered for it so.

As she read, forgetting herself and him, intent upon
her theme, a curious change came over her whole being.
The flame of her spirit burned with a penetrating light,
and seemed to illumine the exquisite vessel which contained it.   The intellect, active and strong, intuitive
and poetic, filled the delicate features with a finer
beauty, and even her body seemed to radiate a force and
a charm at once.   Irresistibly attracted by this unknown
power, which awakened only a feeling as pure yet as
fervent as might some angelic vision, he drew still
nearer and nearer, until at the last words, he swiftly
drew her fair head close to his breast, and kissing her
forehead with a touch of sweetest tenderness, whispered, " Dear heart!"   For a moment this light clasp
seemed to weld them in a harmony too beautiful for
thought ; but Helen, with a face white with emotion,
gently drew away.

"I did not suppose you would criticise it in that way,"
she said demurely, looking at the crumpled paper with a
dubious expression.   " Does that sort of criticism usually
please authors ? " and she smoothed the wrinkles with
a thoughtful movement.

"Helen!" said Ralfe, "I cannot understand myself or you. I wish you would go away. You are not a comrade at all, and you are not a wife, and you are not a friend. I cannot make it out, what you are or I am! How did you know how to write that? And what made you read it to me? Don't you know you tear me to pieces?" He rushed these questions at her in a burst.

"I know I tore your poem that day," she answered with a laugh. "But no! it was only a blank sheet of paper. Maybe," she added consolingly, "you might find an answer to all your questions on it. Almost everything seems to me to be a blank at times. Life itself is a lottery in which we too often draw — a blank. I presume you have heard that rather trite idea expressed before. But it is sufficiently apropos."

"What!" asked Ralfe, amazed and aghast. "Do you allude to me?"

"Be calm," said Helen torturingly. "Ralfe, you do very well. No, not quite a blank, I think, — as a comrade." And she rose in a dignified manner and left him with only one more saucy look.

"If it were not for Sybil!" he muttered, looking after her in half wrath, half delight, "I'd flirt her little head off! Why, by heaven, she is bewitching! But, oh! ha, ha! Flirt with one's wife! By Jove, and feel one's self disloyal to do it! Was there ever such a situation in the world? Confound that Sardia!" For two rich voices rose from the drawing-room, blending in passionate song.

How well he knew them! Sardia's tenor, for which he was famed among all his intimate friends and lovers, and which he scrupulously concealed from every one else. Helen's contralto, divinely rich and as full of longing as the sonnet she had so recently read in melancholy tones of sweetness.

"I do very well for a comrade!" he said aloud, walking quickly to a large mirror. His face did not please him. Illness had taken its bloom; confinement had stolen its fulness. He could fancy he saw the noble head of Sardia bending over Helen as she sang, — and his own face did not please him. It fell into a still deeper shade of melancholy as he looked. "She is right," he murmured. "I am a blank, — what am I beside him ?"

Restlessly he paced the room until suddenly he stopped and opened the door. "I will not stay shut up here any longer," he exclaimed. "I can at least go to the library." The voices had ceased, and as he slowly went down the great staircase, he heard them in a ripple of conversation on a little balcony just outside the library window, "I shall surprise them," he thought rather sardonically, as he approached the curtains.

Helen had added to her costume, since in his room, some great bunches of pink roses. They were fastened in sprays at her belt, they were caught at her throat, a glorious blossom was hanging heavily from her hair, and in her hand were two or three clusters which she was carelessly whipping against her skirts. Her beautifully modulated voice, so easily heard, yet so mellow, seemed continuing an earnest conversation. Sardia was out of sight, but his cane was occasionally tapped on the balcony as if by his idle hand.

"I am being slowly educated to the fact," Helen was saying, "that love is in no manner selfish. I find I can love largely, broadly, fully, and love a good many too. The human idea is to love one and one only ! I believe the diviner idea is to love each with an individual intensity which shall be all-satisfying to them and yet take nothing from any. The limitations of the human idea of division in love have often fretted my soul; for there is a notion among mortals, that if you love one person, it must be all-absorbing, or else it is not loyal!"

Sardia remained thoughtfully silent a moment, and then quietly answered, "Love can never be exclusive with me. It is inclusive, and devotes itself in different degrees to the claims and needs of everybody. Cannot I love my mother just as well and better because I have found my ideal woman? Can I not love that sweet woman better if I enlarge my heart to take in a friend?" His voice grew deep with feeling, his very intonation was a caress.

Helen raised her head and looked straight up at the sunny sky. She heeded nothing but the thought that pleased her. "Love is universal and individual at once," she uttered in a low, reverent voice. "It broods with exquisite protection over the helpless and the sorrowing; it wings its way joyously to the empyrean with the glad and the aspiring. To each, to all, it bears a message of heavenly tenderness, right out of the heart of the Source of love, and he whose cup is largest and able to contain the most, drinks deepest of its nectar."

Both men listened to her with the same conviction. Ralfe, retiring silently to his own room, and Sardia still apparently gazing indifferently at the pretty garden landscape, said each in his secret soul,—

"How beautiful, and how unapproachable, she is!"

Sardia looked up.

"But sometimes we love so blindly, or we find ourselves utterly unrequited! We hold up our cup,—it may be a very large cup,—but it remains unfilled. What shall we do then?"

Helen turned suddenly and looked him wistfully in the face.

"I constantly renew my efforts to care as little as possible for this slow healing wound in the body of

Cupid!" said she, and unconsciously laid her hand on her heart as if she felt a pang.

"O God!" cried Sardia, catching her hand and pressing it between his palms, "I know how to pity you."

The look of pain deepened in each face, and they sank into silence, both falling into one of those distressing states of thought which were the sharp thorns of their rose of friendship.

He so madly loving her, yet with a divine purpose holding himself ever in check. She, woman-like, leaning on his stronger nature, while by so leaning she drew his soul to hers, in bonds unbreakable! And each full of a hopeless and agonized devotion, — mocked by the very nectar they craved, held just away from their lips!

Ralfe, sitting silently and moodily at his window, slowly repeated the last line of the sonnet, which came tripping into his memory. "'Why I have longed and hungered for it so!' What can it be?" he thought. "Out of what despair could come such a cry? Is it freedom? Freedom to love him, — to be loved by him? No! I will not endure the thought! She is mine, mine! Can I not fill her life with joy? Would not my love be worth — something? It must be! It shall!"

Sybil for once was forgotten!

CHAPTER XVII.

IN A NET.

"Much like a subtle spider that doth sit
In middle of her web that spreadeth wide."
Davies.

" Our souls sit close and silently within,
And their own web from their own entrails spin."
Dryden.

DURING Ralfe's illness, one afternoon, Guy and Lulu had wandered across the lawn to a large clump of trees situated quite a distance from the house. They often stole apart from the others, — a proceeding which was smilingly ignored. It was a still, slumberous, mellow day of earliest autumn, following a sudden and unusually cold rainstorm. The sunshine sifted hotly through the trees, which were dropping their dying leaves with the soft, rustling patter so familiar to those who are at home in the woods. The moist earth was teeming with odorous balsamic scents from the unfolding blossoms of wild asters, the spicy smell of the laurel bushes, and all the varied natural perfumes of mingled sea and shore. One light yellow butterfly hovered disconsolately over a budding golden-rod, feebly fluttering his half-chilled wings, but higher in air a great cluster of silver midges danced, swung and circled about each other, as if indeed winter were a thing uncared for and unknown. The rich warmth of the atmosphere made them jolly and light of heart indeed. They greeted each other with sounds of pleasure, and seemed to be having their dance in honor of some gay occasion.

Lulu was a close observer of nature, and now she called Guy's attention to this pretty festival. They watched it with admiration and wonder. How human were their movements! A party would retire from the circle, and then leaving their positions, going into the midst, would to their own music, set their light bodies in motion. Backward and forward, swinging and circling, now in couples, now alone, now in groups of threes and fours, advancing, retreating, and with inimitable ease dropping below or rising above the others, — these tiny insects put the sinuous grace of Eastern dancing girls to shame, and in the natural freedom of every invisible curve they traced could be seen the symmetrical design and harmony in the mind of Him who is the soul and life of beauty.

Far up in the walnut trees, sudden gusts of wind shook the topmost branches, and as the lovers sauntered along, on the yellow leaves about them would fall at long intervals a single decayed nut, with the muffled sound so appropriate to the season. The pine needles were polished enough to be slippery as glass beneath their feet, and here and there hidden in part by a mossy stone, or standing bravely out to meet the day, were scarlet dots of bright-eye berries, with their creeping sprays of round green leaves. They walked along, chatting in Lu's own jolly and childlike way, until, finding an open spot where the grass was dry and warm, they seated themselves on a fallen log which had been formed into a sort of rustic sofa.

The intercourse between Lulu and her lover was of that rare kind which savored more of loyalty than sentiment. Their conversation, although tinctured with a tenderness and sweet courtesy which would instantly have proclaimed them to be lovers, was for the most part, of subjects more thoroughly practical than what in the slang of the day might pardonably be called " intense."

Simple and well-bred. they possessed the negative qualities of human nature to perfection. While the negative
qualities are invariably the finer, more delicate, more
spiritual, perhaps those possessing them are worthy of
but little praise ; for they are always inborn in the individual. There is in the true man or woman a subtle
attribute which stamps each as a lady or a gentleman.
None can mistake it. In whatever situation they may
be, whether of embarrassment, poverty or riches, ovation
or insult, they preserve that one unspeakable grace which
neither a crown can make more beautiful nor rags render
less lovely. These two possessed this distinction in a
remarkable degree, for they added to it many positive
virtues, among which honor was the most prominent.

There was in the Englishman, however, a tone of cool,
phlegmatic indifference which characterized him among
his men friends as "a deuced slow-blooded fellow." Yet
there burned within him a depth of passion which
might have led him far astray, had he not a keen distaste
for the general follies of ordinary fast life. He wished
to be always certain of his moral integrity, and he despised as bad taste the indulgences which others less
manly believed to be even fastidiously elegant. He
was by no means so idle as he appeared. His affairs extended from east to west and from New York to the
continent. But with a keen eye to his investments, a
shrewd judgment and quick decision, he managed to preserve that best of advantages — sufficient leisure to
enjoy both business and social intercourse with a quiet
zest. There was a vein of pleasantry in him that frequently cropped out in his speech, which spoke of the
jovial humor of his heart, and Lulu often found him
sufficiently merry to make the dullest day full of sunshine. To-day he was in one of his happiest moods, and
seemed interested in every trifle as they laughingly

talked. She had a dainty little box of artists' utensils, and as she chatted she sketched, while he, tired of his position, finally flung himself with boyish grace upon the ground. A little scrub oak grew beside Lulu, and as one or two glossy leaves detached themselves and floated away, she let fall her pencil and watched them idly in silence, thinking of little save the blue dome above her, the genial warmth of the sun, and the refreshing odors which, without effort of hers, were blown with all their aromatic fragrance to her nostrils.

"How dear and lovely life appears!" suddenly murmured Guy. "There is nothing in all the scene which speaks of unhappiness. The general beginning of decay is but the precedence of a new birth into gladness. The very winds are tuned to a subdued but tender melody. One might easily believe that wrong, outrage, selfishness, fraud or cruelty had no existence. We are at this moment possessed of a little space

> ' Within whose circuit is Elysium,
> And all that poets feign of bliss or joy.'"

Lulu did not reply. Her eyes were fixed with eager interest upon something evidently within the leaves of the oak.

" What do you see ? " he asked, lazily.

"Hush !" she whispered softly, holding up her finger, "don't look. Let me tell you and see if you can guess."

Thorne turned his head so that the mellow sunshine played on the dark, healthy hue of his cheek and smiling in anticipation, said gently, " Go on, love."

" I see," said Lulu, all her tones indicating the most vivid interest, "a curious little creature. She is gray and spotted and hairy. Her undervest is muddy yellow, and her legs are butternut brown. She has piercing, wary, suspicious eyes. She is a small bundle of observation. There is not a movement of hers that does not show her to be on the alert. She is both on the defensive and the aggressive. Her whole being is made up of unconquerable industry, intuitive watchfulness and supreme cunning. Self-interest is displayed in the very way she twists her hind legs together, and knots with precision and swiftness the web she is weaving."

"Oho, little lady! a spider, a spider!"

Lulu laughed and blushed with amused pique. "To think I should have told right out!" said she.

"Pray go on," urged her lover.

"Self-preservation and self-indulgence are seen in the deep, well-covered cave she has manufactured, into which she can crawl and hide from danger, or sit at ease and view the helpless struggles of her prey. She is indeed a very wicked-looking spider."

"Do you know they can sing?"

Lulu looked incredulous. He went on, "It is believed by many that a spider cannot even converse. But I think I can convince you that to a fine ear, accustomed by long and loving observation of nature's music to catch the faintest sound, she sings a low, tragic, mysterious song. Listen and see if dear old Prince Will does not put her crooning into words;" and in a soft, buzzing tone he half repeated, half hummed, —

> "'Fair is foul, and foul is fair,
> Hover through the fog and filthy air.
> I'll drain him dry as hay;
> Sleep shall neither night nor day
> Hang upon his penthouse lid;
> He shall live a thing forbid.
> Weary sev'n-nights, nine times nine,
> Shall he dwindle, peak and pine.'"

The spider which they had both been watching had until this moment been busily at work enlarging her web, but now Lulu exclaimed, "I believe, dearest, you have chanted that poor victim's death-knell."

While she spoke a very small honey-bee became caught within an inch of the cave. The spider knew it the moment he touched the web, but she had perfect confidence in her work. They anticipated that she would instantly approach him so that she might more certainly ensnare him, but they were astonished to note the coolness of her movements. She stopped weaving, and with that peculiarly angular motion which spiders have, she turned with one straight bound, so that she sat sideways towards the intruder; then, with a sly, subtle, quiet satisfaction, she settled herself well into her airy swing, and began to puff herself out. She watched that unfortunate bee with a fiendish and most deliberate pleasure. As with many a wrathful and finally despairing buzz he endeavored to loosen his feet and wings, but only succeeded in more closely entangling them, she made the whole web about her tremble, whether with malicious laughter they knew not, but certainly with an emotion which set her whole disagreeable little body in spasmodic action. Having seen that it needed no further effort of hers to hold him fast, she shrank to her ordinary size and went again to work as if nothing had happened.

Lulu had watched all this with twenty expressions crossing her face. She now put forth her little hand and exclaimed indignantly, "I will rescue him!"

Guy caught it, however, his face charged with a slow, indefinite scorn. "No, let us wait and see the end of the tragedy. It will teach us its lesson. Look, she has returned to him." It had not taken her spidership long to complete her task. When she had fastened the last rope, with a slow, cautious, apparently timid motion, she crawled towards what was at last to be her supper. She had not arrived half way before he set up a cry of defiance. She stopped and measured his proportions, went around him on her fairy ladder, and satisfied herself that in no wise he could get away; and then, with the insolence of power, sat immediately in front of him and began to swell herself out. This was more than his knighthood could endure. He forgot her sex. He forgot his own desperate condition. He roared out his hatred and contempt with a thousand twirls of his legs and twists of his head. At this she became infuriated. With the utmost ease avoiding his sting, she drew her slimy body over and about him until she had enveloped him with her strong cables, and then, over his very head she wove a nightcap which silenced him forever. The skill and courage she displayed in passing and repassing his fiery weapon, the cool trustfulness in her own ingenious trap, the insolent enjoyment of the anguish of her victim, the prosaic yet wonderfully successful plan by which she shut her enemy's mouth, and her subsequent retirement into her self-constructed castle, there to recruit after her exertion and prepare herself for supper, awakened in the human beings who watched her, feelings of horror and disgust.

"Do you not see a symbol, Lulu, in this scene, of those natures among our kind, who, grasping, cunning, and cruel, endowed with wisdom, power, and efficiency of action, spend their lives in building for self alone?" She crept closer to her lover and nestled her hand in his as he proceeded. "These make of their existences snares, into which are drawn generosity, bravery and innocence, to be insulted, imposed upon, and finally strangled, as was the valiant honey-bee. *These must have their supper*, though it be from the dead body of all that is sweet, benevolent, and manly."

"How bitterly you speak, dear," she murmured. "Can it be that you have known such people?"

"Who has not?" he answered. "If they cover the true soul of themselves with an outward show of sweet manners and professed goodness, underneath is working the real nature of the spider. Do you not know one whose secret being might be appropriately represented by this?" and he pointed with a gesture of aversion to the cobweb.

She shuddered a little and pressed closer to his side. "I know whom you mean," she almost whispered. "Ever since I gave you some little idea of my evening in Sybil's room, you have seemed to hate her."

"Darling, darling," he answered in a strained and unnatural voice. "God forgive me if I do her wrong, but I have watched her closely ever since she came to this place, and I have indeed grown to feel a strong and ever-increasing dislike. Do not listen to her! Do not be alone with her one moment; will you, my innocent love?" He looked into her face with an anxiety which was even a stronger warning than his words.

"She could not influence me to do wrong!" exclaimed Lulu with considerable pride.

"I know, I know," he answered with equal pride, but added gently, "I have seen large brown spots suddenly appear on the most perfect and fragrant magnolia, after it had been simply breathed upon!"

Lulu understood. "I promise, dear. Indeed, I was going to speak with you about it. You must be a mother to me as well as a lover, now that I am so far away," and she lifted her trusting face with a reverent look. "I do not know — but she fascinates, yet repels me. I wish to sit beside her, I long to touch her. Her dark beauty appeals to me with a strange power, and yet, if she touches me, if she kisses me, as she so often does when I least expect it, I become so angry in a minute that I could strike her."

"Avoid her! Never touch her! Do not permit her to kiss you!" cried Guy, earnestly. "But this has indeed been a sober ending to our little walk." He rose and shook himself as if to throw off an evil impression. "Let us go and forget in some sweet deed this strange little drama of the woods."

" Helen wished me to go and carry a large package of wine and delicacies to a poor old black woman she knows in the town. I have been two or three times before with her. Let us go now. Will you order a carriage?" So these two young people who shuddered at the thought of wicked or ignoble deeds, with the soft rays of the declining sun shedding a glory about them, drove along towards the humble cottage where they would carry help and comfort and benediction to one who forgot pain and poverty in their merry voices. They left the small gray spider looking out from her den and gloating over her victim with ever-watchful eyes. They did not molest her. Why should they? She was irresponsible. She had acted out her nature. But forth from the one thing beautiful about her, the gossamer web which she had spun, might easily have been imagined to come the sound of

> "Weary sev'n-nights, nine times nine,
> Shall he dwindle, peak and pine."

Lulu was very thoughtful all the evening, and as she was taking down her glossy brown hair for the night, she nodded two or three times gravely at her reflection in the mirror, and said, confidentially, —

"And Ralfe is the honey-bee!"

Yet she was looking into her own eyes.

CHAPTER XVIII

AT LAST!

"Sometimes we are devils to ourselves,
  When we will tempt the frailty of our powers."
                                    Troilus and Cressida.

"Sufficient to have stood, though free to fall."
                                    Milton.

RALFE'S convalescence was now rapid. Not many days passed before he could go into other apartments, and soon he habitually sought the library, where, reposing in some great chair or lying on an easy lounge, every one vied to render his hours gay with their society, or else scrupulously avoided disturbing his frequent intervals of enforced quiet. Miss Visonti had returned after a few days, and seemed filled with a desire to please every one with whom she came in contact. Even Sardia was half charmed from his suspicion by the gentle, but indifferent, manner she displayed towards Ralfe, and her evident wish to avoid being alone with him, since she invariably managed to be accompanied.

Ralfe chafed and fretted with inward rage. Was it fate, or was it Sybil herself, who put this barrier forever between them? Should he never regain his strength and be able to command her presence for a moment?

She had brought with her, as a pretext for her trip to New York, a superb bas-relief of the head of the elder Delsarte, which she averred had been detained in the custom-house and which for some reason she had had great difficulty in securing. Displaying the portrait on an easel, she stood before it in an attitude of proud humility. "The great master!" she exclaimed. "If I have anything of grace about me, it is from close study of his art!" And with a worshipping abandonment she threw herself on a low cricket and gazed admiringly at the stern, cold, intellectual features. "What an elevation of soul comes to one who can understand, even so slightly as I, the deep mysterious unity of being which underlay all his teachings! And how impossible to communicate to the uninitiated, the subtle fascination of his laws!"

"But what is the result of them?" asked Charlie Vane, who was prone to go straight to the end of anything.

Sybil rose with a grace that could be felt, as well as seen, and stood before him with a triumphant smile.

"I am answered!" he exclaimed, and the others, in spite of their varied feelings towards her, involuntarily admitted their appreciation.

Signor Zante, who happened to be present, with his soft old hand patted her gently on the arm. "Well done!" said he. "I knew both the Delsartes, and I could fancy they had inspired you?"

"You studied in Venice, did you not?" remarked Sardia with the quiet manner of one who knows what will be replied. "Whom did you find there to properly supplement the great Frenchman?"

Sterility of invention was not her fault. "Only his charts and rules, under his son's previous direction," she replied. "I allowed myself to think of nothing else whatever. I devoted myself to study for months," and she turned to the examination of the plaque.

"And your object?" queried Helen. "Did you mean to teach?"

"To cultivate myself," she answered scornfully. "That

is just like you New Englanders. You must always make a practical use of everything. I presume it seems absurd to you to wish to become cultured for one's own sake. You think, perhaps, that if I study the dramatic art, my object should be to go upon the stage, and make money. That only is consistence here. I prefer to be inconsistent!" and her lip curved to an unmistakable sneer.

"But would it not be very sweet to have an object outside of one's self after all?" said Helen, gently ignoring her manner. "To share the delights of culture seems to me a very high object. Sympathetic natures are so few, self-centred ones so many. And you with your intense personality might give such exquisite pleasure by imparting what you may have gained. I think, perhaps, you wrong us when you attribute a mercenary or practical desire in everything. But there is a terrible lack of expression of which an Italian may well complain. We are exclusive of the individual. We give to the world insipid generalities."

"The American is notorious for spending money right and left. Generous with worldly goods, and free with gold, we hug the wealth of our own natures tight to ourselves, and hold our best ideas as if contact with others were contamination. What true conversation do we have here?"

"We are diffident," said Guy. "That is one reason."

Every one shouted, "A Yankee diffident! A Yankee shy! Who ever heard of such a thing! Well, that is delicious!" they exclaimed amidst universal laughter.

"It is a fact," he replied doggedly, "nevertheless. The American may talk and brag and bluster and splurge a great deal; but after all, down in his heart he is as retiring and diffident as a shy child. I mean that the very noblest, sweetest, richest impulses and emotions of his complex nature are hidden under this very exterior. The sayings, ' He puts his worst foot foremost,' and ' His tongue is his own worst enemy,' are very true of him, and he too often covers the delicacies of his soul with a crust of crudeness and folly. It is the crisis that proves the American. Then his stability appears. Then he rings true!"

"Our history proves that, I think," remarked Charlie Vane. "But on an average we mutely plod through life, seldom if ever showing out our souls even to our own."

"There is still an English strain in us," laughed Ralfe. " I am not surprised that Miss Visonti, or any foreigner, should consider the American people purely practical. Why, even our very grief we hold in check! We think it unmanly, if when to our lips is pressed the bitterest draught, we let the tears flow! To make a scene were dreadful. To let the true natural emotion vent itself in appreciative sobs or laughter, in glad speeches or sympathetic applause, were to be pronounced green, countrified, verdant, and unsophisticated!"

"Another thing! We exclude from our conversation all that hints of Heaven. Religion has become nothing but an argument. We do not talk of it to men as we pray it to God. We do not confess that we pray at all, — or, if we do, it is with a tone of apology. All that is sweet and quick within us, we cover with the silks of form and velvets of ceremony, or secrete under a brusque indifference, a rough witticism, or a rigid silence. How much of Eden we lose daily!"

As they talked, all had moved slowly out of the room, excepting Ralfe and Sybil, who still remained; the one lying on the lounge by the breezy vine-embowered window, the other still leaning against the richly draped portrait of Delsarte. She spoke in a cheerfully indifferent tone of the execution, coloring and likeness, and having settled it to her satisfaction, glanced unconcernedly over her shoulder and said, —

"By the way, you can do me a little favor if you choose."

Ralfe flushed with pleasure.

"I shall be charmed," said he.

Sybil laughed.

"Does it confuse you?" she questioned shrewdly; "that is what you always say when you are annoyed!"

"On the contrary. What can I do, what may I do to serve you?"

"Lend me some money," she answered, dropping her eyes. And then raising them and looking straight at him, "I must have it, or I would not ask."

Ralfe felt his whole heart flow out to her in sympathy. The bluntness, the straightforwardness of the request, must cover the keenest sensitiveness, the deepest humiliation. He instantly took out his purse and handed it to her, and then scratched his signature on a blank check.

She daintily toyed with the purse, shook out a gold piece or two in her hand, pulled out some bills, and selecting four, shut the purse nicely and handed it back to him saying, —

"This will do, thanks."

She had taken four one-hundred-dollar bills. He had drawn five hundred the day before, and had used but little.

"How fortunate that I could do you this trifling service!" he said, in a self-congratulatory tone, "I am not always so lucky!"

She passed along to where some of the guests were standing in various costumes, awaiting the carriages to take them on their usual morning jaunts. Some were bound for fishing, some for shopping, one or two for the sea-bath, and Helen was already equipped for a long promised horseback ride with Sardia, who stood holding her horse, not trusting the groom to place her in the saddle. From one of the great overflowing urns, Sybil gathered a bunch of glowing scarlet geranium whose pungent odor seemed to suit her mood, and after waving them all a graceful adieu, slowly returned to the library, where Ralfe still reclined in the soft, dim, morning light, sifted through myriads of leaves. Coming softly behind his couch and bending over him, she repeated musingly, —

"How much of Eden we lose daily!"

Ralfe, who had tremblingly awaited this meeting, was filled with so intense an excitement that he remained silent and motionless. It seemed to him as if the culmination of his life were reached; as if the crest of the topmost wave were rolling over him. All previous existence in instantaneous panorama rushed across his soul's vision, only to make this moment the seeming end and aim of all.

She moved her dark, flower-like face a little nearer, pressing the blood-red blossoms to her breathing bosom, and fixed her eyes full upon him. Those eyes, deepening, expanding, glowing, suddenly grew liquid with unshed tears. He raised his arms with a yearning, eager gesture, and in an ecstasy too deep for words, drew her throbbing heart close to his own.

"At last!" they mutually murmured.

Then dropping on her knees as if exhausted, her arm close about his head, her soft, magnetic fingers twined in his curls, the thrills of her fervent touch flooding him with tropical languor and fire, his heart in a resistless torrent poured out its long-pent worship in distracted sentences, exclamations, fantastic love-words : — the depths of his whole self-contained nature breaking up and yielding inevitably to the spell. From her seemed to fall distilled the charm which mocked the beauty or attainments of all other women ; his thirsty being drank its nectar and became intoxicated with its joy. She sank back breathless, on the low seat by his side, and hid her face in the crushed and broken blossoms as if their scarlet should indicate her shame. But he had no thought of shame or fear, duty or obligation.

"I love you, I love you!" was all he could think or say.

"I have had joys of the thought of Death so often, oh, so often!" she said in a low, tremulous voice, "but I can never think of Death again, save with hate."

"But if he came with me?" he answered eagerly, with all the insistence on extremes of a lover.

"With you!" and she met his gaze with a flashing eye. "I could enslave him. We would live and love forever."

"Tell me, darling," said he, calming himself a little, and taking her hands closely in his trembling palms, "what does this all mean? Why are we separated? Why are not you my wife? What fatal thing has made this barrier between us?"

She suddenly laughed in scornful bitterness. "A wedding ring," said she.

"It might have been yours," he answered, looking strangely into her eyes.

"It *might* have been!"

Her tone had a subtle significance, a hint of some possibility which his intuition caught with lightning quickness. He leaped to his feet, and raising her with a swift movement, held her straight before him, the slight physical separation seeming to be like an interval of time in which he could fully comprehend the true meaning of his thoughts. He looked away and up and out in his spirit, and for an instant high and pure as an

angel shone the clear, calm face of Helen. But the eyes
of his body rested on the seductive, pleading, commanding beauty of Sybil Visonti. Clasping her again with
fierce, defiant grasp, he hid her head in his bosom and,
holding her as if he could never let her go, almost cried
out, " It *shall* be yours! We will be robbed no longer."
An eloquent silence followed, filled with a sense of jubi-
lant heroism for him, a triumphant diplomacy for her.

She had won by neither persuasion, threat, nor promise. She had not even exercised pathos. It had been
fine workmanship. She had neither invited nor denied.
Her vanity, which forever had held a mirror up in front
of her own intellectual subtleties, gave back a satisfactory show of that art which was "an underlying unity"
of her being.

"And do you say to me that henceforth I shall be no
longer lonesome, no longer pine and die in hungering
after you ? " Sybil breathed at last, releasing herself, and
gently drawing him beside her on the couch.

"Oh, this terrible interval, this crushing, devouring,
burning past, of nights of sighs, of tears, — worse, a
thousand times worse, since irresistibly attracted to this
house, I have dared to face your possible displeasure, to
brave your very hatred and scorn just to look in your
face, to know you were near, although — hers ! Ralfe,
Ralfe, can you realize it ? Can you see how even I,
I in my abandonment could throw off my very womanhood and bear the pangs of sight, hearing, touch, in
seeming indifference ? I am tired, worn, dead with this
frightful concealment, this pressing down of my real
feelings. I could not have borne it longer. When you
were ill I tried to go away and stay forever. I said to
myself in unspeakable bitterness that should you die,
she would be the one to take your parting breath; and
should you live, what hope ? I would go then in the

very crisis of my anguish, and hugging my secret to my own breast, let it tear my soul from my body if it would. But I could not. Away from you was greater torture than to be near you. I bound the mask across my face again — but it is past. You will never bid me wear it to you again."

"Marvellous woman!" he whispered. "Can it be possible you love me so? And I! How many times have I lavished on dumb, insensate paper the assurances which I longed with aching heart to give you! As I have thought of you, I seemed to leap towards you. My spirit seemed to leave my body. I flew to embrace you, to take your dear brow — so — between my hands, and begin to kiss you from your darling little curls to your dear feet. I have actually felt my arms around you. I could not curb my imagination. No words can express the surging sea of love which has always flowed to you, surrounded you, swept you along its life-giving current. I could have hailed Love out of the sky to bid him fly on the wings of the wind to bathe you in my caresses, to give your sense the fragrance of a thousand sighs, your eyes the light of a life of smiles. And when in your radiance you came here under my roof, when the very atmosphere was impregnated with the delight of your presence, and I saw you move about in the place where I had meant you to be my queen, I felt as if in a dream — an ecstatic dream which the least movement might shatter, the least word put to flight. Longing for a moment alone with you, I still avoided it, for I knew not what lay beneath your apparent indifference. Your seeming coldness cut me to the quick; your pleasantries with others hurt my pride; your very smile was a mystery too sweet to fathom. Ah, how impossible it is to judge by the hints of one's surface life what lies deep and seething within the soul! With what a history of struggle, pain, hope, fear, trust, suspicion, and a thousand other strong emotions should I overwhelm you, if I should pour forth the fulness of my heart!"

"My true life, too, is always within," she answered, tallying with his mood, "and always how solitary! But in you I shall ever find a friend, a companion, another soul like my own, strong and rich with emotions, exalted in intellectual pursuit, noble in feeling. Oh, promise me that I may rest in you; that in you I shall find that protection, that chivalry which will permit me to battle no longer with the world, but hide me safe from petty misconception, cruel criticism — all human ills! Oh! to be hidden in the depths of an ever-present love!"

Intoxicated with her pleading helplessness, there was nothing which Ralfe was not willing to do or sacrifice to make her happy. His very chivalry aroused him to promise her his devoted protection. Wooing her with words whose eloquence seemed to spring with inspiration from his lips, with but the lightest touches he sketched a future which great wealth should render possible with comparative ease. And she with softest suggestions, and childlike innocent preferences, painted in the picture with colors caught from her own vivid imagination. Nothing should be done unwisely, nothing unadvisedly. They would bask in the sweet sunshine of a mutual understanding through the long bright days of summer; and when all his affairs were quietly arranged and some legal settlements should be gradually accomplished, by which at last he should be free, — free from a bondage which a blind, inevitable necessity had caused him to assume, — they would go away, far from the society which was as nothing to their love, and finding some beautiful retreat beneath foreign skies, forget that they had ever suffered or been parted. Suddenly confronting an unanswered doubt, he exclaimed, —

"But, darling, even now I know not how this terrible mistake came about! Why did you return my letter of proposal in that harsh fashion — torn open, and without one word of reply?"

"What letter of proposal?" exclaimed Sybil, in evident bewilderment. "When? where?"

"Do you mean to say you never received it?" he cried, springing up and facing her with face white to the very throat

"I never received anything from you," said Sybil, with an air of exhaustion, "but flowers."

"On the day before I left Paris I sent you a letter and a bouquet. I asked you to be my wife. That letter came back to me rudely torn open, and without an answer. What was I to think? I was insulted beyond measure. But oh, I loved you!"

Sybil looked at him with a countenance in which dismay, bewilderment, fright, and agony seemed to struggle.

"Who could have done it? Who could have done it?" she repeated in a helpless way as if faint with intensity of feeling. "What motive? What enemy — I cannot explain it. Destiny ruled it. But if your love had been more steadfast, your trust, your knowledge of me more perfect!" and with this bitter thrust, she laid her head on her arms and sobbed piteously.

Ralfe rushed to his desk, and scattering papers right and left, said, excitedly, —

"Here is the letter! Accept it now! By the Heaven above me, I will make that base wretch suffer to his latest day, who dared to intercept it! I will find him if he lives upon the earth!"

But he could not find the letter. He searched in every nook and cranny, impatiently tossing everything aside; but it was not there. In a quiet rage which made him formidable, he pulled the bell, and ordered

the maid to appear whose duty it was to take care of the
library. But, question her as he might, the trembling
girl declared that she had neither burned nor destroyed
anything whatever. That her mistress had given her
strictest orders never to touch a paper of any kind. He
dismissed her, and going to Sybil, who had passed on
into the conservatory, begged her to pardon him this
strange interruption.

"The letter has mysteriously disappeared," he said.
"I will ask Helen if she knows anything of it."

Sybil looked at him as if shocked.

"Would you tell her of this affair?"

His anger had carried him beyond all remembrance
of the consequences. He saw his mistake and smiled a
grim smile.

"That would be an odd episode," said he.

"Say nothing of it to any one — promise me!"
pleaded Sybil, winding her arms about him. "The past
is past, it is irretrievable. But, dearest, are we not
happy, satisfied, content? What is a letter beside your
lips, — a sheet of paper beside your touch? Love came
late, but, oh Heaven, it has come; and let us welcome it
without a cloud!" And with an ecstatic, joyous, triumphant gesture, she seemed to fling aside all annoyance
and claim her right to him with an embrace. "Let us
from this moment dedicate ourselves to joy. If we
have not entered the temple by the door, we have besieged and taken it, and razed the walls! Henceforth
we will be a law unto ourselves!"

She looked so glorious, her queenly figure surrounded
and caressed by the great tropic blooms about her head
that the magnificent audacity of her speech but added
to the fascination which was so wildly sweet. Governed
by an impulse which he could not control, and led on by
the acquiescence which was half-yielding and half-coy,

he madly pledged himself to schemes and proposals which even half an hour of sober reason would have taught him were wholly beneath him, yet under the charm of her alluring tongue took on the hues of honor, chivalry and right. In the midst of their fondest plans, the swift feet of horses were heard cantering up the lawn. With accomplished ease Sybil broke away from Ralfe's detaining hand. With a glowing look, full of unutterable attraction, she turned to go; but suddenly grew white with the intensity of her purpose.

"We are one?" she said, solemnly closing her hand over his.

"One forever."

"Come what may?"

"Be it death itself."

"And meantime, silence?"

"Silence and faith."

"Silence and faith," she repeated, just disappearing when Helen's voice was heard in the hall.

When she was safely in her room, she made a low, reverent bow to nothing; and with a lip of sardonic derision, uttered again the proud words of that morning: "It is the crisis that proves the American. Then it is that he always rings true!"

CHAPTER XIX.

A WEDDING RING.

" No hinge, nor loop to hang a doubt on."

Othello.

WHILE Ralfe sat with his head bowed on his hands, trying to calm the tempest of his thought, Helen softly entered, holding in her hand a pretty ring. Something in his attitude and in his face when he raised it, pale and haggard with the conflict of conscience with inclination, startled her. Her soul found within itself a re-echoing cry, and she advanced white and trembling to his side. He grasped her hands and looked into her great, wistful eyes as he would into those of an angel sent to save him. Oh, the speaking silence of those eyes! What a depth of pure, sweet, holy tenderness they contained! How clean and fair was the look, mingled with an anxious and troubled questioning. Her gentle voice, so vibrant yet so melodious, rich with the harmony of her perfectly attuned nature, seemed to him like a healing, cooling breeze after fever.

"You are sad, comrade!"

Sad? But a few moment ago he believed himself in the wildest delirium of joy! He had clasped to his heart the woman whose very name enslaved him. Sad? He had believed himself trembling with bliss, enraptured with mad happiness! But grasping his wife's hands, looking into her sympathetic face, feeling the heaven of her soul touching the hell of his, and lifting him out of himself into her purer sphere, he shuddered, and drawing her nearer and nearer, clung to her as if he were drowning; and laying his head against her arm, shut his eyes, and with quivering lip answered, " Yes, comrade; I am sad."

They remained thus for a moment without speaking. his hot temple throbbing against her round, white wrist, and his excited brain thinking, "Oh, if she only loved me she could so easily save me! I feel so helpless. If she only loved me! But she pities me."

While Helen yearned to kiss the dear, bowed head, longingly saying to herself, " How I would give my very blood to comfort him if he would have it ! — but, he will not."

He could not speak and tell her of the terrible battle he was fighting. Could he tell his wife, " Sybil Visonti seems to overpower reason, conscience, habit, principle, every noble feeling of my being. and fells me helpless at her feet, a mere animal with an animal's uncontrolled instincts! I crave her, and seem to enjoy paradise in the very touch of her dress. I am lost to everything but her beauty, her magnetism, her glowing eyes!" He shook himself and rose to his feet. "Did you wish for anything, dearest ? " he said gently.

Alas, that "dearest." It was the first time he had ever used it, but she wished he had left it unsaid. She felt it put her far away, refused her sympathy. She saw he meant to be strong alone, and in her tender love. she wondered at his sudden assumption of indifference to his own sorrow, whatever it might be. But it would have been impossible for her to intrude on an emotion which he strove to throw off.

"He will never really trust me," she thought despairingly, then answered, " Yes, I wished you to do a little errand for me when you drive down town. Will it be too much trouble ? "

“To serve you is a favor, always, Helen. Certainly I will do it. What is it?”

“I wish this ring mended. I loaned it to Sybil a week or two ago, but as to-day is the anniversary of my mother’s wedding, and this was her wedding-ring, I requested her to let me have it again in remembrance. When I put it on, however, I found that the largest diamond was loose, and I dare not wear it until the setting is fastened. Can you take it for me to Griffin? He has a little shop, but he is reliable.”

“Can I find the place?” he said, tucking the ring into his purse.

“Oh, Hewston knows. He has been there,” she answered carelessly, and with a smile, turned away.

He appreciated her delicacy. “There is one thing,” said he to himself, “she is the least curious of women. How I hate that invariable, ‘What is the matter?’ which most people ask. They must know all about it before they can even say ‘I am sorry.’” And catching up his hat, he went out to give orders for his cart.

The morning was deliciously fresh and brilliant. He felt better as he drove Bocket and King Cute at a rattling pace, the leader tossing his silky mane and curveting like a skittish colt. Hewston directed him to a small shop set in the corner of a busy, narrow, dirty little thoroughfare in the old part of the town. Throwing him the reins, Ralfe stepped in, to find a gray-haired old man, beautifully gotten up as to linen, polishing with his own hands a tiny lace pin.

“I have a ring here that needs mending a little,” said Ralfe pleasantly, after the usual greeting. “One of the stones appears to be loose.”

“Why, that is odd,” said the jeweller, “I did not think my setting would last so short a time,” examining it closely. “The lady must have hit it a hard knock.”

"Your setting ? " said Ralfe, a little surprised. "Have you mended this ring before ? "

"I set these stones for a young lady only a few days ago."

"Set them ? " repeated Ralfe, surprised indeed at his phrase. "Were not these diamonds set as they are now ? "

"The diamonds were, but these are the paste stones I set in their places."

"Paste ! " exclaimed Ralfe, thunderstruck.

"Why, yes," said he complacently, "and I declared to her that only an expert could detect them. Now I am sure she will be satisfied," and he chuckled with pleasure. "You know," he went on confidentially, "a great many ladies do that sort of thing nowadays. Of course, as she sent you with the ring, she has no objection to your knowing, though of course it is always understood that these little transactions are kept secret. Probably she wanted to test these pretty deceptions," rubbing them smartly, and evidently pleased to see how completely they had deceived the bearer.

Ralfe had somewhat recovered his outer calmness. "I don't think she would care to have you mention it to any one else. Did she leave her name ? "

"Let's see. No, come to think of it, she didn't. She only left her initials, S. V."

"Yes those are the initials of my residence, 'Spray View,'" said Ralfe quickly. "I suppose you bought the diamonds ? " he added carelessly, hazarding a guess at what had become of them.

"Yes. Three hundred and twenty-five dollars was fair, wasn't it ? "

Ralfe felt as if he should choke. The air became stagnant. He clinched his hand to steady himself.

"Is that what you paid her ? "

"Yes, sir. She was a good judge of stones. She wanted three hundred and seventy-five dollars, but finally took up with my offer."

For a moment Ralfe felt as if he must rush out of the place to breathe. He controlled himself, however, and thought, "I must not arouse suspicion. I must bargain for them or he will suspect. What if he has sold them!"

"Did she give you any orders to retain them?" said he. "Had she an intention of buying them back again?"

"Not at all, she drove a sharp bargain for them, and sold them outright."

"I suppose you would not sell them for the same money?" he queried, carelessly.

"Not if I know it!"

"Then you have them?"

"Yes, I haven't done any thing with them."

"What will you sell them for?" feeling all the time as if he were bargaining for his own honor, his life, with an unspeakable disgust and shame.

"I don't know as I want to sell. Diamonds are on the rise. I think I shall set them as a cluster pin."

"Wouldn't you take three hundred and seventy-five dollars for them, unset?"

"Well, no, I don't think I could exactly do that."

"What will you take?" said Ralfe sharply, fumbling impatiently in his note-book. "Come, come, set a price. I will buy them and have them set right back in their places if you make it reasonable; if not I shall go elsewhere," and he picked up Helen's ring and began to put it in his purse. "Oh, if he would say five hundred dollars and be done with it," he thought, chafing at the man's slowness — for what sum would he not gladly have paid to once get away from that place!

"I'll take four hundred dollars," said the dealer at last, looking shrewdly at his customer.

"Very well!" with a sigh of relief. "Here is my check; and I want that ring done by five o'clock at latest. It cannot be so great a matter to exchange these stones. Send the ring to Mrs. Fielding, Spray View."

The loose diamonds, which had now been produced, sparkled in a ray of sunshine which fell across the little velvet pad.

"I rely on you to use the very stones that were in it before," said Ralfe sharply, looking at their modest glitter closely.

"I've been in this place twenty-five years," said Mr. Griffin proudly, "and I never had any trouble yet."

"Pardon me," said Mr. Fielding, going, "it was not for the value of the diamonds. It was for their associations. It was a wedding-ring."

CHAPTER XX.

TWO HEARTS.

"Love took up the harp of Life, and smote on all its chords with
    might;
Smote the chord of Self, that, trembling, passed in music out of
    sight."

Tennyson.

On starting out for their ride that morning, Sardia
and Helen were both in the gayest spirits. She, having
been so constantly confined to the house, had been longing for a gallop in the fresh air, and her guest, who seldom had a moment's *tête à tête* with her, felt that air to
be a breath from Paradise, as they gently cantered away.
Their road stretched inland, back from the frequented
path by the sea, and after two or three miles they found
themselves in quiet woodland ways, crossing occasionally some brook with its willow embowered bridge, or
winding in and out among the pine-clad mounds and
hollows of a rolling country. The fresh smells of the
morning rose like an incense, and, still undisputed by
the sun, light wreaths of mist hung waveringly over
the marshes, tipping the grasses with pearly drops and
making the wide-stretched cobwebs like fairy tents hung
with opals. They cantered a long time without speaking, she drinking in the glory of the early day, and he
drinking in the glory of her beauty, her companionship,
her presence. As they turned into a nook-like bridle
path, whose edges were dotted with tufts of earliest
blue asters, — that rarely modest flower which like a

maiden's eye looks natural love into your own, — a flight
of bluejays made the sun-gilt trees a windy rustle, with
notes and whirs of wings all mixed, and flashing snowy
tips of tails and crests anod!

Both stopped to listen until their strange wild notes
broke the mist far away in a wooded valley.

"I was much interested in a sentence of John Fiske's,
the other day," said Helen, looking around with a comprehensive glance. "He said, 'The material is but the
temporary relations, otherwise unknown, between ourselves and the Infinite Deity.' Yes! to give us an
individual enjoyment He placed us in natural relations,
and then, — how He manifests Himself! How He shows
Himself! How He speaks himself out to eye and ear,
taste and smell and touch! How in that robin's cry He
warbles 'Here am I!' How in those nodding plumes of
wind-bowed grasses He sighs softly, 'Here I am, dear!'
How He comes and floods our senses with those locust
blossoms, murmuring 'Here is your Father, little ones!'
and in that sweep of clouds across the serene heavens,
how He bends down His face to utter the same appeal
for recognition, 'Children, look higher! I am above
you!' He manifests himself in temporary relations to
the finite senses in so grand a way, what do you think
His manifestations will be, — His permanent manifestations, in spirit, not in matter?"

Sardia answered with a smile of perfect sympathy.

"There will be no limit, no end," he said. "The imagination fails to picture it. But oh! Helen, I am glad
we know it beforehand, — many do not."

Helen took off her hat and let the breeze blow her soft
hair in fluffy curls from her flushed face.

Sardia smiled, and dismounting, came and patted the
neck of her horse, looking up at her with so dear, so
exquisite an expression, that she stooped forward and
softly touched his shoulder.

"How good you are," she murmured.

He gave her a grateful glance, but turned and slowly gazed about him, as if to lose nothing of so sweet a spot. Then looking again at her with a thrill of deep joy in his voice, he said softly, —

"Such little scenes in one's life are the rhymes and songs amidst the blank verse of the drama. They come into the melancholy solidity of every-day existence, as some of the refrains in the tragedies of Shakespeare, or take one's fancy a-roaming like the fairy shows of ' Midsummer Night's Dream.'

'I know a bank whereon the wild thyme grows,
Where oxlips and the nodding violet blows,'

steals with kindred poesy into the sensitive mind, and leaves an impress of ethereal beauty."

"Our home has been very sweet this summer, has it not ? " said Helen, allowing her dewy eyes to rest wistfully on his face. "Never in all my life have I been so situated! Never so free from criticism, never so unshackled from the heavy load of conventionalism, — for after all, our party are so delightfully Bohemian, that we think but little of rites and rules! I feel at ease to do, dress, laugh, think, read, play, sing, shout at my own sweet will, — and to my heart's content, and all in an atmosphere of tenderness, good-will and approval, which I find rich with new life! Every one is so kind to me — so considerate! Even Ralfe is kind. Is this freedom the gift of marriage ? "

His cheek paled as he answered, —

"You, grateful for kindness, who make life a joy to every one about you ? Why, who could have the courage to be unkind, or cold, or — Helen, I cannot bear it. I cannot bear to see those unshed drops in your eyes! Yes, to me your home has been the dearest spot of earth! To me the very air you breathe, the ground you tread, the object you touch, are sacred. Your every mood appeals to my soul with articulate meanings. I exult in your joy, and feel my whole being droop when sadness clouds your sweet countenance. I thought not to tell you, — I have striven not to tell you, dear, of what you still must have read so plainly — but — O God, I suffer, and for once am wholly unmanned."

"No, never that," said she, looking into his face with an air of perfect faith, "I know your soul too well for that."

"But I love you!" he answered, returning her gaze with cheeks so white and eyes so strained with anguish that he seemed transformed and ghost-like.

Her own blanched with intense pity.

"Take me down," said she, "and let us tell our whole hearts out."

"I cannot, I dare not," he answered, shutting his teeth. "I shall clasp you to my heart if you do. Get down here, dearest, — I cannot touch you!"

She leapt lightly on to the fallen log, and went to a softly-bedded spot, where, casting aside her hat, she sat waiting for him to come. In a moment or two he flung himself on the ground and buried his face in the cool green moss.

"I have known from the first, dear friend, that you loved me, and you have known from the first that I love Ralfe. Can any one in this world more deeply appreciate what you feel than I? Are there any words you could use to me that I should not use to him? Yet shall this divide us? It has not. All these weeks your heart and mine have been close together in a bond of mutual pain. Our union is a friendship of unspeakable sadness; but it is all we can hope for, since it is our destiny to love separately. Oh, Sardia, be greater than love itself, — be my true friend. Turn love into Christ-like abnegation! You are capable of it, — you will do it!"

"Why do you love him so?" he cried desperately.

"Why do you love me so?" asked she.

"Why?" and his tone seemed to concentrate every grace, and glory, and virtue of womanhood and angel-hood in the one syllable. "Helen, do not! It is almost blasphemous to yourself. What soul that reads the purity of yours can fail to love you?"

"That is just what I say in my secret heart — of him," she murmured wistfully.

"Yet he does not love you!" The retort sprang to his lips involuntarily, but he checked it in time. Should he be deliberately cruel because she was unconsciously so? "Helen," he only said wearily, "what are we to do? It seems to me, dear, that we are the only ones who can unwind this tangled skein. If you knew how willing I am to help you — if you dreamed that even though I love you so deeply — I still — I shall not allow that to make any difference — why, I stumble in my speech like a school-boy! I beg your pardon!"

"You mean to say, that no matter how you may suffer yourself, you desire my happiness most and will sacri-fice your own love to give me content. Is not that it?"

"Yes — but how did you know?"

"That is just what I have planned to do myself — for Ralfe," said she gently. "I read love, your great love, straight out of my own heart. What I can do for love's sake, you will do, noble, sublime soul that you are! Do I not know that? Have I not trusted it? Do I not lean on you as I would lean on my Saviour, were He here to speak to me? Is it possible you think I do not understand you, when not an hour passes that my thought does not leap out to you and feel your sustaining thought respond ? Mine is no light feeling for you, dear, kind one ! If I were to choose the wide world over for a man I could trust to the end, it would be you !"

He heard these words with the glow stealing warmly back into his cheek, the fire into his eyes, the tenderness and resignation into his heart. " How can I thank you, best of all women ! But trust me now. Open your very soul to me. I feel that at this moment a crisis has been reached in all our lives. We must be brave and meet it."

"Sybil Visonti ? " Helen half whispered.

" It is enough. Her name indicates it all. Must she triumph ? "

" But *is* it triumph ? Is it not rather justice ? " questioned Helen. " You know they loved before he saw me; and some slight misunderstanding, some pique, some little estrangement, threw him into my — into his present position. Is it right ? Have I not robbed her of a thousand things ? Can you blame her if she looks upon me as her enemy, and upon him as her natural and proper mate ? How can she help doing her best to keep his love ? Remember her Southern nature, her fiery temperament. His love is all she can keep. I have taken his name ; have become his legal wife ; the mistress of his home; and how did I deserve it or win it ? He did not know me. He had no time to study me. He was almost forced to marry me. It was a question of money, — money !" and the disgust which came into her voice showed how truly she despised it. " Honestly, can you blame her ?"

" Perhaps it is the money which she really envies you ? " said he.

" No !" jumping to her feet. " If I thought that ! But it cannot be. How could she expect to gain his money now? What could be her object? Oh, she loves him. It is nothing else."

"Yet when he had a contagious disease she left him! Helen, would you follow the man you loved into his new home, and try to entice him away from his bride, whether he loved her or not? Don't answer me. So base a thought never entered your mind, or could enter it. But that is precisely what she is doing. She means to rob you of your husband's love, then of your husband's person, and then of your husband's money. She is unscrupulous. There is a passage in her life which she conceals from every one. The Princess Menshikoff knows it, and if I choose to ask her I can know it too. This secret once known might ruin her, so madame has hinted, and when she hinted she frowned like fate. Shall I find out and tell you what it is, that you may guard yourself and Ralfe, perhaps save Ralfe from social and moral destruction?"

"Certainly not!" said Helen decidedly. "Miss Visonti is my guest. Her past is her own. I have nothing to do with it, and have no curiosity about it. If she is evil, God will requite her ill deeds. I will not play the spy. I do not believe in bad means to good ends."

Sardia's face beamed with pride. "How impossible it is to strike a false note in you!" he murmured.

But she did not heed him. "What I wish to do is this. If Sybil is worthy of Ralfe, and their love is a noble and lasting one, I wish them to belong to each other. I wish to annul this marriage which to him is a horrible bondage, and placing her hand in his, wish them God's blessing, and then — go away somewhere and — die." And she broke into passionate sobs.

As she bowed her head to hide her tear-stained cheeks, and the silken hair half fell in flossy folds over her shapely neck, Sardia bent over it, and then taking a little lock in his hand, kissed it. It was a silent benediction.

"Dear heart," he said, when she had become quiet, "most people would laugh at such a Quixotic notion. They would tell you it was impossible, romantic, absurd, ridiculous. But they would not understand you as I do" —

"Then you think I am right?" she exclaimed eagerly, heroism like a flame starting into her looks.

But swifter still than that, a terrible temptation now assailed Sir Sardia. "What if I should counsel her to follow out this wild dream?" he thought. "Supposing she were encouraged to free him and free herself! Where then would she fly for protection, sympathy, comfort, — love? Where but to me?"

To her surprise, instead of answering her, he walked away and sat down on the log, dropping his face into his hands. How could she know what a fierce struggle went on in that keenly smitten soul! How could she dream that behind those hiding hands was a face growing paler and paler as devil after devil of temptation held up before him the bliss, the rapture, the joy of holding this woman in his longing embrace and lavishing on her a love which should drive the thought of Ralfe forever out of her mind? The silence became oppressive. The impatient stamping of the horses, the rubbing of their bridles against the trees, the impertinent hum of a vagrant bee, sounded to both so loud as to be startling. With that strange comprehension of trifles which comes in the midst of supreme emotions, they even noticed the soft rustle of the wind through the long grasses.

"He believes I should do it," Helen was thinking, "and is suffering in anticipation of what I must bear," while her spirits grew even more sad.

"Sustain me, Thou Righteousness!" his heart was crying within him.

At last, raising his head, and looking about in a dazed fashion, as if not sure it was light, he answered slowly, "Forgive me, dear, for keeping you waiting, but I have been trying to think wisely for you. I admire, you cannot know how much, the grand, the generous impulse which leads you to plan so strange a method of righting what you deem a wrong, and if we finally conclude it is a wrong, I am not sure but I should say 'Do as you think best.' But let us be very sure. I sometimes think that no marriage is in vain. It seems to me that God does rule the lives of His children. It may not seem so — it often seems impossible that anything of God could exist in an unhappy marriage, — but, after all, is it not ourselves who make or mar the opportunities which He puts into our lives? If every marriage were made the best of by both, would there ever be a divorce? So in faith that He knew, who separated them and joined you to him, what was best for all, let us be very sure, very certain, that you would be wise in putting the bond asunder. It is Ralfe's best good that you wish to secure, — not so much his happiness as his highest good. As yet we do not know that she is capable of giving him that, or that she is worthy of intimate association with him at all. Will you not wait until you prove her so ?"

These words, spoken painfully, slowly, as if dragged from the very depths of his being, fell on Helen's ears with a promise of infinite comfort. With what a sense of relief, of blessed respite, of almost peace, she thought them over, language can hardly express.

"How you comfort me, how you content me!" she exclaimed, going to his side and lifting up a grateful countenance which sweetly spoke her thanks. " What a true, wise friend you are. How always strong, good and restful you are to me! How I can depend upon you! Do you know what an inspiration you have just given me ?

How hope has blazed into my heart again like a beautiful vision? You seemed for a moment like a great, grand angel who had vanquished something evil. I believe you did." And with childlike openness she looked with rapt gaze into his eyes.

"Earth is no place for you, darling. You see too clearly, and seeing so always brings such pain. Yes, I vanquished something, for I remembered your words: 'Do I not lean on you as I would lean on my Saviour, were He here to speak to me?' I am no Judas."

She could not understand him, but as they slowly mounted and rode homeward, she often glanced at his face, stern and set in a melancholy over which would occasionally flit a tender smile as he looked at her, with a strange sense of loss, as if some change in him had drawn him nearer Heaven and a little more away from earth. Her sensitive nature, touched to the core by his devotion and full of all womanly longing to comfort, soothe and bless him, suffered more in this homeward ride for him, than for herself or all the world beside.

As they neared the town, he suddenly stopped his horse and drawing hers close beside him, took her hand.

"Let us go on patiently as we have been," said he, "believing all will be well in the end. If this woman is unworthy of Ralfe's love; if she simply awakens passion for the sake of the possibilities of his leaving you and giving her a life of luxury and ease, you may depend upon it, she will fail; for she is certain to make missteps which will discover her plans and blast her character in his eyes. No evil purpose can be carried on, week after week, without the betrayal of character. Ralfe is only blinded. He lives in the clouds. Let her show him some trait which will shock his sense of honor, and he will awaken with a start. Besides, I am convinced that there are adversaries on her track with which she will be powerless to contend. As for me, I have been thinking during the last mile or two, what it is best for me to do. I had an impulse to go away, yes, to the uttermost parts of the earth; but I believe that would be cowardly. You do not wish me to leave you now, in the midst of trouble? I will stay right by you, Helen. You may need me. You know me too well now, not to feel that this is all. I shall not pain you after this with words of love. But Helen, remember, I love you. That is as immutable as the laws of God. And knowing that, trust it."

The countenance of beautiful gratitude, faith and affection she turned to him, shook his whole being with a pang that again rendered him silent, but when she softly bent over her saddle and kissed his white ungloved hand with her warm, fresh lips, a thrill of life, a revivification of strength and heavenly peace crept sweetly through his veins.

CHAPTER XXI.

DISCOVERED.

I waive the quantum o' the sin,
The hazard of concealing;
But och! it hardens a' within,
And petrifies the feeling!

Burns.

THERE is an unbought grace of feeling which some rare women possess for their own sex, to which even the word chivalry could not add dignity. And yet no other so roundly expresses the delicacy of honor which borders on generous pride — the fear of intrusion or self-assertion which modestly waives its own rights; or the swift and gracious acknowledgment of another's claims or desires. Not all have that sense of justice "imbued with sanctity of reason," which can brook the advancement of a rival.

Having touched the sublime sharp summit of her own passion, and reached that noble altitude from which she could readily survey her situation, Helen, by her inherent sense of righteousness, determined, unconsciously, her manner of action. She was incapable of double-mindedness, and being sure that her husband was worthy of the highest happiness, she awaited whatever issue might arise, with the sole purpose of furthering his joy. Few could endure with equanimity the presence of the woman who daily robbed them of the love they craved. But, with an invulnerable sense of justice, Helen recognized the fact that this affection had arisen long before she had known her husband, and acknowledged with self-abasement and bitter regret, that she had inopportunely, although so innocently, stepped between two lovers, who doubtless might easily have explained some unfortunate misconception. The more deeply she loved, herself, the more humble she grew, and at times her position as the unloved wife of a man whose whole heart yearned for another, and that other her most intimate friend, was well-nigh intolerable. To Sybil, whom personally she had loved and admired from her childhood, she gave a sweet patience and tender courtesy of manner which would have touched a generous heart to its depths. It was as if she flung her very spirit with compassion and determination around these two, as a protective and salutary power. She equalized their loves with her own, and inevitably made a divine rapport of true gallantry between herself and them which penetrated their souls without presenting itself in words to their minds. Ralfe instinctively recognized her as his silent ally without being able to give a reason for what, in fact, was intuition. Sybil felt it also, but with an opposition and repulsion which sprang from her egotistic pride. It was the natural hatred of a dark and narrow intention for the air-sweetness of wide, clear, high and open motive. But with a certain consistent inconsistency, she enjoyed and accepted all the practical favors heaped upon her by Helen's stintless hand; nor did she scruple to make her wishes known by a hundred artistic methods, any one of which would have appeared the simplest and most casual observation to any one not on the alert to please. Realizing with the intensest sensitiveness the possibility of what Sybil might have commanded had Ralfe's wishes been carried out, there was hardly a fancy which her friend manifested for anything she possessed that Helen did not quietly gratify, — and to Sybil's secret amazement and contempt, she often gave more than was requested.

On the afternoon of the day when she had desired Ralfe to take the ring to be mended, she was in her own room dressing, when Sybil, as was her frequent custom, tapped at the door, and at the same moment, Wilson deferentially asked Miss Visonti if madame was in. Helen spoke pleasantly as she opened the door and said, —

"Ah, Wilson, what have you there?"

"A package for you, madame," and bowed himself away, while Sybil cried enthusiastically, —

"Jewelry, I know! Richest gems in smallest cases."

Helen smiled as she unwrapped the tiny box and answered, —

"Nothing new this time. It is only my ring," and took off the cover. On the top lay a narrow paper which proved to be the bill carefully made out and receipted, which Ralfe in his agitation had completely forgotten. Helen read it with a look of astonishment, but said nothing and continued to examine the box. In the midst of the pink cotton was the ring, flashing its well-known gems in a pretty glitter, and beside it a tiny tissue paper contained the paste stones which had filled their places.

Sybil had breathlessly watched the disclosure of her guilt with a face flushing from dark red to gray, and now, convinced that concealment was useless, sprang to Helen's side and dropped gracefully at her feet, hiding her dark head in the drapery of her skirts.

"Oh, do not condemn me, dearest," she half sobbed, half murmured. "How horribly unlucky I am! If you knew, if you knew the terrible necessity which drove me to it! you would not utter a word to scold me. I dared not ask to borrow such a sum, I was too proud to do so; and you know, dear Helen, how miserably small my pittance of an income is. It was only for two or three days. If you had not happened to ask for it, you would never have known anything about it. I was going to have the stones changed myself this very day." As Helen did not reply she looked up pitifully and anxiously into her face, her tear-stained cheeks appealing more than her words. "Do you not believe it? See, see, I have the money, this moment, — oh, I swear to you I only gave security in that way for a few, few days! Here, take it, take it!" and she drew a roll of bills from her purse. "I am so glad I can confess — so glad you found it out. Was it not rather a clever way? But I felt dreadfully anxious, — oh!" rising and throwing up her arms. "I feel as if a weight were off me!"

Some peaches were on the table. She picked one up and began to eat it. Her hostess smiled. In spite of the shock of disgust and displeasure which this unlooked-for confession provoked, she could not help a sense of scornful amusement at the ever-present, ever-dominant self, the "I" of this unscrupulous woman, who, in the very midst of exposure and degradation, could admire herself as clever, and, thinking only of what she felt, cast not a glance on the moral phase of the affair. She had not brushed the tear from her cheek before she had begun to indulge herself. The fruit looked tempting; why should she not eat it?

Helen as yet had not uttered a word, but stood and looked at Sybil, who daintily ate the peach, with a positively nonplussed expression.

She was mechanically holding the money which had been thrust in her hand, and seemed at a loss how to act or answer.

"What is the matter?" said Sybil brightly, looking up with a childish expression from the fruit. "Haven't I explained enough? Haven't I done all I could? I'm sure I have paid for my folly pretty roundly. I hate to cry! You always make such a to-do over any little trifle like that!"

"It is a question of honor moral and legal," said Helen, speaking for the first time.

"Good heavens!" cried Sybil impatiently; "if I hand you the money to pay the bill, what more do you want? What has honor to do with it?"

Her friend gave a little sigh.

"I think," she said slowly and with an air of quiet determination, "that I shall take this money which you offer me, as an equivalent for what has been paid out. It is but fair. I cannot say how sorry I am that you should have been so unfortunately pressed for money as to be obliged to do something so unbecoming. I beg of you henceforth to make me your confidante and tell me plainly of your needs, rather than to resort to such devices. Pardon me, Sybil, but I do not think it clever. I need not tell a person of your intelligence that such an affair could be made very disagreeable for you if practised on any but a friend. Certainly, it would have been better to have trusted me rather than to have risked my confidence. Have I ever refused you anything?"

"No, but you would have refused so large a sum as that," replied Sybil sullenly, looking askance at the money which her friend still held.

Her ingratitude seemed to close a door in Helen's heart. She folded up the bills and put them away.

"My first impulse was to give that back to you," said she, coming close to Sybil and touching her hair gently. "I thought if you had so terrible a necessity as to cause you to sell my diamonds that you still must need it far more than I. But I still have so much confidence in your intention to have replaced the stones, that I will

not dishonor your integrity by so indelicate an act as
to refuse to allow you to stand squarely with yourself
and with me. But if you find yourself again in similar
circumstances, I assure you that you will find me happy
and ready to help you."

Sybil could not withstand this sweet and healthy
consideration which seemed to be emitted in steady
and limitless kindness, yet which calmly preserved the
rightful measure of its way. With a momentary impulse
of admiration she kissed the hand so softly touching
her and murmured, "How God must love you!" but
added to herself as instantaneously, "But I do not!"

A light knock at the door gave her an excuse to
escape from what she mentally termed "no end of a row,"
and she quickly went out through another chamber,
not waiting to see who entered. It proved to be Ralfe,
who had bethought him of the receipt which he feared
the honest jeweller would enclose with the ring. "If
so, Helen will certainly comprehend the whole thing,"
he thought anxiously; and at last he became so troubled
that he could not help trying to ascertain.

It was but seldom that he appeared in Helen's sitting
room, and now he paused hesitatingly on the threshold,
although her voice told him pleasantly to come in. She
approached the door with a brilliant smile lighting her
features. The excitement of the interview had given
her cheeks a flush of divinest rose. He thought he had
never seen her so full of an inexpressible completeness.
She seemed in her place and moved with a perfect balance. Her eyes were at once bright and tender.

He said carelessly, "I wondered if the man had sent
your ring. I remembered that you would like it for
dinner."

"Yes," she replied almost as carelessly, "and I desire
to be Miss Visonti's agent for the nonce, and pay the

bill which you so kindly settled. She has just left me the money. She said it was a mere matter of a day."

"Did you know of it then?" he asked, very much surprised.

"No, not until she told me just now. But I want to thank you from my heart, not only for seeing that my mother's ring should suffer no harm, but for endeavoring to prevent me from knowing my friend's mistake. Of course I was troubled that she had not saved herself an unpleasant experience by borrowing the money of me. I appreciate your delicacy fully."

"The jeweller sent the bill, I suppose? To tell the truth I forgot it. I did not intend you should know anything about it."

Helen smiled with the least touch of sarcasm.

"No, I suppose not! But you cannot escape my gratitude. Here is the money Sybil gave me. It was doubtless a very trying necessity which forced her to this act. She said she was ashamed — too proud to borrow such a sum, and that she certainly intended to replace the stones." And she handed him four one-hundred-dollar notes.

He started as if stung. He instantly recognized them.

"Does she know I did the errand?" he asked in a low voice, looking at the money with a singular expression.

"No. I felt sure that you would not like to pain her by letting her know that her secret had become known to you. Surely it was enough for her to suffer the knowledge that I had discovered it."

He flushed with sudden emotion.

"It is you who deserve gratitude. We both owe you gratitude beyond words." And with a look that she never forgot he suddenly left Helen alone.

"How strange!" thought she, as she stood gazing unconsciously at the closed door, "how strange, that so soon, so very soon after our determination to let things take their own course, this incident should occur! How clearly Sardia reads human nature! What would he say if he knew this! I know; he would repeat, 'God takes care of His children.'" Then softly dropping on her knees, she clasped her hands and uttered, "But, dear Father, she is Thy child too."

CHAPTER XXII.

A VAMPIRE.

> " Beautiful as sweet!
> And young as beautiful!   And soft as young!
> And gay as soft! and innocent as gay!"
>
> *Young.*

> " Find out the cause of this effect;
> Or rather say the cause of this defect,
> For this effect defective comes by cause."
>
> *Hamlet.*

SARDIA stood leaning against an urn of flowers by the great entrance one evening, while Guy by his side idly tapped him on the shoulder. They stood together in that attitude of unconscious confidence which needs no words to betray a mutual respect and affection. They were both watching two ladies who were gently moving over the grass, absorbed in low conversation.

One was Lulu, who was half encircled by the embracing arm of Sybil Visonti, and her cheeks were dotted by two bright hectic spots, while all the rest of her pretty face was unusually pale. Every moment or two she instinctively half thrust away the little dark hand that lay on her hip, yet she was so engaged in conversation that she did not persist. It was a nervous, unconscious movement, evidently not directed by the will.

Sardia suddenly turned a keen questioning glance on Guy and said, "Do you like to see that ?"

Mr. Thorne looked amused and surprised. "Does a man like to look at the woman he loves ?   At two beau-

tiful women displaying their prettiest charms? Oh,
no! of course not," and he laughed.

"If I loved a woman I would take care of her," his
friend said in a cold, slow way.

Guy started up. "Is it chilly?" and he moved towards the house. "I will get a wrap."

"Stay. It is not chilly. Do you believe in animal
magnetism, Guy? The power of one will over another?
If you do not you cannot see those women from the
same standpoint that I do. But is not Lulu thin, excitable, changed? Where is her blithe laugh? I
miss it."

Guy looked troubled. "So do I. Yet I had not
thought of it. And it is I who love her. Sardia, old
fellow, — tell me, out with it. What do you mean?"

"I cannot better answer you than to tell you to
watch. Open your eyes," and he sauntered off.

Guy fell into a deep revery. The soft chatter of the
voices kept up an accompaniment to his thought. He
earnestly compared in his own mind what Lulu had
been in the early summer, and what she was now.

Sardia's few words had reminded him of his own
vague fears, which, strongly accented on the Visonti's
first arrival, had been lulled to rest by contact with
her inscrutable charm, and he now found his darling
brought before him in a new light. She was no longer
the gay, merry, light-hearted, laughing Lulu. She no
longer spent her days in every possible out-door exercise; "wild" over horseback riding; having a craze
for a tricycle; rowing her tiny hands brown and callous;
only too happy when standing the living figure-head of
his jolly sail-boat and glorying in the rough weather or
stiff breezes that tossed her like a plume. Where was
the shout with which she raced down-stairs, and when
softly rebuked for being not quite lady-like, the smiling

pout and coquettish defiance with which she sprang from his detaining arms? Where were the overflowing life, the madcap pranks with which she had assailed him and tortured him, leading him a dance which only made him adore her more and more? Now he found her lying languidly in the library or on the long seats in the summer-house. She refused the beautiful twilight walks so dear to him, she was so tired. She lay back among the cushions of the boat and gazed dreamily across the waves, instead of insisting on minding the wheel. Her sweet temper had thrown out sudden flashes of anger and irritability, — in a moment atoned for, to be sure, by a melancholy little prayer for forgiveness, — why, had he been blind, deaf, dumb? Fool that he was, had it not been for Sardia how long would his soul have been stupidly unmindful and unheeding? He rose from his seat on the step and walked swiftly towards the young women.

"Lulu, I want you," he said sharply.

The Visonti stopped in her walk, and Lulu gazed at him in a sort of unseeing way, as if her mind was so far off that she had not comprehended. For a moment the man and woman looked into each other's eyes with a singular intensity. If she read anything that was in his thoughts, it elicited only defiance in Sybil. She drew her arm closer about Lulu with a sort of possessive pressure and looking softly into her eyes, slowly moved her away, saying gently but significantly, —

"Lulu, *I* want you."

It was a mockery so delicate and so well done that it left Guy standing there, unable to utter a word, although he literally shook from head to foot with a sudden tide of hot yet impotent rage. Yet what could he do? Here were two ladies chatting, and one playfully retained her companion. Was he to murder her on the spot?

He felt like it. He went into the house and to his room, threw off his coat, put his heels on top of a chair-back and smoked. It was a long time before he rejoined the party. He did not know, — why should he? — how in spite of the little episode of her first visit to Sybil's room, Lulu had almost immediately overlooked and forgotten her sudden disgust. The very next day she had been made so conscience-stricken by the extreme kindness of Miss Visonti, and had been so quietly laughed out of her "pretty anger" by her new friend, that she felt she had been absurdly annoyed. Sybil was so exquisitely thoughtful, so delicate, her devotion to Lulu was so unpretending, yet so certain, that it exercised a singular influence, a soft flattery to which her innocent heart yielded with gratitude. She began to know the charm of being sought, — sought persistently, patiently, humbly. She began to feel that her love and friendship to this one woman at least was invaluable, — possessing an exceptional preciousness. She felt that she possessed the key to a thousand times richer nature than her own. The magician made her believe that she herself held the wand.

"You cannot get rid of me," Sybil softly whispered, winding a sunny lock of Lulu's bright hair about her fingers. "Nothing shall drive me away. I will hang on until you love me whether you want me or not. I will have you love me in spite of yourself," and every tone was a caress, every syllable a tender tyranny. And there were so many lovable things about her! Her conversation, rapid, caustic, witty, filled with personal description and anecdote, kept the mind on the *qui vive* to attend, while the ear was soothed by the rare modulations of her trained voice. And intellectually, Lulu did love her, agree with her, appreciate her and delight in association with her. It was but seldom that she was

again surprised by a moral lapse, — and then, how graceful was the apology. How small and illiberal the moral
side of the light sensualism appeared.

Lulu felt but one exaction in all this rosy intercourse.
Sybil insisted that she should trust her. "Believe me
true, true to the very core, darling. It is all I ask. Look
deeper than the surface. Read the core of my heart. In
you I see my salvation, my hope of better things. Life
has in its way been bitter to me. By some strange mis-
chance, I seem never to have been understood. My quality
is so different from the American fibre, — yet I recognize
in you its counterpart, — a quality so subtly deep and rich
that the world can never fathom it. Let us fathom each
other. Let us prove to ourselves if to none others, that
there can exist between two women a love, holy. pure,
exalted, which no change of circumstance can alter, no
selfishness or jealousy can make less true. Let us enter
into a sweet secret together of undying faith and mutual
help, that for once in all this great sceptical world we
may bring out the possibilities of womanly character, —
a loyalty so belied, so scouted, that but to admit it exists
is to be scorned." Her flashing eyes and indignant attitude supplemented their eloquence to the appeal.

And remembering with pity the sad tears, the aspiration she had overheard by the sea; her imagination
filled with crosses and sorrows which were all the more
terrible because so mysterious; Lulu with all her sweet
soul tossed by varied emotions, sprang into Sybil's arms
and sealed the compact with a long, clinging kiss, the
first that she had voluntarily tendered to her woman-
lover.

As time went on the pressure of this exaction began
to be felt. Yet so supreme was her loyalty, so self-sacrificing the purity of her intention, that Lulu neither
understood nor analyzed her position.

With the enthusiasm of youth which had been so gradually yet surely awakened, she longed to do anything, to give anything, to be anything to show the intensity of her devotion, the unadulteration of her friendship. Fired with the thought that she in her girlish inexperience, had still in her some magnetic "quality" which held this magnificent woman of the world in the mesh of her lightest will, she abandoned herself mentally and physically to the fascinating pleasure of giving that joy which thrilled the Visonti with visible emotion. Many and many a time when taking their afternoon siesta, Sybil, capturing her hand, had gently drawn it to her own brown throat, her very heart, where, beneath its light pressure, Lulu could feel the blood leap in an ecstasy she could not understand.

"I feel as if I were floating on white clouds, dearest, when you touch me. My body is light as air, and my soul seems to drift into a fairy realm. What magic lies in these precious finger-tips to give me such an unknown happiness!" And murmuring sweet poetic phrases, she would still entice the pretty hand.

Taking advantage of a sudden influx of visitors, Sybil had begged to be allowed to share her large apartment with Lulu, and although Helen in her thoughtful hospitality had endeavored to leave each guest undisturbed, the assurances of both that it would be only the more agreeable, decided her to arrange it in that way, and soon the two friends were associated far more intimately than before.

And if, with an occasional access of her original tendencies, Lulu deserted Sybil for a whole day, or went away with Guy to spend delicious hours of chat and fun, regaining in his wholesome presence, the strong, fresh vitality, which was her constitutional condition, she would soon be made to feel how lonely, how sad, how longing for her had been the time for Sybil, who, although occupied with her own affairs, protested that in her heart all was dreariness without the light of Lulu's smile.

Then too, the little demons of vanity and jealousy, which lurk in every heart, were roused by the comparison of Helen's constancy. For Sybil claimed all that was to be claimed from that source.

She was made to feel that Helen was so tender, so generous, so loving, so comprehensive, — not like her, cold, sarcastic, indifferent, cruel, irresponsive or careless of the ever-increasing love she had awakened.

That love seemed to close around her, cling to her, fall about her like a beautiful gauze, through which she could hear and see the outside world, but which enveloped her so perfectly as to net her in.

It was the shimering film of a soft veil which seemed to shut her in, body and soul, to this enthralling friendship, against which she had but spasmodic inclinations to struggle; and having struggled with a vehement, passionate, nerve-shaking revolt, like a sudden fury of anger, suspicion, or unspeakable horror and hate, left her in a weakness, a dulness and indifference, which was only chafed or soothed into passive acceptance again by the soft sarcasms or softer persuasions of her companion.

Of the growing familiarity of this association, Lulu said nothing to Guy, although she daily declared to herself that she would confess, — what? That although he had warned her to beware, she had left his desire unheeded? That she had, although he begged her not to stay one moment alone with the Visonti, for several weeks shared her room?

Perhaps that would seem to throw some blame on Helen, and besides, was she in duty bound to run to him with every little thing? Was she not capable of ruling her own affairs, if she could rule this lovely woman with a frown? Her pride, her shame, her sense of the pleasure of her secret, all led her to keep silent, while Sybil had often with pricking pleasantry scorned in a general way, the idea of masculine intrusion.

"Must we make our lovers our father-confessors, our guardians, our popes infallible?" she cried one day when Lulu said, "I had better ask Guy," about some intended excursion. "Are you at the knee of your future husband, or is he at yours? The attitude of self-abasement would not be pleasing to me, no matter how much I loved a man. And mark me, sweet, what now you offer, after marriage he will exact. But, of course, go, tell him the whole of your dear little heart out. Even if you will, tell him of my bondage to you, and let him sneer at what he would call a woman's passion. Subject even the sacred beauty of our love to the cynical criticisms of his man-like analysis. Oh! I am not jealous of him. Do not believe that. I have never intruded myself between you one hair, have I? But, Lulu, my Lulu, do not let him intrude between us," and with a wild, hungry look, pitiful in its seeming intensity, she pleaded as if for an almost lost treasure.

The young girl felt her brain whirl with a sense of her subjugation of this woman. She assumed an expression which infinitely amused Sybil, while it pricked her to sudden wrath. Murmuring her promises and assurances as a mother soothes a nervous child, "Why, dear Sybil," she said, "are you so fearful that my noble Guy could not understand your tenderness for me? You wrong him, I know you do. Should he ever again intimate that he — he — wants me all to himself, I will tell him frankly, that your love and mine is something totally different, — so impossible to contain the same elements that are in his love and mine, that they are quite distinct, — quite unapproachable by any comparison." And with all the loyalty of her soul aflame, she determined to let nothing so much as cast a shadow over so high and fine an union.

"So he has intimated that I am trying to take you away from him?" said Sybil reproachfully, looking at her as if with still an unsatisfied doubt.

Lulu blushed, remembering his saying about the magnolia. To hide her confusion she left the room, flinging her answer gayly back. "Oh, he was a little jealous too."

Sybil grew dark as the cloud-rack that was driving up the sky. As she pushed wider the blinds, and felt the first cool drops beat on her up-turned forehead, her stormy brow seemed to invoke the thunder which suddenly rolled across the zenith with tremendous echoes. Casting a long look down the dim hall through which Lulu was passing, she shook with scornful laughter. She tossed her arm lightly towards the retreating figure, and then gazed at its luxurious display of round, soft curves with a sensuous admiration. Tapping the wrist lightly with her fingers and nodding her head towards it gently and slowly, she murmured, "But her young life throbs here."

CHAPTER XXIII.

A STUNNING ANNOUNCEMENT.

"Thoughts, that voluntary move
Harmonious numbers."

"On a sudden open fly
With impetuous recoil and jarring sound
Th' infernal doors, and on their hinges grate
Harsh thunder."

THE heavy shower settled into a steady rain when evening came down, and as it happened that no engagement of any importance had been made by any of the party, after dinner they all went into the great drawing-room which, with a crackling wood fire and many wax candles, looked surprisingly inviting. As if it were winter, and the "cosey" feeling had fallen on the guests, all gathered about the blaze; and that softly confidential mood which seldom extends beyond two or three in a group, crept over even the most reticent, and produced a charming chatter from one to the other, filled with playful banter and trifles of wit which sparkled like the hickory. Snatches of conversation were caught up and commented on with pleasant laughter, and never since the first breath of the "home" atmosphere on their arrival, had they all been so thoroughly careless and at ease.

"The more I read, the more I wish to," Lulu was saying to Sardia. "What an insatiable appetite is this craving for knowledge! But I always congratulate myself on the Eternities, for then we shall not be hampered by days, hours, and weeks. Then, the great angel of the Apocalypse shall set one foot on sea and one on land and declare that Time shall be no more. But I always wondered how he was going to set his foot on the sea, for St. John said, ' There shall be no more sea,' you remember."

Sardia smilingly put by her incorrect reading and answered, "If one were inclined, one might easily fancy that the saint of Patmos was preaching a grand annihilation, so many majestic things he makes ' no more ' with a sweep of his pen."

" And do you remember how he ends up his gospel ? " put in Charlie Vane. " He said, ' And there are many other things which Jesus did, the which if they should be written every one, I suppose that even the world itself could not contain the books that should be written.' That always seemed so delightfully naïve, so innocent, to me! He did not know of the possibilities of nineteenth-century publishers."

" I suppose the surface story of a whole life could be condensed into a column — look at our obituaries of great men," Guy answered. " But the life of the soul — the inner being — what volume could contain it ? "

"People have smiled over and again at the seeming ignorance of that divine old writer," Helen remarked thoughtfully, " but I have no doubt he referred to things done in the spirit — the actions of the soul of the Master, which were boundless in conception and intent, compassing the whole earth indeed and intimately connected with its past, present, and future. And time may prove that the world itself is a book, whereon shall be written the eternal result of just ' those things that Jesus did,' to the exclusion of all lesser matter."

" The literature of materialism is doing its best to put in a chapter and teach the efficacy of present and eternal

death. There is an annihilation for you which knocks
out old Father Time the first round," exclaimed Guy,
rather slangily.

> " ' The revelations of Devout and Learned
>   Who rose before us and as prophets burned,
>   Are all but stories, which, awoke from sleep,
>   They told their fellows and to sleep returned.
>
>   Ah, make the most of what we yet may spend,
>   Before we too into the dust descend;
>   Dust into dust and under dust to lie
>   Sans wine, sans song, sans singer, and sans end.'

So Omar wrote seven hundred years ago, and who shall
say him nay ? "

Sybil's low, melodious voice melted into the silence
like a shadow into the moonlight, the cold, sad scepti-
cism of the lines taking on a new poetry from her tones.

"I am not dust ! " cried Lulu, standing up and flashing
her youthful defiance against this dry philosophy. " I
will not have it so. Such a belief casts a pall over the
face of Hope."

Ralfe looked at her appreciatively, and spoke for the
first time. He said, —

> " This hath been found in rubric letters writ
>   By some old monk of piety and wit,
>   Who set upon his missal's well-thumbed page
>   These verselets, not unmeet a later age.
>
> I am the golden corn, my body is the husk ;
> I am the gleaming star, my body is the dusk.
>
> I am the silvery pearl, my body is the shell ;
> I am the water bright, my body is the well.
>
> I am the emerald, my body sets it round ;
> I am the love i' the word, my body is the sound.
>
> I am the sympathy, my body is the tear ;
> I am the loving thought, my body makes it clear.

I am the hearing, sight, my body ear and eye ;
I am the will to go, my body wings to fly.

I am the meaning sweet, my body is the rhyme ;
I am the tune i' the bell, my body is the chime.

I am the subtle scent, my body is the flower ;
I am the maiden bride, my body is her dower.

I am the architect, my body is the stone ;
I am the crowned king, my body is his throne.

I am the lesson taught, my body doth but teach ;
I am the eloquence, my body is the speech.

I am the germ within, my body is the seed :
I am the deep intent, my body is the deed.

I am the charity, my body is the act ;
I am the wider truth, my body is the fact.

I am the chrysm of love, my body is the kiss ;
I am the finer grace, my body is the bliss.

I am the enemy, my body is the wrong,
I am the praise to God, my body is the song.

I am communion full, my body is the prayer ;
I am the living soul, my body I but wear.

Immortal, what need I my body to love much ?
When it lies dead, I see, I feel, I touch.

Eternal, then and now, to-morrow and for aye !
I shall be I, unchanged, — my body scattered clay.

> Ah, wise old man, who centuries ago
>   From his soul's joy thus simply penned the truth !
> Long hath his dust been flower or stream or snow,
>   But he ! — How glorious his perennial youth !"

Helen had listened with the rest, but oh, with what
an expression ! She had not heard but a few couplets
when she became convinced that they were his own.   He

caught her gaze as he finished and thrilled with an intellectual sympathy so fine that he was for a moment deaf to the questionings, the guesses as to the authorship, and finally the accusations and congratulations which his evident embarrassment called forth.

"So that is what you have been doing all these mornings," cried Guy, giving him a glance of happy pride, "flirting with the Muses! The whole nine, I'll warrant. Ladies, you might as well put up your pretty arrows. He has already been struck with a divine weapon. His especial fancy in Muses will henceforth appear in public, and when he rides Pegasus she will play ring-mistress. Come, we will superintend your mental gymnastics henceforth, now you have made your *début.*"

Ralfe stood the fire of their badinage with his usual imperturbability, yet resorting to his defensive little catchword, "I shall be charmed." But his whole being was alive to the strange inspiration, the glow, the spiritual harmony, which seemed to infold and uplift him as his eyes again sought Helen's. Had they been alone, he must have inevitably approached her, touched her, drawn her to him, so strong, so irresistible was the attraction of this silent comprehension.

It was as if flesh was forgotten of both, done with, thrown off for the moment, and only their "I am" remained, mingling in mystic and delicious union.

The wind which had been constantly on the increase gave a sudden sigh about the house, and drove a gust of drops against the broad panes, which startled Lulu, whose timid fancies of late had grown almost pathetic. She crept close to Guy, looking fearingly at the window and trembled slightly, her cold fingers clasping his wrist with a nervous pressure. For in the avenue were two lights like giants' eyes speeding up the darkness, and soon three prancing ghosts of horses seemed to leap along the driveway and draw up with a plunge under the *porte-cochère.* There was an imperious tap of the gong, an opening of the great doors, a rush of cool air, the musical tinkle of little silver bells, and as they all involuntarily started up, the deep voice of the Princess Menshikoff calling, —

"Madame! Monsieur, — ah! but it blows! and the ponies, — what shall be done with them?"

The rotund James who had let her in, and had in spite of his rigid determination to be astonished at nothing, nevertheless stood in mute bewilderment gazing at the unwonted sight of three small, cream-colored horses, harnessed abreast, Russian fashion, to a light phaeton and held by two lackeys whose rubber coats streamed with water, at last came to his senses and signalled to the stable, whence soon appeared the head groom.

The Princess was glittering with drops which rolled from her long cloak, and as the maid took it off, she laughed with vivacious pleasure.

"What a run," she exclaimed. "I liked it! A close carriage? Faugh! No! I drove myself of course. You did not expect me? I am glad. That makes me one of you, not one of all the place! Come, madame, I am ready. You do not mind my *dishabille?* You see it was sudden. I felt that this house was just at this moment the best spot in the world, — I felt your harmony, — so I rushed!"

Her "*dishabille*" was a long trained garment of scarlet brocade, shot through with great arabesques of gold, and flowing back from a skirt of black satin. The sleeves, long and open to the shoulder, were lined with black, and her arms were entirely covered with the favorite mitts of red and gold, with a fringe of tassels from elbow to wrist. On her head was a gauzy cap of some embroidery of gold and scarlet with the favorite fez-like tassel.

So simple yet so completely apropos to her odd person was her costume, that despite its rich beauty, one would hardly remark it. Her personality dominated everything, even her eccentric environment.

As they all rose to greet her she suddenly frowned in the midst of her greetings and murmured to Sybil as she passed her, —

"I did not feel you! Strange! I fancied all was well," and she shrugged her shoulders with an impatient movement instantly hidden by some laughing remark.

She was soon the centre of an interested group. To Sardia, she had given the strong hand pressure of one comrade to another, and she accepted the large chair he wheeled forward with evident satisfaction.

"Your house has a chair big and strong enough for me," she said to Ralfe. "Not always I find one! I strew my path with wrecks of that sort!" and she pointed to a dainty, gilt-legged affair, which was occupied by Lulu.

As she sought the young girl's face she suddenly showed a keen light in her eyes, — a light that seemed to pierce the very soul of Lulu, who looked back at her as if fascinated. "You too?" said the Princess under her breath, and in a moment she was begging to see the foreign photograph which had almost dropped from her hand.

"Ah!" she then exclaimed, looking at the picture which she had taken, "This is singular! What a coincidence! It is the very town in which I was born!"

"Madame is a native of Valdai then?"

"Yes, the Valdai Hills were the glory of my childhood. But I was a child. What could I know? How could I tell that they lifted themselves from a soil stained with every persecution, every crime, to which liberty was an unknown word and peace an unknown blessing!

Over the Valdai Hills rose a solemn sun which stung our helpless sorrows."

"Then you do not love them still," Lulu said in pathetic surprise. To her, not to love the dear old home where she was born, seemed nothing short of sacrilege.

"Russia is a bitter draught to me," answered the princess grimly. "She was a cruel mother to us all. I had a gay, good brother once. He was keen of wit and brave of soul. He saw persecution stare in at every window of his village. He felt his free spirit chained, and he spoke out. He has been long dead. I saw him after he had worked in the Siberian mines for twelve long years. He was still brave of soul. But not until he proved it to me, his sister, did I know him. Read a chapter of horrors from the history of the Inquisition. Siberia is worse. Russia has many debts to settle. But I escaped her wicked clutches. I go to India. India! I love it. It is the country of my heart, my soul. Born in Russia of Russian parentage, my body may be claimed as of that country; but the land of my desire, the home of my affections and ambitions, is grand old India, ancient of days."

The sparkle, the enthusiasm, of her mood was catching. Conversation was for a moment quite hushed. The eloquence of her intense emotion was felt to breathe itself from eye, lip, and hand.

"Signor Zante will accompany you when you go back, I understand," remarked Ralfe as he joined the group. "What an enthusiast he is. He tells me that he is now allowing himself but four hours sleep, and eats nothing but bread and milk. It is astonishing to see with what joy he looks forward to being able to live upon bread and water alone."

"Yes," answered the princess in a matter-of-course way. "We must all go through the discipline."

“But tell me, what will this utter subjugation of the body to the will produce?”

“Nothing here in the direction he desires. The West does not present the same conditions as the Orient. There, the very atmosphere is impregnated with vital forces unknown to the dwellers of this hemisphere. What has been contemptuously termed Paganism was and is ancient wisdom, replete with Deity, and he who will, may become one with higher powers before he casts off this mantle,” touching her smooth white hand. “Signor Zante aspires to being an adept, and if purity of life, intensity of will, self-sacrifice of inclination, patience and faith, can make him one, you will yet hear that he stands amidst the ignorant, humbled and wronged masses of India as another savior. But I had forgotten to say that he will join us this evening, although he is attending a reception at the present moment.”

She had risen, and Lulu with girlish confidence had stolen her arm into her sleeve and moved along beside her to a distant sofa. “But what is an adept?” she asked curiously, having listened with awe to this conversation.

“If you had told your lover that you have placed his magnolia where the very miasma may blow on it; if you had shown him that the magnolia is already almost visibly stained, would you not have found in him a dear protection? Is this the confidence of true affection?” She breathed these words so softly that none else could hear.

Lulu turned pale to the very lips. “How could you know? Who told you? What is this?” she whispered in terror.

“I have answered your question,” said the princess soothingly, “and I hope I have warned you at the same time. Such are the powers of the human spirit if one knows how to use them. An adept knows," and she turned away to Helen who was offering a glass of wine with her own hand. "We were speaking of invisible powers," she said lightly. "Those powers which by most are seen as through a glass darkly; but which adepts in the art of self-control claim to see face to face; intuition, clairvoyance, for instance."

."Of course it is positively useless for me to try to understand the invisible in any practical way," said Charlie Vane, who had followed Helen, and addressed the princess. "But this peculiar preparation for things so out of ordinary comprehension, as if it were the most every-day fact, impresses me profoundly. Signor Zante evidently believes that after a certain course of study and self-discipline, his spirit will so dominate his body that he will become almost as if unhampered by it, and able to do those things which certainly seem supernatural."

"Nothing is supernatural, not God himself," declared madame.

"It may be so. To follow out idea after idea in sequence through the minds of opposite races or nations has always been a singularly agreeable study to me. It enlarges the range of one's opinion to find that the English, French and German conception of the same idea has a similar basis, but always deviates in detail. For unless people can understand that a thing can be looked at from all sides and present itself in different lights, yet still remain the same, true charity is impossible. We are all so apt to gauge things by the way they look to *us!* If we have been educated in one way we look in one way, and we forget that some one else is looking from exactly an opposite standpoint. How grand is the knowledge that God can see from all points at once, precisely as it is. Therein lies His power of impartiality."

"I wish I might become an adept," said Lulu, suddenly recovering her courage. "I too would like to read minds and see things as they are," and she gave the Princess Menshikoff the sweetest look of mingled submission and gratitude.

"Ah! keep your own sweet wits, that's enough. There are queer things and people in this world of ours! I say ours meaningly, for, my dear, no other world is ours yet, until we shed 'the vile body,' so don't you live so much in any other as to make you worry over or disdain this, as I have often been tempted to do to my own discomfort!"

"Is it possible?" murmured Helen, who looked at the form before her with an incredulous expression. For that form so seemed to be the embodiment of a reserve strength, a calm, unbiassed will, resistless, self-poised, eloquent of itself in every gesture, every look; the soul, like a strong flame, seemed to so illuminate it with hidden wisdom, the overshadowing of something untranslatable so appeared to give its ungainly contour a commanding grace, that to hear of the petty worries and discomforts of the world from those lips, seemed utterly incongruous. Her thought may have betrayed itself in her eyes, for madame gently took her hand and pressing it, said softly, —

"No one is exempt from vexation, from suffering. Exalt the spirit as one may, earth drags it back. But all the joy we know is here. Let us cling to it, while we grow above it."

"But how does this exaltation of the will, which Signor Zante is trying to gain, set towards our submission to God? In so perfecting the action of the human will, would not one forget the compliance of the prayer,

'*Thy* will be done'?" earnestly asked Charlie Vane, still pursuing the train of his thought.

The princess turned to him sympathetically. "I do not think of God as a personality," said she, with a smile, "although it is easier to speak of Him as such. But certainly an adept could in no wise be in opposition to Him. I have found it to be an absolutely practical truth that, if we are willing, God can do a great deal for us. But He is too honorable to rule our wills. He gives us our freedom. We are not slaves, but children. If we are not willing to let Him order our lives he does not compel us to do so; but if in faith and love we ask Him to take charge of us, will and all, we begin to be in instantaneous harmony with His designs, rather than in direct opposition; and thus we gain all the advantages of His power, instead of kicking against the inevitable. With God we have the backing and helping of every force in nature, visible and invisible. In our own way we may 'hit it right,' as you Americans say, or we may not; and certainly if we do not, our puny powers must inevitably be thwarted by the carrying on of that eternal process, which tends unchangeably towards the greatest good.

"As in an orchestra, those who tune their instruments to the right key and follow the leader explicitly, make a grand harmony of music, and find themselves on the wave of beauty lifted to a perfect success; so we may enter into the general choir and be one with the power, the grace, the victory of the Divine intention; or we may choose to flat the key, play according to our own ideas of time, plan that a bar shall end there and a new passage begin here, and find ourselves at last, hopelessly out of the work, a discord to others, and a failure to ourselves. An adept seeks continually to keep himself closely within the limits of God's design, as then he attracts to himself all the ministering agents of the universe, spiritual or material."

"Then he must inevitably be true, pure, and good?"

"Or he will fail," said madame.

"One would think you were a Christian instead of a Buddhist," said Guy, coming forward and laughingly taking her empty glass.

"I am a Universalist," said she, but seeing their looks of surprise, she added, " Am I wrong? Do I not mean what you mean? My creed is short at any rate, it is this: Let Love and Wisdom uplift the whole world forever unto Perfection. I care not who teaches that, or what race claims the idea; I know my soul responds to it, and I mean to do my part."

At this moment Signor Zante entered, his usually pale cheeks a little flushed with the wind and rain. He was soon comfortably ensconced beside his hostess, for whom he had instantly shown a preference. His venerable locks of silver, under which the dark, kind eyes glowed pleasantly, crowned his massive head with a wintry beauty, as if age had brought her season in a loving mood.

The conversation drifted on through ordinary commonplaces until some one made the quotation:

> "Though the mills of God grind slowly
> Yet they grind exceeding small,"

and Signor Zante looked up to say, " That is doubtless true, but sometimes Justice seems blind indeed. I heard something to-day which interested me very much as an instance of the varied vicissitudes of human destiny. Some years ago, I knew in a casual way, a young man who was at the time one of the 'bloods' of Paris. He had a romantic history behind him of travel, adventure and fast living, which, in a way, captivated the imagina-

tion of his companions. He had the graces but not the
morals of a gentleman, and he managed to carry himself
into very good society, although he had no visible
means of support. The fact is that while he kept up
an appearance of considerable wealth, but few knew
his real position, which financially was most of the time
very precarious, and not many dreamed that he lived
by his wits in a very crooked way, which often put him
to various straits out of which he made most narrow
escapes. But certainly I found that he allied to an absolute lack of scrupulous feeling, an instinctive ambition,
and he concealed with diplomatic art, what perhaps were
not absolutely crimes, but certainly nothing of which to be
proud. I remember I often regretted that he existed, as I
knew only too well how dangerous he must be to others,
for withal, he had a singularly fascinating manner and
handsome face.

"He of course, passed entirely out of my memory until
I was reminded of him to-day by the unexpected mention
of his name and what has recently occurred to him. It
seems that but a short time ago he was actually reduced
to poverty in London, and also very ill, when a man
hired for the estate, and who is a professional detective,
discovered him and announced that he had long been
sought for as the heir to an immense property. My
friend briefly narrated the circumstances to me of what
I consider a decidedly romantic affair.

"It seems that this young man had, in his early youth,
committed some breach of honor which so affected his
family, that his parents actually left their Italian home
and hid their shame in a foreign land. Precocious,
headstrong, and proud, this son had left the home of his
birth, cursing the father and mother, whose unstained
name he had disgraced and whose pardon he rejected,
and as years went on and he never made himself known

to them, they deemed him forever alien or dead. On arriving in America they banished his name from their lips, every token of his existence from their home, and as it appeared, every vestige of remembrance of him from their hearts, for no one here ever dreamed that they had a son until their will was made known privately to their lawyers. But in this, title, race, name, blood, parental love conquered, and they gave him the larger portion of their fortune, provided he appeared in person to claim it in the course of five years."

He paused to whisk a spark from his coat, and some one curiously asked, "And what was to become of it if they did not find him ? "

" It was to go to the daughter, much younger than he. One of the executors of the will is an old friend of mine and happened to tell me the story. The limit of time is nearly up. I believe the date is the twenty-third of this month. Of course there is no doubt that the heir will appear. He has been legally notified."

" No doubt at all," said Guy cynically.

" Well," pursued Signor Zante, " it seems that in renouncing them, this heartless young fellow really gave up his parents forever, and leading the life of a reckless roué, had no idea that across the sea was accumulating for him a sum of money, which doubtless would have attracted his keenest attention had he known of it. But so it was, and I am informed that he seemed as if stunned when he heard of it. What made it of especial interest to me was that I presume he must be some distant relative of yours, Miss Visonti, although if it prove so I wish I might have given him a pleasanter record."

" A relative of mine ? " said Sybil in a languid way, turning a proud glance on him, " I fancy that is not probable. The Visonti family were few. My father, I have always heard, was the last male descendant, and I am the only representative of our race. What was the person's name ? "

" It was Julian Savelli, — or rather " —

But Miss Visonti had half arisen from her seat and was looking at him with a gaze in which wonder and delight were blended. "Julian Savelli !" she repeated, with so subtle a mixture of emotions in her voice that when she sank back in her chair, as she did almost instantly, she seemed to have taken on a new sense of power   For her mind had caught like lightning the possibilities in store for her.

" I meant to say," said he quietly, " that Julian Savelli was the assumed name under which he had hidden his identity. His real name was Visonti."

"Strange," murmured Sybil, abashed at this disclosure, which assured her that he must indeed be some relative of whom she had never dreamed. " I suppose there must have been another branch of our house. And his parents came to America? It is incredible! We must have heard of them. Pray what and who were these Visontis ? "

While speaking these words, a dim intuition began to grow into a vague reality in her mind. It seemed as if a cold hand was slyly and softly being clutched about her throat. The firelight grew nothing but a dim glow, and the silence between her own slow words seemed to throb in her ears with a dull hot thrill.

" I anticipated that you would ask me that question, my dear young lady, and so I made sure of answering it," replied Signor Zante, and smiling at his own sagacity, he drew a note-book from his pocket and leisurely began to look through its leaves.

To Sybil the suspense of every second seemed a crisis, and the answer which the old gentleman finally read with considerable decision seemed to beat like separate strokes upon her brain.

"Their names were Juliet and Baptiste."

Sybil sprang from her chair and looked wildly and piteously around.

Death seemed to wring her heart. "My father and mother!" she gasped, clasping her hands towards him as if for mercy. "Then Julian Savelli, — Visonti — is my" —

"Yes. If they were your parents, I suppose they were also his. I fear — I did not dream — oh, forgive me! How could I know that he was your brother?"

She leaned against Helen, who had quickly gained her side, and now with warmest compassion and sympathy, supported her with a strong, tender arm.

"Do not be so shaken, dear," she said gently. "Be brave. Surely this may be a blessing in disguise. He may have been wild for the very lack of a sister's influence, a home and parental love. No Visonti can go very wrong. A noble work is given you in this discovery."

But Sybil looked from earth to heaven, from heaven to hell, in the depths of her soul and found no comfort. Clanging through her brain like harsh bells crashing out an alarm, rang the terrible words over and over again:

"He was my brother, my brother, and he knew!"

CHAPTER XXIV.

THE TRAIL OF THE SERPENT.

> "She moved
> Like Proserpine in Enna, gathering flowers."
>> *Tennyson.*

> "The palpable obscure."
>> *Paradise Lost.*

HELEN was walking in her garden. It was a morning full of the glow of early autumn. Every blossom, every shrub, the velvet grass, sparkled with drops of dew. At intervals, stretched like fairy canopies from twig to twig, were gauzy cobwebs studded with opals and pearls, while underneath some broad green leaf hid the cricket, who crustily gave good-morrow to the rasping grasshopper. Nature was full of busy sounds. Overhead birds twittered and called, while in a soft, muffled rumble, the sea beat its giant drums along the shore. A mist had enveloped the dawn as with a veil, loath to yield up its beauty to the sun, but now day stood blushing and radiant in the light of his smile.

And Helen walked in her garden !

Petrarch, in those old days when his soul was ever pierced with tender woe, wrote of his lovely Laura, —

> "As o'er the fresh grass her fair form is sweet,
> And graceful passage makes at morning hours,
> Seems as around the newly awakened flowers
> Found virtue issue from her delicate feet."

And when Helen gently moved from rose bloom to rose bloom, culling a bouquet of velvet blossoms, her beauty seemed to give the lawn a newer loveliness, and leave behind her as she went, a brighter charm.

There are some natures so clear, so pure, so crystalline, that one may only liken them to a mountain brook, a stream full of joyous vitality, cool, sweet and health-giving to all who touch it.

Such was the soul of Helen, and her fair body with its chaste outlines, her skin white and spotless, her deep, deep eyes filled with the light of noble thought, made an atmosphere about her which was curative to others, physically and morally. In her presence only good ideas seemed to arise in the mind. Anything low shrank back aghast. Only the most evil nature could pursue its ends unchecked when in contact with her genuine and generous spirit. Unconsciously she laid her hand of healing even on the vilest, and uplifted such, at least for a moment, into a better sphere.

Now, for the first time quite alone in the great plateau surrounding the house, her guests having all gone out to enjoy an especial entertainment given on board a Russian man-of-war, she from preference had remained at home to enjoy a day of rare solitude, in the midst of so gay a season. She breathed in, with unusual vivacity the fresh breeze, and lingered beside the hedge-rows, plucking a dead leaf here or straightening a crooked vine, forgetful of all save the singular delight of being once more alone.

Slowly approaching the great gates that opened on the avenue, she was surprised to see a woman come through them, and run rapidly towards her, holding by the hand a little child who was almost lifted off the ground by the speed with which they came. She ran straight to Helen, and panting with fatigue and evident fright gave a cautious glance behind her and exclaimed in French, —

"Oh, madame! Is this right? Is this where Madame Visonti is staying?"

"Madame Visonti?" exclaimed Helen, "why! Madame Visonti is dead. She did not live here. She died in New York."

The woman lost every particle of color and sank to the ground.

"Madame Visonti dead? Oh, my God, what shall I do? Oh, madame, at least you knew her. Save me, I beg. Hide me! I am pursued. I have been pursued by a man who is bound to steal this child. Will you not hide me in your house a little while?"

She almost knelt as she clasped her hands and implored with her streaming eyes. Helen was struck by her evident despair. Her French was provincial, yet touched with an accent of refinement. The child was seemingly weary and miserable. She instantly said, "Follow me," and walked rapidly to the house. For some reason undefined to herself, she led the way to her own apartments, and giving the woman a seat, stood patiently waiting until she could recover her breath and senses.

"You knew madame Visonti?" she then queried.

"Ah, yes, madame! I dreamed not that she was dead. Alas! when, when did she die?"

"Why, she died four or five years ago, my good woman," said Helen.

The creature started up with joy and cried rapturously, "Then she is alive, she is alive! for I heard from her only a few weeks ago, — I saw her only a few months back. I was directed here to see her. She told me if I were ever absolutely obliged to telegraph her, I must send it in care of Madame Fielding."

"You mean Miss Visonti," said Helen. "I supposed you meant her mother, the old lady."

"She is not an old lady," said the woman staring; "she is young, beautiful, dark as night, and wonderful in style, — a Parisian, madame, Sybil Visonti."

Helen was perplexed and annoyed. She spoke sharply.

"Then why do you call her madame? I tell you she is unmarried and a Miss, not a Mrs."

As if to convince without another word, with an expressive gesture the woman thrust the little boy forward, and pulling off his velvet cap said decidedly, "This is her child."

"What!"

"This is her child," said the Frenchwoman doggedly, "and it is to her that I have brought him. Although he bears my name, I know his true one, and as I was compelled to use it, have done so."

Helen felt faint. She poured out a little glass of wine and drank it, then, reminded of her guest, gave her some also, courteously begging pardon. For a few moments not a word was uttered. Helen felt incapable of putting her thoughts into language. At last however she questioned, —

"Who is pursuing you?"

"I do not know, madame. Since Madame Visonti sent the last money to me, a man came to our village and began to ask my neighbors about me and the child. He then called on me and tried to induce me to sell my darling to him. I finally became so afraid of him that my little boy never went out of the house save with me. One day I left him for not more than ten minutes, and when I came in I found the stranger about to take him from the crib. I called for help, and the fellow walked off; but then I dared not stay any longer. I had pledged my life to take good care of the child. I ran away. I went to Paris, I went to Liverpool, I came to America, I am here. He, also, he too came. He soon traced and followed me. He was on the same steamer, he haunted me in New York, he took the same train, he too is here! I am afraid he is at the very door. Ah, what I suffer!"

It was French, it was dramatic, almost tragic, but it was genuine excitement, it was real.

"Tell me about yourself," said Helen calming her. "Tell me all about Madame Visonti. How do you know this is her child?"

"I was her nurse," said the woman simply; "I was with the little darling when he was born," taking him on her lap and soothing his cries which had now become rather alarming. "Yes, pet, nursey will find him his breakfast. We have not breakfasted," she said humbly to Helen. "We went from the train to a hotel, and I was sure I saw not the man who pursued, but the moment we were about to go to a room we heard the dreadful voice in the lower hall. I caught the child and ran down a back passage and so on, on, until I reached you."

"You shall have breakfast immediately. But how do you come to have Madame Visonti's child?"

"Why, madame, she left him with me in the country in my little home to stay until he could go to school. I was his nurse, I was faithful, I was a widow; I had lost a little one, and I was poor."

"Ah, I see. She was a great lady in society and did not wish the care of her baby, so she left him with you, for the country air and milk. Many French ladies do that, I fancy. We seldom do so here. Is she a kind mistress?"

"Oh, yes, madame, she is generous, liberal, too liberal

to me, and she lavishes riches on the little one's clothing,—ah, the neighbors smile when he is called Dantin!
But I had enough to make this sudden journey and even
more."

Helen had a sense of being in a fantastic dream.
Was this woman honestly stupid or excessively cunning,
or was there really nothing to conceal? A feeling of
strangeness with all earthly things stole over her brain
as she looked at these two beings so strangely appealing
to her sympathy.

"Where is Monsieur Visonti?" she asked abruptly.

"I don't know," replied the woman mysteriously.
"I never saw him. He is never mentioned, and I am
never to say the word 'Papa' in the boy's presence"—
whispering. "But I believe he was a wicked, cruel
man, and that is why Madame Visonti conceals her
name. I believe he lives, and I have thought it might
be he who follows. But may I not see my mistress?
Cannot I present her with her child? Every moment
is agony to me while I still keep him. What if that
man is in the house now? Take me to her, I beg, I
must see her!" and again she looked about with evident
dread. Helen took her into an inner room and showed
her that it had no outlet save into her own chamber.

"Have no fear. No stranger can enter here. Madame
Visonti is away for several hours, but she will be at
home before night. You shall see her immediately
she returns. The child will be perfectly safe here with
you, and we will keep him in this little room, locked in.
But no, perhaps it will be best to serve your breakfast
in my sitting-room, and I will take care of him myself.
You will both be more comfortable. Say nothing to
the maid who serves you. When you have finished,
come back here to us." She rang the bell, and the
woman now almost fell on her knees again for gratitude.

The little boy had watched Helen with childish admiration, murmuring to himself in his baby French, and now when she took him on her lap, smoothed his curls and spoke gently to him in the same language, he chattered like a little magpie, and calling for his breakfast in an imperial manner, ordered his weary nurse to bring his milk.

The maid appeared, but not until Helen had taken the child into her dressing-room and left him to amuse himself with a pretty toy.

Giving her orders, she soon stood alone, looking in a dazed way out on to the lawn, where half an hour before she had been so happy. There was the same gay sunlight, the same freshness of the morning.

"But the trail of the serpent is over them all," she murmured. "Sybil disgraced!" she kept thinking over and over. "Sybil capable of concealing such a secret as this? Living the frivolous life of a woman of fashion, with this child in the background, its father unacknowledged, its very name a lie. Sybil passing for a maiden, when she must be either a married or unmarried mother! What a ghastly thing in one way or another her past must be! And yet with what cool bravado she comes here to mingle with our pleasures as of old! Oh, it must be that she has contracted a secret marriage. Duped by some villain, and discovering her mistake, she has fled from his cruelties, hidden her child, and saved herself by — but she keeps her maiden name! There is no concealment in that! I am confused. What can I think? This woman seems to believe every thing is correct. She speaks freely, as if she had received no lessons, — what can I believe? What can any one think of this?"

She was not allowed to think. An imperious little hand rattled the knob of the dressing-room door, and as it did not yield, as lordly a little foot hit it a smart kick. Then a scream, "It pricks, it pricks, the horrid rose!" and opening the door she found the baby boy stamping angrily upon the cluster of roses, which she had gathered, and holding out a tiny thumb, on which a little bead of blood stood out. She caught him up and comforted him, in spite of her half-aversion, for she loved children, and he was beautiful.

Beautiful! He was a dream of beauty. His head was a mass of tangled curls, golden as the sun; his eyes and brows were dark, glorious eyes, flashing and glooming, — oh, so much like Sybil's. His features and form, strong, healthy, and remarkably developed for three years, his scarlet lips so curved and pouting, — he might have made a delicious model for a Cupid, and already bewitching in his baby wrath, his sudden smile full of angelic sweetness captivated her heart.

"Whoever you are, I shall surely love you," she murmured, and was glad to think again, "Whoever you are, you are a child, an innocent little child."

CHAPTER XXV.

AN ACCOMPLISHED ACTRESS.

"But all was false and hollow; though the tongue
Dropped manna, and could make the worse appear
The better reason, to perplex, and dash
Maturest counsels."

Paradise Lost.

THE day seemed to pass very slowly. The woman and her charge were quietly waiting in the little dressing-room, which Helen had taken the precaution to lock. No one had seen them that she could discover, and in view of future possibilities she believed it wiser that they should remain concealed. How the hours dragged. The house seemed so still, so ominously still. The intense heat of the summer noon, tempered by only the lightest breath from the sea, was full of weariness to her, yet she could not sleep, and vainly tried to read or write.

This strange presence in her home, of so doubtful a mystery, seemed to cast a shadow wherever she moved. She wished to attain justness and clearness of thought, but she was baffled by her own determination. Her mind seemed full to running over with past, present and future. It seemed impossible to grasp the dominant meaning of all the incidents connected with Sybil.

This indecision was the outgrowth of a fine trait. She was invariably slow to believe evil. She was also invariably quick to forgive, and with her, forgiveness was no half-hearted work. It was positive, unlimited, unfeigned. She forgave, and she forgot. That was the end of it. And now, brought face to face with a new and terrible deception, in spite of herself all past deceptions ranged themselves before her memory and against her will, thrust themselves prominently into view. Every trifling vanity, every little trick, every "white lie," and every black one; the sly and ingenious excuses, the selfish acceptance of undue favors, the bold requests, the flattering hypocrisy, the painful lack of honor!—honor!—that was the word! No honor, in great things or small. No honor in speech or act,—always self, self at the end of all doing, at the bottom of all planning, at the top of all being!

Helen felt sick to the very soul. "Oh, how hard it is to be honest with one's self, to be true to others," she murmured. For in her heart was welling up a mighty disgust for this woman, whom she had fondly and truly loved. Even the episode of the ring had not made so deep an impression on her mind as to obliterate this affection. Like Ralfe, she had thought, "Sybil could never have intended to let the stones remain changed. She had a very sudden and pressing need for money, no doubt; and either was too proud to ask it, or was held in the bondage of some secret." Now it became plain to Helen what that secret was. By the light of this event she understood the other. "It was for her child," she thought. "Poor mother! it was for her child." And in connection with that ring remained the sweet, the unspeakably sweet remembrance of Ralfe's gratitude, which inevitably counteracted at the time, and even now, any contempt or bitterness she may have felt.

But here was a culmination of unfriendship. Whether married or unmarried, the assumption of her old position in society, the coming audaciously to her friend's arms with all the apparent innocence of past years, the entering into every gayety, the light flirtations, follies, and indiscretions which had marked her whole stay, seemed so utterly devoid of true womanliness, so bereft of the ordinary modesties of a pure heart, that Helen grew gravely and thoughtfully cold and resolved, as the hours went on. The more she considered, the more she could not believe Sybil to be a married woman. Yet she compelled herself to reserve her judgment. "I must not presuppose anything. If I were in the same position, I should require absolute faith from a friend until the friend knew the truth. But how shall I get at the truth? She lies so easily!" and Helen blushed. It seemed so low to her, so cowardly, to lie.

Strange to say, she did not once think of Ralfe in this connection. She did not analyze the effect upon him of this sudden relationship. The fact of his existence seemed to have gone from her. The first thought of most women under the circumstances would have been one of exultation, for in any case, such a revelation would effect a great change in the feelings of any man. But Helen was too direct. As yet, this secret was not hers, and it might so turn out that it would never be made known to any but herself. She simply studied the bare facts of the case. What might come of them she left to the future. Her mind was eminently judicial. But she was nervous, excited and almost irritable. She longed to have it over.

At last the welcome wheels came rolling up the avenue. Gay voices and low laughter came stealing to her window. Light feet ran up-stairs, doors were opened and shut, she heard her name spoken in pleasant accents. But a sudden lethargy seemed to have stolen over her limbs, she felt as if carved of stone. She tried to determine whether she should go to Sybil, or if Sybil would come to her before dressing for dinner, as she nearly always did. She sat with a face gray with suspense, — waiting and waiting.

Sybil came. She knocked lightly, called out, "Helen darling, are you awake?" softly opened the door, and seeing her sitting there, rushed in with her deep, melodious laugh, and cried, "Dressed already? Oh, why didn't you come with us? It was the best affair of the season. You have no idea," — and she had almost clasped her friend in her arms in the usual passionate embrace, when Helen rose with a countenance so cold and stern, so white and sad, that she was astonished, and sprang back, stammering, "What — what has happened? What is the matter?"

Helen's voice was very calm and still. She spoke as one who mechanically repeats a lesson. "Sybil, I am told that in France you are called madame."

Sybil grew equally white. "Who tells you so?" she finally uttered.

"I am told," went on Helen in a measured way, "that you are not only called madame, but that you are called mother. That you are a mother."

Sybil had a little recovered herself. "Who tells you so?" she demanded this time angrily.

"I am told," continued Helen as if no interruption had occurred, "that your child lives, that you provide for it, and that the father is never known, never seen, never mentioned. Is this true?"

Sybil's eyes blazed with fury and her cheeks were like a flame. "No!" she cried. "It is a lie, a base, horrible lie, and you should know it. How dare you question me thus, — you who have been my friend for so many years! How dare you take advantage of my absence to see the Princess Menshikoff, and listen to her false, malicious tongue? This is your purity. This is your loyalty. Even you gossip when you have a chance. Do you not know a friend would have cast the lie back in her teeth?"

"The Princess Menshikoff!" murmured Helen abashed. "Does *she* know anything about it ?"

Sybil turned like a snake. She knew in an instant that she had made some fatal mistake. How had she betrayed herself ? "My vile temper!" she thought. But she braved it out, and said sullenly, "About what ? She knows she hates me, and I know it too. Hates me enough to murder me."

"It is singular," said Helen in the same strained voice, "that you have always declared that she was an utter stranger to you until you met her here. But I did not hear this from the Princess Menshikoff or from any one whom you have met at this place. You have had two callers to-day who informed me."

"They lied, and they knew they lied when they said it. I do not care who they were or what. They either maliciously lied or were entirely misinformed. Who were they ? I demand to know."

"Then," said Helen suddenly changing her manner, and coming towards Sybil she gently took her hands and looked with her truthful eyes straight into those beautiful, wicked orbs, "then you are not a wife ? "

"No."

"And you are not a mother ? "

"No ! so help me Heaven. Helen, let me go. You act as if you were crazy."

Helen stepped to the door and locked it. Then she opened the dressing-room door, and the woman, who had been impatiently awaiting her summons, rushed out and threw herself at Sybil's feet.

"Oh, madame, madame !" she cried, "I have brought him safe and sound. I have found you, and I give him to you safe and happy."

For one instant Sybil wavered, then her stupendous will forced her to be calm. She haughtily drew herself up, and looking scornfully at Helen, said, "What kind of dramatics are these? Are you rehearsing for a play? Who is this woman? What is she doing here?"

The woman clung to her dress. "I am Dantin, Dantin!" she exclaimed in French. "Do you not know me, dear Madame Sybil? I could not let you know. I was pursued. A man tried to steal the child. I ran away. Oh, God! I have suffered such fear."

"What child?" asked Sybil still haughtily, and drawing herself away. "Woman, I do not know you, and never heard of you or your child. What an impostor you are! What do you want here?"

"O Heaven!" said Dantin, and with a spring she passed into the dressing-room. She caught from the lounge the beautiful boy, who, sound asleep, was rosy and lovely as a flower. "Do you not know *him?*" she asked triumphantly, placing him in his mother's arms, who instinctly held them out lest he should fall to the floor.

Sybil looked down on him an instant, and met his now open eyes, his eyes, so like her own. Mother and child gazed at each other as in a trance.

"Oh, my God!" she breathed, sinking down on her knees, "have mercy upon me."

The sight was touching. Helen's eyes swam with tears. She bade the woman go back into the other room, and having shut the door, said softly, "Rise, Sybil. You are a mother. And now trust my love fully. Surely you know its kindness. Tell me truly, are you also a wife?"

Sybil closed her eyes. The baby hands played with her ear-jewel. In a moment he cooed softly, "Pretty lady, pretty lady! I love 'oo, pretty lady."

Sybil covered his head with passionate kisses, and looked at him with an impulse of unutterable pride and

joy. "My beautiful boy, my noble boy," she murmured
with all a mother's happiness in her handsome, healthy
child.

Helen watched her with a keen sensation of sympathy
and compassion. Surely the heart could not be all bad,
the soul all false, which could so fondly express maternal
emotion.

Sybil suddenly shook herself, and set the boy on his
feet, and rising, took him slowly to the dressing-room,
and gave him to the nurse. "Take him," she said,
unheeding the painful bewilderment of the woman, and
sharply closing the door. She then turned to Helen.
Her face wore an expression of cool audacity. "Since
circumstances have betrayed my secret into your hands,
I suppose there is no longer use in denial. I expect
no mercy from you. You are a woman, and no woman
yet had mercy on another whose destiny had brought
her to my pass. You ask me if I am a wife? I told
you no, and I tell you no again. But if I had been a
wife you would not have been one. Shall I tell you
more, or is your curiosity satisfied?"

Helen could have struck her to the ground. She
towered above her in terrible anger. "Madame," she
said, "mercy is due to the repentant, not to the defiant.
My heart is open to the appeal of sorrow, but I am
human enough to resent insolence. I understand but
one thing. You came into my house as a virtuous and
single woman. You are a mother and are called
madame. Yet you say you are not married. You do
not say it humbly and with shame. You do not confess
your sin with agony and tears. You seem conscience-
less, for you utter it as with some lurking threat to me,
your friend and hostess. Now, madame, you will
explain fully, or the disgrace you seem to merit will
fall upon you. What is the name of that child?"

Sybil put on a sardonic smile, a smile which meant the subtle triumph of a long hatred. It was a look which seemed to thrust and stab its way into Helen's soul. She felt as if a death-blow was coming. It warned her beforehand.

“Ralfe,” said Sybil.

As a great ship at sea trembles and reels for a moment when struck by a tremendous storm wave, but then gallantly rights itself and unerringly pursues its course, so Helen shuddered for an instant at the sound of this beloved name. But her natural strength, her healthful mind and body, carried her on with continued courage.

“Who is the father of your son?”

“Your husband.”

Helen was too incensed for words. Her indignation shook her from head to foot. She gazed upon Sybil with a face like some great Greek goddess, full of unutterable scorn. Before her just wrath Sybil shrank. Her eyes sought the floor, she bowed her head. She sobbed. She caught the hem of Helen's dress and clung to it in seeming anguish.

“Pity me, Helen, my friend, my darling childhood's friend,” she murmured. “It is too true. It is true, but I never dreamed you loved him so! It was before you knew him, only think. It was more than three years ago. He wronged me, he injured me. He swore he loved me, and he made me believe it. I was young, ardent, and I loved him with my whole soul. Oh, Helen, do not be too hard upon me! Think if he had flattered you, if he had breathed vows of tenderest love to you, if his kisses had melted on your lips, and his eyes full of passionate devotion had pleaded with your own! Would not you have yielded? Could you have resisted — even you, chaste and cold and calm as your Northern blood must make you? Then think of me, a child of the South, with every pulse on fire, with every fibre of body aflame! Have mercy, Helen, have consideration!"

These words, which fell on her heart like drops of molten lava, each with its own keen pain, did not affect Helen's mind. Her imagination was stung into unspeakable bitterness; but her reason remained steadfast. She answered sternly, —

"Sybil, you are an accomplished actress, but you are dealing with a clear eye and an honest soul. Beware how far you carry these inventions. You know that there is not one word of truth in what you have just said. The man you accuse is incapable of the least dishonorable action, much less the shameless crime which you attribute to him. Choose a less noble being to assail! You can never prove a single statement."

"Can I not!" almost screamed Sybil, rising and pulling at something in the bosom of her dress. "Can I not, madame! Well, what is this but proof, absolute proof?" and she drew out a letter and placed it firmly in Helen's hand. It was addressed to Sybil in the unmistakable handwriting of Ralfe Fielding.

CHAPTER XXVI.

PROBATION.

> "Abashed the devil stood,
>   And felt how awful goodness is, and saw
>   Virtue in her shape how lovely."
>
> *Paradise Lost.*

A STRANGE haze seemed to gather before Helen's eyes as she held the letter open before her. She tried in vain to see the words. They swam together and were lost in a blot and blur. But she knew her enemy was watching her with malicious pleasure, and with a mighty effort she controlled herself, and slowly read, —

PARIS, March 16, 1882.

MY DARLING SYBIL, — You know I have long loved you with all the ardor of my soul. Even at our first meeting you must have seen with what power and passion love awakened within me. Has not every act of mine since, proved a constant homage and devotion? Even my acts of folly, my impulse, my rashness, but assure you of a passion which nothing checks, nothing lessens. Your caprice, your coldness, and again your maddening kindness, have driven me almost to desperation. Why hold yourself aloof from me now, when once we were so near! Again I beg you to be my wife. Throw aside these foolish scruples. Have no fear that anything you have ever done, or ever may do, can alter the affection which seems to be a very part of my being. Am I faultless? Am I blameless? Have not I too sinned? Ah! who has not? Be one with me. Are we not one already? What remains but that little ceremony which will make me blessed beyond expression! You love me as I love you. I have read it in your eyes, felt it burn in your touch. I have been ravished with the perfume of love in your hair, gone mad from the pressure of your lip. Do not tear me from myself! You are in me and of me, one and indivisible. The very blood in our veins leaps in rhythm, for I have felt it throbbing in your pretty wrist. Be mine, be mine! Let nothing influence you to deny me. The past is past. Let it sink into oblivion. Once my wife, our past is one, as will be our future. I will never reproach you, you shall always trust me. Thus shall the secret be doubly guarded. I will protect you from every evil. I will surround you with every comfort. The million — I neither need nor want it! How small a sacrifice for so supreme a reward. I am able to earn with ease sufficient for us both. Darling, you shall never lack your accustomed luxuries. Give me your faith. Unite our destinies and make Heaven a visible truth. Oh, answer me quickly!

RALFE.

The torture of these lines to Helen was so terrible that her being itself seemed to faint and die away. She stood motionless, holding the paper, while thoughts like great pangs of physical pain shot through her brain.

"This, then, is how he can love. So no doubt he loves her still. And he is tied to me. Bound in a horrible thraldom which he loathes and hates, while this woman tears his heart with her cruel presence. What suffering his true soul must endure. What temptation is constantly before him. Oh, I pity him, I love him, I pity him! And I would give my life to have received such a letter! If she now be miserable unto death, she once was supremely blessed — while I — I " —

She sank into a chair and closed her eyes.

A solemn silence fell upon the room. The setting sun cast a mellow light across one corner of the now half-dark apartment, and touched her pale beauty with a melancholy glow. Sybil did not move. She simply waited. Finally, Helen turned to her and said in a cold, penetrating voice, —

"You received such a proposal from the father of your child — the proposal to make you an honorable wife and mother — and you did not avail yourself of it! You permitted him to break his heart and marry me; to leave you still dishonored and disgraced, when you had but to say one word to be this good man's wife? Why, your tricks are laughable. You are not even clever. You should have kept this communication to yourself. Do you think to make me believe you after this? This letter is no proof of anything save the generosity and manly faith of Ralfe Fielding in the woman he adores. It states nothing positively. It only alludes to secrets and scruples. I will show him this letter," quietly putting it in her pocket. "He shall identify his writing and explain its meaning."

Then, indeed, was Sybil baffled. She looked as if she could spring upon Helen and tear her limb from limb. But in a second she was the tearful hypocrite again, fawning at her feet.

"Would you be so cruel to me as that? I could not marry him, I dared not tell him. Can you have the heart to disgrace me forever in his eyes? His happiness too — you will ruin it forever! He knows nothing of this child! I have kept the secret for three years, hidden as if in the grave. Have I not been brave, good, merciful to him, to hide from him the miserable extent of his folly? Did I not do my duty when he wrote me this letter, to return it unanswered?"

This slip of the tongue was instantly perceived by Helen. She smiled in superb contempt. "If you returned the letter," said she, the slow disgust making her voice stingingly quiet, "how does it happen to be in your possession?"

Sybil was silent. She knew not which way to turn. Finally conjuring up another falsity, she answered, —

"Since I came here I begged him to give it to me again, and he did so. You know he loves me." Her tones rang out defiantly, "He gave it willingly, yes, willingly. Why do you try to battle with me? You can only gain sorrow by it. He loved me from the moment he saw me. If he wronged me it was because he loved me too well. And I? I loved him too much to stand in his way. I have seen life, I know the world. Money means power, and to him money meant you. Without you he would be a pauper; with you he is a millionnaire. What would any woman do who thought nothing of giving her life for the man she loved? Sacrifice herself. Yes, sacrifice herself. Men do not, but women do. I did. I buried myself for months, I bore his child in a garret; I hid it, as I believed, for many years to come in the country, far away from Paris, and I refused to marry him because to marry him would be to take away his fortune. Will you curse me for thus loving him whom you love, whom you own, whose allegiance you can claim, whose life must be held to yours with bonds of iron, whose children may be yours? Will you denounce me to him and show him his child and bring this horror and disgrace on yourself? For the love of Heaven and justice, do not do this bitter thing."

Helen looked at her coldly.

"Is it not just possible that you refused him because it would take away his fortune to accept? Is it not just possible that you remembered money was a power, regarding yourself? I believe poverty would not be agreeable to you, madame. I think you prefer laces to rags. If by marrying him you would have gained instead of lost a million, you perhaps might have given him a different answer. And now, now that he has become master of his property by this supreme sacrifice of yours, where do I find you? Wearing out your heart away from him? Killing out a bad passion by honest endeavor, or turning to some other pursuit than the vain and reckless follies of a woman of the gay world?

No! You are here, under his roof, the guest of his wife,
enjoying his hospitality, hiding from him his true relationship to you, accepting his favors, torturing him with
the person which beguiled him, exercising all your wiles
and graces to win his noble heart away from the right
path and to steal his soul away with your infernal arts.
He has his money now, and what may not be your scheme
to finally make it yours? You are here, as you claim,
the injured woman whom he wronged, the mother of the
child he never knew, for what? He loves you, you say.
What then? What do you intend? What do you
propose? With what seductive charm do you mean to
entice him, and when you have captured him what shall
you do with him? You will lead him down to perdition."

She poured this torrent of words upon Sybil with
overwhelming intensity and solemnity. She seemed to
burn with them. Sybil sat as if stunned. Was this
the cold, the gentle Helen? Was it possible that this
magnificent anger which lit up her beauty until she
gleamed like a lurid star, was a part of the woman
whom she had sneeringly called "tame"? She became
cold and horribly afraid. She could not answer. She
felt a strange sense of moral fear. If a great angel of
God had drawn a flaming sword before her and called
her "Sinner!" she could hardly have experienced a more
singular feeling of awe. Her spirit was struck a blow
which searched it to the quick. Her very mind seemed
congealed. A long silence followed. At last Sybil
shudderingly asked in a low tone, —

"What shall you do?"

" I shall do what is right and just to each and every
one of us, regardless of consequences. I do not believe
this tissue of paltry lies, but I will give you the benefit
of the doubt. You may be telling the truth. I shall

take every honorable method to find out. But since
you plead with me so earnestly, and since at last you
shed tears of entreaty, humbly begging instead of defy-
ing me, I promise you to reserve my judgment until
later, and that I will not take any step towards enlight-
ening my husband as to your character, until I have
given you fair warning. But of one thing rest assured;
if you have been wronged and have made this sacrifice
truly and purely from love of my husband, I will do
you full justice. The wrong shall be repaired, the love
and sacrifice returned fourfold. You shall be repaid
with joy ten times what you have suffered. But if you
have accused him wrongly, — Sybil, God pity you!
Meantime the child is mine. I shall adopt him. He
will be my charge. If he really belongs to my husband
it is right that he should, consciously or unconsciously,
live under his father's influence. Certainly, you had
abandoned him in person if not in purse. He was being
no comfort to you, and you were giving him nothing of
a mother's attentions. In any case, you cannot own
him. He is orphaned of both parents. You cannot
claim him. You are not in Paris now. You are not a
madame here. You are a young, virtuous gentlewoman,
associating with pure and honorable gentlewomen. You
are a lady, here. You are a maiden, madame."

"And so are you," almost shouted Sybil, in a mad,
triumphant burst. "And so are you!"

Helen looked upon her with a quiet dignity whose
calmness seemed the very chrism of chastity.

"That is true," she said gently, "and my sense of
justice will be all the more unbiassed in consequence."

"Oh, that some power would strike her dead," thought
Sybil, a murderous desire seeming to stifle her. "How
dare she plunge the dagger into me with such a cool,
scornful, delicate hand?"

For one spark of human feeling yet remained within her; one bright, beautiful enthusiasm, one fond ambition, one lovely passion, warm and tender, still flooded her treacherous and selfish heart. It was her love for her little child. She sobbed out loud. She wept tears of agony which she could not stay. This time the anguish was too terrible to be feigned.

"What, take my baby from me? Never let him know his mother's face? Bring him up to love, respect, admire *you?* To give you the beautiful name of mother? To give you the caresses of his little arms, the love of his beautiful eyes? My child your child! My rights your rights, my love your love? Oh, no! this is too great a punishment. It is too hard. I shall never live to bear it. You will kill me. You cannot, you shall not do it." And dashing forward, she fiercely caught Helen by the arm. "You shall die first!"

"Very well," said Helen quietly, "I will take him down to dinner and introduce him as your son."

Sybil could bear no more. She went to the door and turning, looked with baffled and merciless hate upon her hostess. But she simply said, "And I?"

Helen unlocked the door and opened it for her to pass.

"You will dress for dinner and be the wittiest and gayest of the party. You are on probation."

CHAPTER XXVII.

THE ROSE BLOOMS.

"The utterance of these things is torture to me, but so, too, is
their silence.   Each way lies woe strong as fate."

Prometheus Bound.

"I cannot speak
Of love, even, as a good thing of my own,
Thy soul hath snatched up mine all faint and weak,
And placed it by thee on a golden throne."

Portuguese Sonnets.

HELEN had disappeared very soon after dinner, and as
she went to her own room, she sent an order to her
butler.   James appeared before his mistress in a twinkling.   Her servants loved her.   "I am about to send
you to New York, James, to accompany a lady to a
foreign steamer.   I have ascertained that a steamer sails
for Havre to-morrow at noon.   You will take the midnight train, and in the morning escort her directly to
the office of the line, where you will buy her a first-class
ticket.   Accompany her then to the steamer and see
that her state-room is agreeable.   Secure her a good
seat at table, and speak to the stewardess about her comfort.   When you have done this remain on the dock
until the steamer sails, and do not come home without
being able to assure me that she has sailed also.   At the
last moment, before you leave her, hand her fifty dollars,
and tell her to remember what I have said to her.   Here
is sufficient money.   Come home at once when the
steamer is under way, and if any one questions you,

either now or later, here or there, you can answer simply
that I permitted you to visit New York. Treat the
lady with perfect respect. She is French, and cannot
talk with you. And James, the carriage will be at the
side door, nearest the stable, at about eleven. Be prompt
and keep your instructions fully in your mind. Do you
understand me ? "

"Yes, I think I do," said James, respectfully. "My
old master, your uncle, Miss Helen, as you well know,
trusted me with a good many of his affairs, and, Miss
Helen — I mean madam — I am sure you know, well —
I'll do all you say, ma'am, and not make a single mistake."

"You are a good soul, James," said Helen, smiling very
kindly at him, "and I trust you fully. This matter is
important. James, you may be somewhat astonished to
find a little boy in this house when you come back. I
am going to adopt one."

"Well, ma'am," he said in answer, turning to hide a
chuckle, "I 'ope as it won't be the last little boy we
shall hever see around here, not presumin' too much."

"Say nothing of this, James," said Helen, quietly;
and the door was delicately closed behind him.

"And this French lady is the little feller's mother,"
thought James, cunningly. "She's sold 'im, the frog-
eater! Hah!"

"The little feller" was sound asleep in the inner
room, all unconscious that his nurse had forever left him,
when the morning sun crept softly across his pillow and
touched his silky head to shimmering gold. A pretty
young maid stood gazing upon him with wonderment
and delight. Helen watched the expression of her face
and said pleasantly, "I promised you a surprise yesterday. How do you like it ? "

"Oh, ma'am, isn't he just a little love, a little darling!

And am I to wait on him and take care of him, ma'am, all the time?"

"Yes, Kitty, he is a poor little boy who has no father or mother to protect him, so I thought I would let him live here with us as our own. I hope he will prove a good child. I hope you will always treat him with patience and kindness, Kitty. Do you promise?"

Tears leaped from the great, generous Irish heart of the girl to her bonny, blue eyes. "Indeed I will. I will never say a cross word to him."

"Very well, when he has had his bath and breakfast, you may send one of the maids to me and I will take him down-stairs."

"I have a little surprise for you all," said Helen, entering the breakfast-room, where Ralfe and most of the guests had assembled. "Somebody said the other day that this house would be perfect if it only had some children playing about. I am determined to make the house perfect, and so I have secured a pretty little child. Shall I bring him to you?"

A shout of glee went up at this announcement. Guy brought forward a remarkably natural earthen pug dog and queried, "Is it this kind?"

"Or this?" said Charlie Vane, pointing to a cunning cupid on the ceiling.

"Or this?" smiled Sardia, lifting a porcelain hen from her dish of snowy eggs.

"Is it alive?" cried Lulu, with wide eyes, "really and truly alive?"

"You shall see," answered Helen, smiling, and in a few moments coming back through the door, she was seen leading by the hand the sweetest, manliest little man of three that they had ever met.

Every one was speechless with astonishment. Then a perfect chorus of voices demanded to know who he was, where he came from, who was his mother, who his father, if he was to stay, and if she had really adopted him, and finally Ralfe said gently, "What is his name ?" Helen parried all these questions with infinite tact, while the boy, glancing his dark eyes about from one to another, seemed solemnly to consider his new surroundings.

"His name shall be that of the person to whom he shall voluntarily go. You may all coax him." So then, one and all called and coaxed, held out their arms and begged him to come to them. Helen bent down and said softly in French, "Go to the one you like best, dear," and he slowly released his hand from hers and marched straight into Ralfe's arms.

"I am charmed," articulated her husband with a deep flush rising to his forehead. Then looking into the bright, trustful little face that was gazing in sober baby-fashion into his own, he lifted the little lad up, kissed him, and swinging him to his shoulder, marched up and down with his trophy really delighted, while the others laughed, "Victory, victory! his name is Ralfe."

"Oui, oui !" cried the little chap, hearing his familiar name, "Ralfe, Ralfe."

"Was not that a slight innovation of our mutual comradeship ? " said her husband to Helen later, when the boy had been taken into the garden by his new nurse. "Should you not have told me ? " a little reproachfully.

"I did not suppose you would be especially interested," she answered. "I can amply provide for him," and she dropped her eyes with a sudden loss of color.

"Helen," he cried passionately, "I am interested in everything you do, say, think ! Do you imagine I can have lived so long in your presence, and remain cold and dispassionate ? No, no, it is you, always you who are not interested in me. Had you been, had you read me, understood me, this might not, — I mean that I always feel a comradeship — a partnership, at least, in all that concerns you."

They had followed the nurse and child slowly down the path, and now stood near that clump of oaks, under which Guy and Lulu had learned the spider's lesson.

"You flatter me," said Helen coldly. "I had not supposed you capable of deviating a hair from the true line of your devotion."

A dark flush crimsoned Ralfe's face, and he angrily crushed an oak-leaf in his hand. "I am used to being believed," said he.

"Then if it is true, and you really take an interest, I will answer your question. You wished to know if I did not think I had made an innovation? Well, yes, but under the circumstances a most natural one."

"I do not understand you, but I wish to return to my protest. I wish you to know, Helen, how deeply, how richly you have impressed me with your consideration, your goodness, ah — I cannot, I dare not say — nay, I am too proud to say what I wish. Why cannot you see, read, feel all that is growing in my soul?" clasping her hand fervently yet impatiently, and gazing into her face with wistfulness and strange passion, as if something was dawning with a flush of rosy light in the dark night of his troubled being.

"You can love, how deeply you can love, I know full well!" answered his wife in a soft, sad tone; "but it is not me. Do not speak," as he tried to interrupt her. "Let us have an understanding, since you desire it. You love, you have always loved Sybil Visonti with your whole being. You wished to marry her. You wrote her so in words that seem to burn where they are written. She is here, and you love her more madly than ever. Would you not say the same words over to-day if you could?"

"What do you know of that letter?" asked Ralfe, looking at her with infinite surprise.

"Here it is," she answered, drawing it from her little bag, and placing it in his hand. "I restore it to you."

Her husband looked at her with a face growing more and more white and dazed.

"So it was you, you, who took that letter from my desk. Curious and dishonorable! Who would have believed it? I thought, at least, my private papers, my own writing desk, would be held sacred by you. By Heaven! Is nobody on earth true?"

As he uttered these words, Helen raised her head higher and higher until righteous pride flashed on him from her eyes, and her lips set themselves in a stern, strong curve. "Sir," said she, "you are speaking to *me.*"

The dignity of that quiet word of self-assertion caused him to stop short.

A moment of silence ensued, when Helen said quietly, "Miss Visonti placed that letter in my hand yesterday."

"Oh, I see!" uttered Ralfe, starting as if shot. "It is Miss Visonti who is to bear the blame. Well, madam, it won't do. I *know* positively that she never saw that letter, never so much as saw it in Paris when I sent it to her. I searched for it myself, in order to show it to her, and although I am certain I left it in my desk, *I could not find it.* I suppose you had been before me."

Helen stood as if transfixed before his scornful looks.

She trembled a little, as if a rough wind had sent a blast of sleet against her.

"Nevertheless, the first time I ever saw or heard of it was yesterday, when, to prove her assertions that you had always loved her, had wronged her, had tried to repair your wrong by an offer of marriage, which she from self-sacrificing love refused, because she knew you would lose our uncle's bequest should she accept, Sybil Visonti gave me that letter to read, and told me of the awful secret between you for so long."

"When did I wrong her?" slowly asked Ralfe, after a strange silence, in which he had taken time to think this extraordinary statement over, and meantime had leaned heavily against the oak.

The letter fluttered from Helen's outstretched hand to the ground, and she half turned away her head. "About four years ago," she answered in a low tone, a blush creeping over her face and neck.

"How did Miss Visonti come into possession of the letter, did you say?" went on Ralfe in a voice half-indifferent sounding, it was so soft and tempered.

"You gave it to her yourself since she came here willingly, because she asked you for it."

"And how did I get it back from her in the first place?"

"She sent it back, and without an answer, on purpose to drive you away, and pique you to come over here and secure your fortune by marrying me."

"Where is James?" suddenly and loudly spoke Ralfe, stepping forward with a terrible look. "Where is James, your spy, James?"

Helen faced him in amazement. "James!" she faltered, thinking quickly and with horror, "Is he crazy?' "James," she repeated with a frightened air, "I have sent him to New York."

"Oh!" ejaculated Ralfe with a laugh of infinite bitterness and scorn. "Oh, you have sent him to New York! Madam, you are not much of a strategist. You should have suspected that I would hit upon your plot and the way of it. You should have had him here, well coached. It looks suspicious to have him in New York. Well, what else did he hear?"

Helen had recovered her calmness. She saw Ralfe was not crazy, and she was certain he was entirely ignorant of the truth. "Ralfe," said she, "I do not know what you mean about James, and I intend to explain his absence. But you force me to plain measures by suggesting that I am not speaking facts. Miss Visonti told me yesterday that as the result of the wrong done to her was utterly unknown to you, and she had kept it as a sacred secret from you all these years, that you could not understand, and it would be cruel to tell you. But I cannot permit such complications to arise. I am ready, as I told her, to do all in my power to set this terrible matter right. If you still love each other; if she truly made this tremendous sacrifice for you; if she has concealed the results of your folly from her devotion to your happiness, you and I will repay her tenfold what she has suffered. It is useless to conceal it, the truth is always best. Ralfe, the child you see there, playing by that flower-bed, is rightly named. He is your child, and his mother is Sybil Visonti."

Ralfe looked at the child, then at Helen, and again at the child, finally breaking into a laugh, — such a laugh! He laughed first as if the comicality of the whole affair was too delightful for anything, and then laughed with a growing satiric scorn until it fell on Helen's ear like drops of flame.

"Madam," he finally answered, his quiet being more impressive by contrast, "that is an unmitigated falsehood. I am a man, but I am not ashamed to say that I am pure."

When a rose is just about to open its rich petals to the sun, yet still hangs heavy and hesitating on the stem, and a sweet, clean, fresh breeze sweeps along, catching its fragrant leaves with a quickening vibrant force, the blossom suddenly turns its beautiful self upward, and displays in an instant its heart of ruddy gold.

So Helen, caught by the sweep of this unexpected speech, divinely clear and simple, driving away every evil and heavy thing out of her soul, and giving her its life and force of truth, looked up.

And, as he gazed into that heart of gold, lying open before him, breathing its beauty, its fragrance, its exquisite essence of invisible sweetness, purity, and goodness upon him through her illumined face, the deadened, darkened, netted, ensnared spirit within him leaped with an impetuous rush for freedom. Responsive to that wonderful attraction, which for the first time was fully put forth to draw him, his being answered as does the harp to a master-hand, and he recognized in one keen, ecstatic instant the dual, the only mate to mate his soul.

Without another word, both trembling with the hidden, heavenly peace and joy which both knew had come to each, and was shared by each, they moved apart to meet a maid who was hurrying towards them. She hardly stopped to make her little courtesy before she burst out, "Oh! madam, would you not come quickly to see Miss Visonti? She went to bed very soon after dinner, and it seems she has been ill ever since. And, madam, I am afraid, — I am afraid, — and Jane is afraid, something very strange is the matter with her. She seems to not know us, and she keeps saying, 'Tick — tock, the clock on the stairs,' and then she will say, 'The moon, oh! the moon, it will follow me, follow me and kill me, it will ride over my grave.'"

CHAPTER XXVIII.

REVELATIONS.

"A worthless woman ! Mere cold clay,
  As all false things are ? but so fair,
She takes the breath of men away,
  Who gaze upon her unaware.

I would not play her larcenous tricks
To have her looks ! She lied and stole,
And spat into my love's pure pyx,
  The rank saliva of her soul."
                                        The Nightingales.

"That door could lead to hell ?
  That shining merely meant damnation ?
What ? She fell like a woman who was sent
Like an angel, by a spell! She who
Scarcely trod the earth turned mere dirt ?"
                                        Mrs. Browning.

As they approached the entrance, they perceived Signor Zante, who was standing on the great steps awaiting them. A groom was just taking the Princess Menshikoff's white horses around to the stable, which indicated that he had come to make one of his unceremonious little visits which had grown to be a pleasure to all. He watched with his keen old eyes the expression resting on the young faces coming toward him, and their joyous confusion seemed to cast a slight shadow over his own.

"I wanted to see you, — both," he hesitated, "as I had something important to say, — but I see there is something unusual going on. Why are you so agitated?"

"Miss Visonti is ill," replied Helen, "and I must hasten to her. She did not appear at breakfast, and from what her maid says, I should judge she has a fever."

She went by in continued haste to the telephone, and was soon heard calling up her physician.

"You, at least, can listen to me," said Signor Zante to Ralfe. "I beg of you to come at once to the library, where we shall not be disturbed."

Ralfe had watched Helen move along into the morning-room with a curious look in his eyes, but now turned with alacrity to his guest.

"Certainly," he said, "but first will you not have a glass of wine? You look pale. Have you had bad news?"

"I will take a little brandy, please. Thanks. No, I am many years beyond personal troubles," he answered with a smile. "But I am never beyond feeling my old heart quake for my friends," and as he seated himself in Ralfe's "workroom" he gave him an affectionate glance.

"There is hardly anything more bitter in life than its disillusions. To pull down our idols and examine them microscopically causes us the same pangs that we might fancy an insect feels when denuded of his wings. He can fly no more — and our goddesses become poor earthy creatures, unable to crawl any more into our regards. I am sad, this morning, because I propose to disillusion you. I am going to strip your goddess of her wings."

During his speech Ralfe had flushed a deep, dark color, as if some intense emotion, strongly controlled, was playing within him.

"You speak of Helen?" he said.

It was now Signor Zante's turn to flush with surprise. A sardonic smile, however, crept over his lips, which he could but half conceal.

"Since when ? " he said simply.

Ralfe looked up with a manly candor.

"It should have been always," he answered, rising and looking his old friend straight in the eyes, "and it is, — now."

"I congratulate you on coming to your reason," grasping his hand warmly. "Now, my task will not be so trying. Ralfe, do you remember seeing a very beautiful ornament worn by Miss Visonti in her hair? It is a dagger, and the hilt is set with fine rubies. She sometimes takes it out and plays with it, as if it were a paper-knife ? "

"Oh, yes, I have often seen it. She wore it last evening."

"Did she ever make any remarks about it ? "

"Nothing save to say that it was a gift."

" How long has she had it ? "

"Oh, of course I don't know. But I remember she had it in Paris more than a year ago, for I cut my hand on it one evening."

"I do not *know* who gave it to her," said Zante thoughtfully, "but I am pretty sure. I think it was Julian Savelli."

"Her brother ? Visonti ? " exclaimed Ralfe. " Why, she has never yet met him."

"I think she has," replied his friend decidedly. "I think she has."

" She seemed astounded the evening you mentioned him. Don't you remember how she did not know or dream she had a brother ? "

"That is true. She did not dream Savelli was her brother, but she had met him all the same, and I am confident her agitation arose from far graver causes than the mere surprise of discovering a new relation. But let me tell you all I know of Savelli, or rather,

Visonti. The Princess Menshikoff was a life-long friend of Signor and Madame Visonti. Their palace in Venice was in their early life, as homelike a resort for the princess as for themselves, — in two words they were most intimate friends. The little boy Julian even called the princess 'aunt,' and always considered her as one of the family. In those days the Visonti family were fairly prosperous. They were infinitely proud of their long genealogy, and devoted to idolatry to the young heir of all their glories. He became 'a spoiled child,' and at fourteen was quite as mature as some youths of twenty. He became almost ungovernable and was always in the midst of mischiefs which kept his parents in a state of terror for his and their reputation. One day he did not return to dinner nor at night, nor the next day, and upon search of the most rigid nature, nothing could be discovered of his whereabouts. But the shock of his disappearance was supplemented by something even more terrible to the heart-broken father and mother. The princess was visiting them at the time, and her jewel case was found to be gone. It contained ornaments and family gems which were invaluable for their historic associations, and the value at the lowest estimate reached forty thousand pounds."

Ralfe made an exclamation of surprise.

"It seems almost impossible, in these days of sordid calculation, that a woman should part with such a fortune in jewels without making an effort to discover and punish the thief, but the Princess Menshikoff had a nature unlike most women, as you know. Her love for Madame Visonti, whose prostration was alarming, led her to abandon the thought of making further sorrows. Very wealthy, the sum was not of so stupendous a character as to embarrass her, — indeed, she would have always preserved the gems for her heirs intact, and she could not claim of a man whose whole estate would not cover a quarter of the amount, any reimbursement for her loss. It was decided that nothing but appeals to the boy's heart should be made. No complaint to officials should ever disgrace the old name. For some weeks personal notices, worded in such a manner as to convince Julian of silence and forgiveness if he would return, were scattered through the press of Europe, but if he saw them he spurned the proffered kindness and never replied. His father and mother, stricken by so great a grief, could not endure longer the associations of their youth. Banishing from their lips forever the name of their erring son, they left the old Visonti palace to be inhabited by tenants, and emigrated to America, to begin a new life in a new land.

Singularly enough, fortune took a turn in their favor, and from some excellent investments and speculations, it was not long before they began to enjoy something of the old prosperity and luxury of their ancient state. Then awoke a desire to have some representative of their name, on whom to bestow their later gains. Their urgent offers to the princess to pay her from time to time sums which should reimburse her for her financial loss, had always been steadily refused. 'I shall outlive you both,' she would say with a confident smile, 'and then you may make a provision in your will. Maybe through such an act your Julian may even at a late day be reclaimed and brought to a noble manhood,' and she would smile her wise, deep smile which seemed to prophesy the far future with its serene power.

A beautiful little Italian girl was accidentally brought to the notice of Madame Visonti, when in the rush of Broadway, the carriage wheels almost crushed her, — barely escaping with a slight bruise. The little one's screams brought to her side an organ-grinder, who had sent her across the street on her perilous errand of collecting pennies. A mere baby of four or five years, her extreme loveliness attracted the most marked attention, and Madame Visonti at once felt her heart beat with sympathy and affection. Without ado, she told the father that she would like to adopt his child, and as he did not demur, an appointment was made at once. The result was that the man signed papers by which he conveyed Sybil, his baby, irrevocably to the Visontis, and they legally adopted her at once, bestowing upon her their name, and as we are all aware, their devotion and protection."

Ralfe sat white and motionless on hearing the latter part of this narrative. Slowly he said, —

" She is not a Visonti at all, then ? "

"No, and not of noble blood. She comes of the people — and even the lower class of people. Her mother died at her birth. She was a peasant, and her family had all been peasants before her. The father was a native of Ravenna. A barber-shop was his birthplace and his ancestry were of the same calling. I am sorry, but it is the simple truth."

" Yet she is so proud, so intellectual, so refined," murmured Ralfe.

" Why not ? " asked Signor Zante. " Has she not had every possible advantage of education ? Manner may be acquired. Morals are of deeper and more frequently hereditary origin. Character may be improved upon, but the deep passions rooted in the being, control the nature after all. She is all you say and it is the polish on the surface. But she is more, and the stronger part she conceals."

" You speak as if she were all evil," cried Ralfe indignantly.

" How can you suggest it ? " answered Zante quietly. " No one is all evil. But do not let us stumble here —

let us continue the story. You remember that the Visontis were well known to your uncle, and that your wife became a schoolmate of Sybil. At the end of her convent life both parents died within a few months of each other, and Sybil was left quite alone without relatives. An opportunity to travel was offered by a trusted friend, a fashionable widow, and Sybil went with her abroad. She had been to Venice with her parents once, when a child. They had sold the old Venetian palace. It was not long before by a strange fatality her guardian fell ill and died also, exposing her to the necessity of self-control and self-protection, — for she had no one apparently, to whom she could properly go for a home, unless she returned at once to her home in America."

"She was 'the only Visonti in the world,' she used to say," murmured Ralfe, "'the last of the race.'"

"It is almost pitiful," said Signor Zante, "to have such pride debased. But she had already found a protector."

"What?" cried Ralfe leaping up, "a man?"

"Yes, a man," replied Signor Zante with a sympathetic look. "She had met Julian Savelli."

"My God! her brother?"

"Yes, — her adopted brother. Whether they both, or either, knew their relationship in law, I cannot tell, — but I presume without doubt, he did, while she did not. In any case she became deeply attached to him, and, — I dislike to tell you, — she became his " —

"Do not say another word," groaned Ralfe. "I know what you are about to say. Her child is in this house."

It was now Signor Zante's turn to look up with astonishment.

"She told you?"

"No. I was told this morning. She has shielded her lover by accusing *me*."

Both men stood mute and trembling with excitement. The complication of affairs was astounding to each. At this moment Helen entered, bearing a small glass of wine. She too was pale with excitement and sank into a large chair, taking all the wine with a single breath.

"Is she very ill?" the men exclaimed, one grasping a fan and the other relieving her of the glass.

Helen burst into tears. She gave one appealing glance to Ralfe, as if she dreaded to tell him the truth, and then said in a low voice, —

"She has brain fever. She is raving with delirium, — and I am afraid I am to blame, — I was too severe."

They looked at her with surprise and sympathy, when Signor Zante patted her head in most fatherly fashion.

"That could not be, my child," he said. "Your severity even, would be kind."

"No!" exclaimed Helen, rising and flashing her beautiful eyes from one to the other in sudden cold hauteur, which startled them. "No kindness, simply justice remained. She had accused my husband of a great crime. I punished her with my whole wrath. I put her on probation."

Signor Zante smiled.

"How many women would have tempered their anger in that way?"

"You did not believe it?" cried Ralfe eagerly.

She looked at him with a half-deprecating, half-appealing expression.

"I did not know," she answered. "I waited."

"I cannot think your severity caused her fever," now remarked Signor Zante, ignoring this little scene between them. "There must have been a terrible pressure of anxiety on her mind from the moment she discovered Savelli to be Visonti. But, madam, you do not yet know the real story of your guest. Let us tell you."

They then on perceiving her growing calmness, rapidly detailed their past conversation. Even as Ralfe had been amazed and overwhelmed by the revelations, so Helen listened with a changing countenance, full of keenest feeling. As Signor Zante came again to the point where he had been interrupted, Ralfe was thrown into a state of agitation almost equal to that of Helen.

"Is that all?" he exclaimed wildly, rising and pacing forward and back with rapid strides. "Is that all? Go on, go on, signor, I wish to hear the end."

Helen ceased weeping and watched both men with a strangely dismayed countenance.

"May I finish, madam?" said Signor Zante, noticing her intense pallor.

"Go on by all means; do you not see how much he suffers?" and that she suffered also was only too plainly visible.

"The Princess Menshikoff knows of the birth of her child, because Miss Visonti went to the old Visonti palace when her condition became known to her. By an accident, the child was even born in the apartment of the princess, who, as usual, had taken rooms there, during her stay in Venice. That dagger was in her hair when she was borne unconscious into the bed-chamber, and at once with little difficulty, Madame Menshikoff ascertained the name and station of her unbidden guest.

Astonished at finding her own jewel in the possession of a stranger, a small mark on some of the linen, which was perfectly well known as a part of the Visonti crest, to their old friend, easily led her to suppose that she must be the adopted daughter, of whom she had often heard, but had never seen, and with her usual wisdom, she suspected that the brother and sister had met, since otherwise it would have been too strange a coincidence for Sybil to possess the jewel. Lending her own maid to the unfortunate girl, it was her design to take Sybil under her protection as soon as she could properly announce herself as an old friend of the family, when in the night the young mother with the maid and child, stole away without so much as an acknowledgment of her care. Subsequently Madame Menshikoff ascertained all that I have previously told you, and has always known the true situation of affairs from the time she arrived here, called by the counsel of the Visonti family to be present on the final opening and settlement of the will. To-day, you remember, is the twenty-third, the day appointed when Julian Savelli is to appear in New York to claim his estate in person. To-day, also, then, the Princess Menshikoff has arrived there, to meet him and to secure from him either a statement of where the jewels may be and how recovered, or to obtain the sum set apart for her by his parents. It is supposable that he will be there, and even now, the matter may have been adjusted."

"When did she start ? " asked Helen suddenly.

"Last evening by the midnight train," answered Zante. "I accompanied her to the depot."

"And should Visonti not appear, what would be the result ? " asked Ralfe, stopping in his restless walk.

"Sybil would be sole possessor of the estate."

"He shall marry her!" cried Ralfe savagely. "He shall marry her, by God!"

As he uttered these words, a faint knock at the door was followed by a slight opening, and James, hat in hand, red in the face and covered with dust appeared. Seeing the gentlemen he looked dubiously from one to the other until Helen said quickly, —

"Come in at once and shut the door. Well, what have you to say ? "

He hesitated and looked again at the gentlemen.

"Speak," commanded Ralfe, "answer your mistress."

"Madam Helen," he began, "I fear you will be very, very angry, ma'am, but I could not do as you ordered. The French lady did not sail, and I had to come home without doing one thing you told me to. But I'm not to blame, ma'am, I did my best a-persuadin' and a-persuadin', but she wouldn't listen to me, and away she went."

"What do you mean?" exclaimed his mistress in surprise. "Where did she go?"

"Well, ma'am, the Princess Menshikoff took 'er, and told her as how she must go with her. She came into the train just after I got her seated, ma'am, and in a minute the Frenchwoman she give a scream and called her something in her houtlandish landgwige, and first I knowed, I was hordered hoff, and when we got to New York, they told me that I could go home, as I wasn't wanted. So I had to come, Miss Helen, hi never was so hagitated hand put hout in all my life, and I couldn't 'elp it, ma'am, I certainly couldn't."

"Do not disturb yourself, James," said Helen quietly, "matters have come up since you left which make it quite as well that the Frenchwoman should remain in this country. On the whole, all has happened for the best. You may go."

"What Frenchwoman?" asked Ralfe, the moment James had disappeared.

"I, too, have a sad story to tell," answered Helen. "While you were all gone yesterday, a Frenchwoman who called herself Dantin, came running on to the lawn " —

"Why, that was madame's maid," exclaimed Zante, "the maid who ran away from Venice with Miss Visonti."

"She had a little boy with her. She inquired for Madame Visonti and seemed in great fear, saying she was pursued. She said a man was trying to steal the boy and had followed her from Paris even to this place. She had escaped from the hotel and believed he was immediately behind her. She claimed my protection as the friend of Miss Visonti. I took her at once to my room, and there ascertained that Miss Visonti was a mother — but whether a wife the woman did not seem to know. I kept them quietly in my room and waited, — all day. It seemed a year. On Sybil's arrival I brought them face to face. At first Miss Visonti denied all knowledge of them, but finally said the child's name was Ralfe, — his father's name. I then spoke with intense anger and told her I should adopt the child as mine, — that she certainly could not claim him, and that if he were Ralfe's, he should be under his father's protection. Upon this she pleaded so earnestly that I should keep her secret, that I assured her I would do the very best I could for all concerned, while she was to be silent and wait. I saw no necessity for the complication of an unknown Frenchwoman in the house, so sent James to New York with her last night. You have heard the result."

"But the man," exclaimed Ralfe, "the man in pursuit? Who could he be? Did he come? Did you see him?"

"No."

"It was Savelli of course," said Signor Zante, "it could be no one else. He doubtless has now left town and gone to New York. Perhaps he went by the same train with the princess. How strange!"

"We shall see," said Ralfe, with suppressed passion. "We shall see."

CHAPTER XXIX.

AVENGED.

"Wherefore let him that thinketh he standeth, take heed lest he fall."

Corinthians.

THE words, "You are on probation," had scathed Sybil's proud heart as few could. As she slowly left Helen's apartment, her hatred seemed to flame from forehead to feet. On the dressing-table of her chamber were quite a number of letters, and as she entered, pale and trembling from her recent interview, she took them up and mechanically read them over, glancing at the handwriting with eyes which saw not, and taking in the name "Miss Sybil Visonti" with unheeding mind. She opened none, and was about to drop them when a note, as yet unnoticed, really attracted her quickened attention.

With an exclamation she tore it open and read the signature which she already divined would be there.

I am arrived and must see you at once. At once, I say. Do you understand? Leave your garden at nine to-night, and walk on the narrow path above the cliff. I will be there.

JULIAN SAVELLI.

"Lordly as ever," she murmured with a low proud laugh. Then, suddenly struck with a horrifying remembrance she shuddered and thought, "Why should he not be? A Visonti!" With what a maddening mixture of emotions had the thought of his name filled her since that dreadful night when Signor Zante had so unconsciously struck his deadly blow.

"Was it unconscious?" she suddenly cried out to herself.   Did he, did not the princess know?   Was it not a bitter, a fiendish revenge, following naturally the warning of madame?   How many now, knew the secret of her past!   How many, openly and secretly, were leagued together to expose it to the world and cover her with shame!   But who, who knew what she knew — the most appalling secret of all — the fatherhood of that child!   She seemed enmeshed in a very tangle of fatal forces, which she could neither comprehend nor control.   Yet with a few moments' intent study of the present situation, with a rebound from the crushing sensation of Helen's scorn and the certainty of ultimate disclosure, she quietly resumed her usual diplomacy and proceeded to dress.

Every movement of that elaborate toilette was one of subtle meaning.   Her plastic body, trained by long habit to interpret every thought of her mind, seemed speechful even to herself, as she caught a sudden gesture in the mirror and read it like an exclamation.   The cheek burning with a deep red glow beneath the determined, set eyes; the teeth strongly shutting upon each other until the lips were pursed into a chiselled firmness; the grand globes of the lace-shielded breast heaving slowly, but with wonderful underthrobs of the heart which bounded with her busy, teeming brain, and shook her of its own deep beating; the limbs which moved more and more majestically from point to point, as with a rounded plan and purpose she steadily approached the moment when she should begin her last play in the miserable game, were a language unuttered and unutterable, for they each contained a volume.

Robing herself in a silken gauze-like gray gown,

touched here and there with splashes of scarlet, and thrusting a keen-bladed dagger through her hair, its tiny hilt covered with rubies like drops of blood, she at last descended the long staircase — a magnificent mass of flame and smoke, as if she had arisen from the very gulf of Hades. She entered the drawing-room as lightly as if a smoke-wreath had stolen through the doors, but the soft lights deepened her crimson, fluttering, waving ribbons into a fiery glow. Even Sardia involuntarily gave a soft cry of admiration.

No incident marred the charm of that dreaded dinner. Half weary from the exertions of their pleasure trip, conversation was carried on in a desultory fashion, and after coffee some sat down to a quiet game of cards, some lolled in the luxurious smoking-room, while Lulu softly played for Guy, whose constant attendance had of late renewed the roses in those too pale cheeks and revived the brilliant spirits so strangely clouded over.

"I love my little room up in the turret all alone," she murmured innocently over the keys. "Helen changed the furniture on purpose for me. It was a surprise. It seems she wished me to room with Sybil for a while, just to make all the delightful decorations to suit my own taste! And it is such a sweet room, Guy! I can see the stars as if I were in the sky myself, and some way, since I went up there, my thoughts have seemed to change. Mornings I wake so fresh and happy, because the sun creeps through the soft blue draperies, as if through a tender mist; and then at night, I feel God very near, His moon peeps in so, and I pray and forget all trouble."

"Trouble, little one?" answered Guy wistfully, "what trouble can you have, dear heart?"

"That is just it," said Lulu with a puzzled, weary air, "I don't know what it was, but when I was down-stairs

I felt sad, and wicked." And she gave a quick little crashing chord on the piano and rose.

Guy followed her to a great cushioned window and began to talk of the future. Soon a sunny smile chased away the fleeting frown and she was coquetting with him as sweetly as he could wish.

"How happy papa and mamma look!" said she, glancing at the whist-table where they were seated. "Was it not kind of Helen to invite them here to spend this last week? You know she never met them, as I came with her simply as her bride's-maid. How strange that she should have selected me, Guy! But I am sure she knew how truly I loved her, — how happy it would make me! And to think to-morrow will be the last day of our visit!" she ran on. "Don't you hate to go, dear?"

"Yes," he answered, a soft cloud fleeting over his kind face. "But most because I am sure we leave poor Helen unhappy. I had thought the season would end with a happy *dénoûment* — the villain brought to justice and the lovers united — but we must leave everything in a muddle, it seems."

"Foolish Ralfe!" sighed Lulu.

Wrapping a soft shawl about her shoulders Sybil had stolen unperceived down the garden walk and out along the cliff. At the point where the great rock guarded the little cave so familiar to her, she saw standing awaiting her the man who was her love, her curse, her fate, and so much more, that a sudden faintness almost overpowered her as she felt the touch of his hand.

"Come in here, out of sight," he said gently, leading the way into the rift of the rocks so often used by lovers as a happy trysting place. "Sybil, it is long since we met."

"You missed me then?"

"Enough to follow you."

"Oh, no," she answered with slow scorn. "Do not utter any more falsehoods. You came for a fortune."

"And my child," he said distinctly.

"Our child," answered Sybil.

"We shall see about that," said Savelli roughly.

"Julian, Julian, my God, what can you mean! Not our child? Not mine? Are you mad? Do you know who you are and who I am and who he is? What have you come to do? How can our secret be hidden?" and she dropped on to a rock, clasping her hands in an agony of suspense.

"Why, simply give up my boy to me, and I will hide the secret fast enough. You have Ralph on hand, haven't you? The child would be inconvenient."

"Are you a fiend?"

"No, I am a Visonti."

Sybil rose and put both hands on his shoulders, holding her blazing eyes close to his own. "And my brother," she uttered in a blended sigh and hiss which seemed to be the escape of her very soul.

"Certainly not," said Julian cheerfully, "nothing of the kind."

Sybil sank back on the rock as if stunned. Her face was gray against the dark rock, and the dim light from the sickle-moon but gave it a deadlier cast.

"Oh, no!" went on Savelli, flipping a bit of ash from his cigar, "I am not so bad as that, my dear. If I had truly had a sister, maybe I should have been worthy the old name. You have been awfully proud of the old name, haven't you, Sybil? I never could bring myself to disillusion you, and I never would have done it if I had not become heir to the property. But you see *I* must take it now, and spoil your pretty pride in being 'the last Visonti of the race.' My boy is the last Visonti now, and a very clever little chap he is."

"And who is his mother?" asked Sybil in a tone whose indifference seemed the apathy of death.

"Oh, you! what? by blood or adoption? By blood you are some obscure person's daughter, no doubt; by adoption you are legally a Visonti,—my adopted sister."

"Did you know this when you met me?" she asked.

"Oh, yes, I couldn't help it, you know. But you told me the old people only left you a paltry sum, the income of which was just enough to keep body and soul together in these days, and I fancied it was no use saying anything. You see you were not a Visonti, and you were devilish handsome and fascinating. They were dead, and what harm could it do?"

"What harm could it do?" repeated the dazed woman, looking at him in despair. "What harm could it do?"

"Why do you sit there repeating my words like a parrot? Why don't you say where the boy is, and when I may have him?"

"Are you going to marry me?" said Sybil, suddenly rising and standing in an attitude which suggested the panther.

Julian laughed a little, half-inaudibly. "A Visonti doesn't marry that kind," he answered in a low tone.

Quicker than a flash of light, the jewelled dagger with its keen, keen point had cut a curve of silver in the darkness. Quicker than the sword-thrust of an expert, it had struck home; straight through that cold, false heart. Savelli with a smothered shriek fell backwards and down. The tide was nearly high, and the water deep. Sybil stood with the little blade poised in her hand. It did not drip with blood. There was but a slight stain upon it. She listened breathless. There was not a sound. With a great sigh she slowly moved away, on, up, over the rugged pathway, stooping when she reached a little mound of earth, and thrusting the dagger in and out, in and out, until it glittered in the scanty moonlight like an icicle. Back in her dark locks again, who dreamed, as she softly crossed the garden, what its home had been for one brief instant, — a living human heart?

She sped up to her room unnoticed, and grasping the little note, burned it in the gas-jet to ashes. Then, looking out of her casement on to the gloaming sea, whose waves would soon be on the ebb, she said under her breath, "You will not claim the Visonti estates in person on the twenty-third," and sank softly to the floor in a death-like swoon.

CHAPTER XXX.

GOOD-BY.

> " As travellers oft look back at eve,
>   When eastward darkly going,
> To gaze upon that light they leave
>   Still faint behind them glowing, —
> So, when the close of pleasure's day
>   To gloom hath near consigned us,
> We turn to catch one fading ray
>   Of joy that's left behind us."
>
> *Thomas Moore.*

SIGNOR ZANTE, after their trying interview, having taken his departure, saying that nothing could be done until the Princess Menshikoff's return, the house fell into that strange, waiting silence which always accompanies sudden and dangerous illness.

Fortunately it had been planned that the few remaining guests should spend the day fishing in Sardia's yacht, that the preliminary arrangements for leaving the villa for the season might more easily be made.

The engagement of Lulu with Guy Thorne had drawn her father and mother to Spray View, and another engagement, which had not been formally announced, but which was tacitly understood between Charlie Vane and sweet, quiet Jo Millard, had netted all the friends in a mesh of sympathy and pleasure which Sardia had delighted to enhance.

The advent of two trained nurses, the coming and going of two physicians, added to the whispered suspense

and awe of the servants, made a dreary day in the hitherto cheerful mansion. The occasional cries and moans,
which issued from the sickroom, the sudden and terrible
bursts of anger followed by still more sudden silences,
as of horror, filled all hearts with pity for the woman
whose beauty and grace had ever swayed her associates
with bewitching charm.

The sight of Helen seemed to aggravate the intensity
of Sybil's delirium, and she was forced to leave the
room, much as she desired in any way to soothe and calm
her. Ralfe had hurriedly driven off immediately after
Signor Zante, and the little boy, taken by his new nurse
to the beach, no longer filled the halls with his childish
chatter. To-day it had been arranged to break up the
whole party. The end of their happy summer had
come. Already many of their friends had flitted to one
of those interior towns, where they would prolong their
fashionable gayeties far into the autumn. The wedding,
which might prove a double one, of Lulu and Guy, would
take place at the bright Christmas season, and it was
hoped that many would then be reunited under the
holly.

Helen had decided to go up to the old farm, the
homestead of that uncle whose liberality to herself and
Ralfe had endeared to them every spot he had ever
loved. The Princess Menshikoff also, who had simply
waited for this day, had long been eager to return to her
beloved India, accompanied by Signor Zante, and, as she
hoped, by Sardia. Her whole influence had long been
brought to bear upon him, to convert him to that magnificent scheme of the revival of the ancient wisdom
religion, which she believed would be the salvation of
modern India.

"They will never embrace Christianity," she argued;
"let us give them back in its purity, its truth, its noble-

ness, the original, untainted religion of the Light of Asia."

To him, now, any part or place in the world was indifferent. Sardia's soul was filled with its hopeless love. His immense wealth was useless to bring him true pleasure. His culture, his taste, his manhood, might as well be given to his fellow-man in India as in any other country. "I must live my life," he would sigh, thinking with painful intensity of his utter loneliness, "and not as a coward, but as a man. It shall be a life that shall praise her. She shall feel that I have lived it in the sight of God, and the memory of her."

But not until he saw her happy, — not until Ralfe stood awakened and repentant by her side, could he endure the thought of leaving her to bear in silence a grief that matched his own, and which was aggravated by the continual agony of seeing her love ignored for the capricious fascinations of another.

The intimacy of thought between him and the venerable princess had ever been that of a genuine comradeship. She read his heart with the ease of a mother, the tender sympathy of a loyal friend. Not until yesterday, however, had she deemed it wise to detail to him the full story as she had ascertained it of Sybil Visonti's life. Before her departure to the train, she had called him into her curious boudoir and given him the details of that episode which had culminated in the belief of the illegitimate union between the adopted brother and sister. "Say nothing!" she exclaimed, rapidly giving the facts. "I have always promised you, have I not, to make your Helen happy? I have bided my time, but I will not spare. Julian shall marry Sybil; their child shall inherit the estate, or the disgrace of that early crime shall blast him on the very threshold of happiness. Do you think, then, that Ralfe will be still infatnated ? Or will he recognize in all its fairness and generosity, the character of the wife who loves him ? "

She went to the train, leaving Sardia in a singular state of melancholy.

"My desire will be gratified, — she will be blessed. But my desire, my desire! never will it be mine, never in all the world!"

With gracious courtesy he had joined her guests in the early morning, and taken them for their day of pleasure with courtly kindness. With knightly grace he had sent her a message of good-by, at the very moment when with angry words on his lips and a flame of passion in his heart, Ralfe had suddenly stood convicted of the true love of his life.

His yacht had hardly spread her white sails to speed along the glittering waters of the bay before the desire of his soul had been answered in a flood of purest joy in hers, while the last ray of hope, which might have brightened the horizon of his future, faded out into clouds and darkness. But not in vain are such loves given and renounced. Abnegation, who goeth in sackcloth and ashes on earth, hath in Heaven seamless garments, white as no fuller can white them.

The return of the gay party at evening was saddened by the news of Sybil's illness. They had not particularly noticed her absence from breakfast, as she often indulged in very late hours, her hostess never failing to have her served with some dainty, when at last she came, elaborately dressed and imperially smiling, into the breakfast-room. The evening thus somewhat clouded by anxiety, and the soft shadows which inevitably fall upon the ending of any joy, although we are sure it will soon be renewed, was spent in quiet talk, the lights turned low, and the conversation full of reminiscences of this or that hour which had been spent in agreeable diversion or pleasanter repose.

"We can never forget any part of it, dear," said Lulu, clasping Helen's hand with her little fingers. "We owe you and Ralfe a halcyon summer, — a dream of paradise."

"May I say also, how deeply indebted I am to you for so delightful a season?" queried Guy, joining the two, and clasping both hands in his. "I think none of your friends will ever count in all their lives a happier visit."

The others joined them in expressions of genial thanks, and urgent invitations were offered to homes which would always be open for their welcome.

"Of course we cannot go with you to-morrow," said Ralfe in a quiet tone. "We may be delayed indefinitely. Sardia, you have no engagement, have you? You do not mean to rush off to India at once, do you? I know it will be a dull house here now, — but could you not stay with us a little longer? I shall feel lost without any of our old friends. Helen, ask him to stay."

"It would give me infinite pleasure," she answered, looking truthfully into his eager eyes. "I fear it will seem very lonely and quiet, but I am sure you will not mind it; for if you can help any one, you always forget yourself."

The color flushed his face gently as he turned to Ralfe. "I will stay with pleasure, if I can deserve so kind a compliment. Signor Zante and madame do not sail until next month. They have decided to go in my yacht," he said modestly.

"To India!" exclaimed a chorus of voices.

"Why not?" with a smile, "she has been around the world."

"And do you go too?" said Lulu tearfully, her pretty

face clouded with real sorrow. "Shall you not stay for my — for our " —

"For your wedding, little one? I can only send you my blessing across the waves. I shall go too."

The pouting lip curled into the innocent lines of childish grief, and the quick tears fell at once from her limpid eyes. She ran out of the room, and could be heard sobbing as she climbed the stairs. Sardia was her girlish ideal. Not her love, not her joy; but the grave, grand gentleman who had won her supreme respect and reverence and admiration. The beautiful feeling which her tears represented was shared by every one whose hand he had grasped, whose life he had daily touched with some delicate attention, or lifted by some noble thought. The silence which followed Lulu's steps was throbbing with a responsive sympathy, which drew them around him in a saddened group.

After some further conversation, there was a general movement towards their rooms.

"If you don't mind," said Charlie Vane, "I believe I will bid you all good-by to-night. I go very early, and some way, I dislike to say 'farewell' at the last moment."

"Yes, let us all say good-by now," they exclaimed softly, standing in the broad hall, while Helen, Ralfe, and Sardia formed an accidental group against the velvet portière, "we shall remember it all so pleasantly, — your faces like a portrait-painting against that background. Good-night, good-night, we will not say good-by. Heaven bless and keep you." And one by one they stole up-stairs, each turning friendly and loving faces down upon the fair uplifted heads and answering eyes that watched them on their way.

CHAPTER XXXI.

AVOWALS.

> " It is not meet for thee to voice
>   Thy impotent longings to the skies,
>   And vaunt thy feeble sacrifice
>   As if thy fate had been thy choice.
>   Thy duty deep in silence lies;
>   Thou hadst thy will, thou payest the price;
>   Thou mayst remember, not rejoice."
>
> *Charles G. Whiting.*

" I AM very glad you invited me to remain," said Sardia the following day. " I have long sought an opportunity to speak with you on a subject very near to me."

The great house had sunk into seeming slumber. Although open and sunny, although garnished as usual with flowers and in that exquisite order which ever pervaded its refined atmosphere, it seemed lonely and dreary. No gay voices laughed and chattered from room to room. There was no swish of silken skirts, no odor of cigars just lighted, no manly whistles resounding in the bed-chambers. Occasionally a sound of cries or angry remonstrance came from the direction of Miss Visonti's room, where she lay in dangerous delirium, attended by her two nurses and the frequent calls of her physicians. The little boy had made an hour's divertisement in the morning before he had been taken to the beach, but now, Helen, weary with excitement, had retired to her room.

" Yes," said Sardia, repeating his remark a little louder

since Ralfe seemed absorbed in thought and did not answer, "I am glad you asked me to remain."

"Anything particular?" said his host looking up with that dazed aspect which brings people back from wool-gathering.

"Yes," said Sardia, "very particular."

"Well?" courteously and with now awakened interest.

"I wish to speak with you about the woman I love."

"A confession?" smiling with a kind of pain in it.

"A confession of what you already know," replied his friend, coming nearer and seating himself quite in front of Ralfe. "I love your wife."

The expressions of anger, amazement and amusement struggling in Ralfe's countenance would be the despair of a painter.

"I am charmed," he finally uttered, with his sarcastic soft air.

"Yes," went on Sardia, coolly and slowly, "I have loved her from the moment I first saw her at your uncle's house, the year he sent you to Europe and took her home to him. She was only thirteen, and I was twenty-four — but I loved her — and I love her now."

"Why didn't you try to win her?" asked Ralfe, a dull red mantling his countenance, and a dull glow creeping into his eyes.

"When your uncle died, you remember, you and I were doing the Pyramids. You told me of the terms of your uncle's will. To save your fortune, it was necessary you should marry her. On the very night you told me of this situation of your affairs, I intended to tell you of my love. I meant to ask your permission to address Miss Gray, as you had really stood nearest to her uncle and would be his heir. But of course, when you informed me that you had been selected for her husband, I kept silence."

"Sardia!" exclaimed Ralfe, grasping his hand, "can this be possible?"

"It is true," he answered simply. "I thought," he continued in a low, retrospective tone, "that perhaps you would not comply with the terms of the will. I thought that perhaps when you met, you would not love each other. But I could not interfere between you. I kept away, — waiting, hoping; yes, longing to hear that you had mutually, or one of you, had refused to be governed by a dead will, — but I heard of your marriage. You invited me to come. Why should I refuse? I longed at least to see her, for I loved her. When I saw you, — when I saw Miss Visonti, I knew I had not come in vain. You did not care for Helen, — she was your wife but in name. Your heart was bound up in that woman up-stairs there. Helen had been deceived."

The growing sternness of his voice and features, the bitter contempt which, modulated by the ever-present grace and courtesy of the man, only shaded his tones with anger, struck Ralfe's easily touched nature with keenest blows.

He sprang to his feet and cried, —

"You insult me."

"No, I only tell you the truth."

"And have you told Mrs. Fielding 'the truth' likewise? Have you told her you loved her?" giving him a terrible look.

"I am human," said Sardia. "I could not see this noble, generous, beautiful woman, this heart of heaven neglected, ignored, insulted, without pouring out my whole soul at her feet. Yes," said he rising and standing in all the dignity of his pure purpose, "I told her I loved her. I told her that my only wish was to make her happy; my only desire to see her where sorrow could never again reach her; where she might forever lean upon the faithful breast of her husband."

During these words Ralfe became half frenzied.

"By God! Sardia, be careful. I believe I shall kill you if you say another word."

Sardia waited a moment, still looking into the quivering face before him with his strong, fearless gaze.

"She offers you a divorce," he said.

Ralfe started as if a rifle-ball had struck him. He looked at his guest with wide, frightened eyes, as if he saw a pit beneath his feet.

"A divorce?" he murmured.

"Have you not desired it? Have you not planned for it?" said Sardia sternly.

With a low cry, Ralfe flung his arms into the air.

"Great Heaven! Yes," said he.

He sank into a chair and buried his face in his arms. Sardia resumed his seat, and in his usual calm tones continued, —

"When I told your wife of my love, and offered her my whole being for her happiness, I knew she loved you. Every action, every look, had told me, over and again, of her deep, abiding, wonderful, silent passion. I hoped for nothing, I asked for nothing but to serve her. In the mutual sympathy which arose from this confession, she told me that she too had given her very soul away, and to you. Then, when her beautiful eyes wept such tears as would blot out the sins of the meanest creature, she asked me if she could not in some way give you your desire.

"'What is my anguish?' she said, 'if I can only give him the joy he craves. If I suffer, what must he suffer, with this beautiful woman whom he loves beside him, yet with a barrier of iron between them? Oh, I am to blame, to blame. I should have seen he did not love me, and have guessed he loved another. I found it out the first night of our marriage, when I inadvertently overheard a few sentences spoken to Guy Thorne. From that moment I have wished to do this. If Sybil is worthy of Ralfe, and their love is a noble and lasting one, I wish them to belong to each other. I wish to annul this marriage, which to him is a horrible bondage, and placing her hand in his, wish them God's blessing, and then go away somewhere — and die.' "

A silence followed only broken by the soft wind blowing the leaves. Then Ralfe looked up.

" Sardia," he said humbly, looking at his friend with entreating eyes. " Will you forgive me? Will you take my hand? How loyal you are. Let me tell you. Your soul will comprehend it. Yesterday, in the very midst of angry revelations about Miss Visonti, I looked into Helen's face. Do you remember the conversion of Saul recorded in the Bible? A great light came out of the sky, and he saw his Lord and Master in its shining. Sardia, in Helen's face, I saw a light which drew me into heaven. My spirit grew clear-eyed under a seeming sun of flooding light. With a joy unspeakable I felt my spirit mingle with hers. Old things were forgotten, the past a blank, the future uncared for. I awoke a new creature. I became my true self. I threw off my bondage of sin, — I loved her."

His speaking countenance reflected the glory of that remembrance. Ecstasy beamed from his eyes.

" It is enough," said Sardia.

Wringing his hand, Ralfe swiftly left the room, and was soon heard riding rapidly away.

Sardia, left alone, sat silently in the shadow of the wind-blown branches that swept the low window, for nearly an hour, and then made his way out of the quiet house down to the sea, where, in one of the hollowed chambers of the cliffs, he listened to its sad, soft monotone, until, soothed and broadened by contact with its

measureless expanse, across which he was so soon to
pass never to return, his face took on a semblance half
divine. There he gained that harmonious peace which
comes to the soul that has no boundaries to its benevolence, but god-like, sweeps the universe with its patient
wing.

CHAPTER XXXII.

SELF-CRITICISM.

"When all my life was wounded and forlorn,
  It felt the sacred influence wrought by thee,
As when sweet airy couriers of the morn
  Fling rosy prophecies o'er shadowed sea.

And now, though manlier force yet droop and fail,
  Though deathless memories haunt me past control,
Dear spirit of peace, thou art the nightingale,
  That warbles amid the darkness of my soul."

Edgar Fawcett.

RALFE rode away from the town with its beautiful suburbs of villas and cottages, and turned into a road that followed a stream out into the country. As soon as he found himself alone on the way, he became oblivious of his surroundings and sank into deepest thought. His horse took his own gait, now ambling along, now stopping a moment to crop a clover-head, or trotting up a rise with pleased freedom, while the master whom he loved held a steady rein, but never gave a sign of command, or moved in the saddle.

Singularly enough his thoughts turned first upon himself. He went over in mind the life which had been his since he had grown beyond boyhood, and entered upon the experiences and emotions of a man.

"How I have sighed for a companion," he mused. "I need one so much. I am so solitary. I am solitary in my affections, my intellect, my spirit. Sweet as is the intercourse of my immediate friends, there is an unsatisfied longing in the heart of every man of culture for a companion for his mind, his soul! Not that I am a man of any culture, — but I am a little different, — a little more thoughtful than most men, in things not of absolutely practical importance, — and am I to blame? It would be very sweet to have a leisurely companionship which would be an elevation, an inspiration to both. It would be a heavenly thing to feel that close beside me might beat a heart, patient, noble, tender, sympathetic and comprehensive." With this he drew a long deep breath, as if drinking in a finer air. "Can it be that this great joy is to be mine?" he went on, speaking to his own soul. "Out of the darkness and blindness and ignorance and wickedness of an unrighteous passion am I to be lifted to the white heights of a righteous love? I do not deserve it. I can never be worthy of it.

"And yet, while I believed in her, what was Sybil to me, but the one ideal perfect soul that matched my own? God knows that false as she may have been, I was never so. While I loved her she was the dream of excellence which put all other women out of sight. I was true to my ideal. Perhaps it was this very intense longing for comprehension and sympathy which made me cling so long to her, — whose beauty drew me, whose wit charmed, whose soft appealing eyes said worlds of sweetness and yet mystically hid a deeper meaning. I cannot fathom it. Now I cannot see her beauty. I only remember her hours of passionate languor and fascination with a shudder. How can I have ever felt my very being sick for a touch of her hot, scarlet lips? I would not, I could not now endure them.

"And even at the moment of delirious joy when we were first left alone, she was plotting my ruin! Coldly, carefully, she arranged to drive Helen to desperation — and a divorce — by accusing me, and while I supposed I was plotting with her to the same result, she was securing both ends of the noose, in which to net her dearest friend and bind her lover at once! I am appalled at my own stupidity. I can never plead that I had not enough hints to open my eyes. The borrowed money — the diamonds — her pretence of improvising Helen's poem; and yet, love found such easy excuses, — her smile was so full of trust, which misled. But the letter. How did she get it — and when? How could she dream I still possessed it, or where I kept it? My desk is always locked, — by what means did she contrive to obtain it? I must find that out. Helen looked very strangely when I accused James. I will ask James.

"But Helen! If I have been stupid as regards Sybil, what word can express my blindness about my wife? Thank God, thank God, she is my wife, and I can show her by long years of perfect tenderness how deeply I value the unasked, unnoted treasure of her love. To think that all these weeks and months this silent, exquisite, melancholy self-sacrifice has been going on for me, loyally, hopelessly, patiently. To think that her kind heart, suffering its own secret sorrow, has held for me nothing but sweetness, in return for all I have heedlessly heaped upon its sensitive and trembling strings.

"Oh, since she married me at all, with her keen and delicate sense of honor, it was because she loved me from the first, and hoped to win by her great devotion a response which would satisfy her longing. Vain hope! Vain fool that I have been! With what ceaseless care she has tried to give me every advantage! To think that on our wedding night, — the moment when every girlish fancy was sweetest, — she should have heard me say that I did not love her, and presumed she was upstairs planning some bit of dress. No wonder her modest soul sought refuge in her scheme of becoming a

comrade! Anything else would be prostitution in her
pure eyes. Thank God I agreed! Yes, thank God I
had sense enough to agree!

"And since? A series of patient, gentle, persevering
courtesies, and charities, and self-sacrifices, which have
made my life a freedom, an uplifting, a joy. So well
has she guarded her secret, that at this moment nothing
she has ever said or done could prove to me anything
more than an unalterable friendship. Dear woman, won,
yet never wooed! How shall I ever dare to approach
the sacred shrine where lies hidden this wonderful
wealth of affection? Only its supreme outpouring can
hide my past from her clear gaze! Only its own strength
will grant me the grace of being worthy to be hers. It
is like the lavish love of the Father, which seeks nothing
but love in return, to blot out the transgressions which
have defiled and stained the human soul beyond all recognition.

"And I have thought she loved Sardia. When she
sobbed in my sick-chamber, after her long watching, I
fancied it was from longing for Sardia. Longing! Why,
that was the name of her poem! There she spoke her
heart out! There she told me in lines of melancholy
beauty, that she 'hungered for it so!' And I believed
it was for freedom and Sardia! This was pure wickedness. If my mind had been filled with anything but
wickedness, I never could have misread that plain appeal.
My heart was hard, my eyes were darkened, because there
was no light in me. Had I repudiated the woman who
tempted, I should have known the woman who loved. Sin
smothers the spirit!

"I will go home, bravely, faithfully. When God wills,
He will find a time to put my wife in my arms, close to
my heart. I will tell her all. Lay my soul at her feet,
bare of all its superficial coverings, with all its earthy

stains. If she will raise me to her side, I will bless her. If she justly refuses her pardon, I will bless her. Never came culprit before a truer judge. My wife, my darling, my Helen!"

.　　.　　.　　.　　.　　.　　.

On his arrival home he called James into the library. "James," said he, "I have lost a letter. Did you know it?"

"Yes, sir."

"How did you know it?"

"Poor Anne, sir, was weeping in the kitchen, sir, when I came home that evenin', sir, and she said you were angry with her, sir."

"When you came home in the evening, James? Where had you been?"

"Why, sir, you sent me yourself to see to that mortgage on the Rowley farm, sir, and it was a good twenty mile. I couldn't get home earlier, sir."

"Ah!" thought Mr. Fielding with a contented sigh. "Yet I could accuse Helen of setting him as a spy! James," said he slowly, "I have always trusted you, ever since I was a lad. That letter was very important to me. I have never found out how I lost it. Don't you think you could manage to get some clew to it?"

"Yes, sir, I can. I know who stole it."

"Stole it!" exclaimed his master, jumping up.

"Yes, sir, stole it. I saw it done."

"Tell me at once!"

"The night it was stole, sir, was that 'ere queer kind o' doin's you had in the drawin'-room, when Miss Visonti fell asleep in her chair, and you folks went in to hear the mistress sing. You stayed in the library, sir, as you may remember, after all of 'em had gone to bed. After I got to bed myself, I happened to think, sir, that I had neglected to wind your wallable clock in

the hall, and so I slipt on somethin' or other, and crept
down to wind it. But just as I was a-goin' to, I saw the
missis "—

"Your mistress!" cried Ralfe in a voice of pain.

"Wall, no, 'twarn't her; I was sure it was at first, but
it warn't. When she come down by me into the light,
I saw 'twas Miss Visonti, sir, — and you was a-settin'
a-readin' of a letter. She crept up behind you, unbe-
knownst, and would a' done somethin', — I don't exactly
know what, if she hadn't a' caught sight of the letter.
She just come backards like a crab — as smooth, sir, as
if she'd a' been oiled, and when you tossed the letter in
the desk, and slammed down the cover, and went out of
the winder on to the lawn, she skipped back like as if
she was a bird, and grabbin' the letter, she run up the
stairs as if the Devil was arter her, and I do' know
but he was."

Ralfe kept silence a moment, thinking of his walk in
the garden. In an instant he remembered seeing Sybil's
silhouette on the curtain. She was reading a letter.

"Why did you not tell me of this at the time?" he
queried sternly.

James fumbled with his coat and picked at his cuff.
Finally he answered in a low tone, "I feared it would
cost me my situation, sir, if I spoke against Miss
Visonti to you."

Ralfe turned away. In a moment he faced around,
and said, "It shall not. You were quite right in con-
sidering it none of your business. You knew your
place, and have again won my respect. The guests of
this house must be sacred from the tongue of gossip.
But I also thank you for your honesty in answering
when questioned. I shall not forget it, James, — you
may go."

"And so," said Ralfe to himself, as he took the letter

from his pocket, and with a lip of scorn, tore it into tiny fragments, "this letter, which in surprise and tears, Sybil Visonti swore she had never seen nor even ever so much as heard about, was in her possession at that very moment. Stolen by her to further her vile ends!

> ' Long is the way,
> And hard, that out of hell leads up to light.'

But I stand in God's sunshine at last !   The whole is as clear as day."

CHAPTER XXXIII.

CONDEMNED.

> " For murder, though it have no tongue,
>   Will speak with most miraculous organ."
>
> *Hamlet.*

"HE did not appear!" was Madame Menshikoff's first exclamation, as she entered the drawing-room that evening, whither Signor Zante had driven her immediately from the depot. "We waited until six o'clock, and the heir did not come to claim his rights."

Helen helped her to take off her fur-lined mantle, while Sardia carefully closed the doors. Ralfe, having given her a great chair, replied, "He is not here, at any rate."

"Of course you all know"— The princess hesitated. "You have told them the whole story, signor?"

"Yes, of course. We have been awaiting your arrival with the utmost anxiety."

" And Sybil is very sick, — delirious?"

" The physicians are puzzled," said Helen. "She seems to have no great fever, yet does not recover her senses. She is gradually becoming more violent. They talk of acute mania."

"What has done this?" exclaimed Madame Menshikoff in tones of intense surprise.

"That is it! What can have done it? She was as sane as possible Monday evening," echoed Signor Zante.

"I have told you of our interview," answered Helen in a low, troubled voice, "I fear I am the cause."

"You!" they all exclaimed.

"Oh, the cause lies deep. It is something more than even her knowledge that Julian Visonti is at once her adopted brother and the father of little Ralfe," said the princess. "But let me tell you. When I boarded the train, your man James came in accompanied by a woman. In a moment I saw it was my maid, Dantin. At once I compelled her to sit beside me and give me the history of her life from the moment she stole away from me, three or four years ago. It was as I had imagined. She had taken charge of Miss Visonti's child, and had now, in terror of some one, crossed the ocean to place him in his mother's hands. I made her describe the man who followed her, and came to the conclusion that it was the recreant Julian. I took her with me and ordered James to return to you, as I knew you would understand and pardon such an action when Signor Zante had made you acquainted with the truth. We went to the office of the lawyer who has always had charge of the Visonti estates. He had always known my claims, as I had been quietly introduced to him by his clients for that purpose."

"Why, have you ever visited America before?" exclaimed Ralfe in surprise.

"Secretly, yes. Of course you did not know it! Well, we expected to see the door open at any moment and Julian Visonti come in. The will — all the documents were on the table. The hour set was noon. You cannot imagine the suspense of the last few moments! At ten minutes to twelve, I thought out the history of the whole matter. At nine minutes, I foresaw what would happen if he came! At eight, I foresaw all the consequences if he did not come. At seven, I went over the whole method of becoming an adept. At six, a window in another room was suddenly shut, and I went through the feeling of an earthquake. At five, I truly began to tremble. I cannot tell why. I was not calm as usual. I felt a strange chill in the air. All these interminable minutes, in which I had lived lives, seemed concentrated into a palpable, horrible sense of the unnatural, the uncanny, the weird. At the third minute before twelve, I suddenly became conscious of a strong pressure on my shoulder and a breath in my ear. I concentrated my whole will on my hearing, and at the last moment, just while the clock was whirring to strike, I heard a voice say as plainly as my voice now: 'I shall not come. Good-by.'"

The absolute silence which had reigned during this narrative was painfully continued.

"'Let us give him a few hours' lee-way,' I proposed," continued Madame Menshikoff. "They agreed. And we sat there six mortal hours. When the clock struck six, the gentleman handed me a check for an amount which wholly covered all my loss in the jewels, and then formally announced to me, as the oldest and best friend of the family, that Sybil Visonti was now sole heir to the estate, which would amount to nearly three-quarters of a million of money. They then said that immediately on her return from Europe, she had told them of the birth of an illegitimate child, and had then caused them to draw up the papers for the legal adoption of her own boy. After that, she had made her will, leaving everything of which she died possessed to her son, and bestowing on him the name of Ralfe Visonti. The child, then, is the heir of all my poor old friends had gained. But, nevertheless, he is their grandchild, if not in law, by the still stronger tie of blood."

"But where can Visonti be? Why did he fail to appear? He certainly had crossed the ocean for that purpose," cried Signor Zante.

"I have made the most careful inquiries," said Ralfe,

"and I am certain that he was in this town on Monday. He came to the Argyle, registered his name, left a small satchel in his room, and went out of the house almost as soon as he entered it. He dined early, at about three o'clock, and then sauntered out. At seven, he was in the billiard-room for a few moments, and lighting a cigar, went up the avenue. That is the end of my information. No one has heard of or seen him since. Of course he went to New York on an evening train. But why he did not pay his bill and take his satchel, I do not know."

"I conjecture," said Sardia, "that he intended to return at once. He had ascertained that Miss Visonti was here, had found out that Dantin had taken the boy directly to this house, and, confident that they would not disappear before he could come back from New York, after claiming his property, he decided to leave at once, and return to either offer marriage to Sybil, or to demand the custody of his son."

"But if he went to New York, why did he not come and claim the estate?" again asked Madame Menshikoff.

"It is inexplicable," murmured Ralfe. "I cannot see any reason why he should not."

"He may have been arrested," suddenly remarked Signor Zante. "Who knows if he may not be a criminal? A detective may have followed him even from Europe. He may even not have left here at all, but is in hiding, having caught sight of some one whom he feared. Such a man is capable of anything, and it may have been God's will that at the very moment when he may have been entering the door to announce himself, the hand of the law grasped him and led him away. There are many things that may have detained him. Perhaps, on the whole, it is a thousand times better that he never can touch a penny of the money earned by the parents he dishonored and deserted."

"In any case, he is too late now," said the princess with a grave smile. "But I shall never forget that voice. It was that of a spirit."

"Let us go to dinner," said Helen. "You must be tired and hungry."

"I am," answered madame.

Ralfe started as if from a dream. "If he is alive, he shall marry her!" he exclaimed.

"We all agree with you," answered Signor Zante soothingly. "We all agree with you, rest assured."

At that moment a knock was heard, and one of the physicians entered. "Excuse me for intruding," he said, "but I am in real trouble. One of the nurses was called to the death-bed of her mother this afternoon, and I am at this moment called to a most urgent case. The other nurse is absolutely fainting with fatigue. She has not been relieved since very early this morning. I wish her to rest for half an hour, at least, and I have no one to stay with Miss Visonti until another woman, for whom I have telephoned, can arrive. Have you any trustworthy servant, madam, who could remain in the room for a short time? One who will be silent, and who will not repeat what she may hear Miss Visonti say?"

"Our women are all young," said Helen, hesitating. "I will go myself."

"I will accompany you," said Madame Menshikoff.

"Oh, thanks, ladies, nothing could be better! Miss Visonti is now asleep. She drops into short naps, and then awakens,—sometimes calm and sometimes talking very strangely. But I think there is no fear for a short time." And he rushed away without another word.

"Let us go at once," said Helen.

"Let us all go," said Madame Menshikoff, in a clear, low tone. "It will do no harm for us each to observe her, and try to solve the secret of her strange condition."

In a moment the party found themselves in Sybil's great chamber. She was lying on a broad lounge, enveloped in a soft silk dressing-gown which swept the floor in billowy folds. Her hair, knotted high on her head, was fastened with an amber comb, and her hands were devoid of the jewels that usually glittered on her dark little fingers. She was breathing heavily, and constantly moving her head from side to side, while her half-opened eyes gave her an almost frightful expression. They gazed on her with varying emotions, involuntarily falling into a close group, and almost leaning on each other.

Suddenly she gave a short sharp cry, and sprang to her feet. Ralfe stepped forward to catch her, when she looked him full in the face, and cried, "Are you going to marry me?"

He stood as if thunder-struck, and made no reply.

"If I am not a Visonti, who am I?" she went on, glaring at him with insane rage. "If I am the mother of your child, are not you the father? Don't you know the moon is looking at us both, and can witness that you wronged me? Julian, beware!"

Ralfe stepped forward to utter some soothing word, when she assumed the curved, crouching position of a wild beast making ready to spring. "Julian, will you marry me?" she cried again in a terrible voice. And then, as if listening to an exasperating reply, she suddenly tore the comb from her hair, and would have struck him on the breast, had Sardia not grasped her arm. "Die, fool, and tell no tales," she muttered, looking at the floor, and bending down to gaze upon it.

"Sink deep, and be quiet. I cannot hear anything. Ah, ha! you moon, you wicked murderous moon. Now aren't you happy? Now haven't I pleased you, Moon-Devil?" and she flung herself back on the lounge, shaking with maniacal laughter, and subsiding into a low moaning.

They had all listened to her with unspeakable, fascinated horror. In the minds of each, sentence by sentence, dawned and grew the same thought. A chill seemed to settle down upon them, their faces becoming drawn and white with emotion.

"She has killed him," breathed the princess in a whisper of intense awe.

And not one but re-echoed, in their soul of souls, the terrible words of condemnation.

Ralfe felt Helen lean more and more heavily on his side, and looking down, found she was falling in a dead faint.

CHAPTER XXXIV.

UNITED.

> "I said to the rose, ' The brief night goes
>   In babble and revel and wine,
> O young lord-lover, what sighs are those
>   For one that will never be thine ?
> But mine, but mine,' so I swear to the rose,
>   ' Forever and ever, mine.'
>
> For a breeze of morning moves,
>   And the planet of Love is on high,
> Beginning to faint in the light that she loves,
>   On a bed of daffodil sky,
> To faint in the light of the sun she loves,
>   To faint in his light and to die."
>
> *Tennyson.*

WHEN Helen awoke to consciousness, she found herself in her husband's arms. He was holding her gently against his breast, and her head rested upon his shoulder. His eyes were looking into hers with an expression of unutterable love,—a devotion which was more expressive than she had ever seen arise in any human countenance.

For some time she reclined there, passively trying to realize what it was that had brought her to such weakness, such helplessness. But a delicious rest and comfort, a sense of infinite content, soothed her into a moveless silence. Ralfe finally changed his position, and said quietly, while a slight tinge of amusement crept into his voice, "This is an odd situation for two comrades ? "

Helen started and withdrew herself, leaning back on the couch.

He had carried her into her own room, and carefully closed the door. A few simple remedies had revived her clouded senses. Now he drew an ottoman beside her, and added, " But we have grown to be something more, have we not ? "

She flushed slightly, and turned her head away.

Then with a voice trembling with emotion, her husband caught her hand. " My dearest," he murmured, " tell me, tell me if we have not grown to be more ? Can your heart deny its sweet discovery, when mine glories in it, and feels the ecstasy of heaven ? Oh, say, say the words, the precious, beautiful words which I crave to hear as a thirsty man craves a draught of cool spring water ! Be generous ! Do not deny me, even although you know so well that I deserve nothing, worse than nothing, from you ! I am at your feet in all humility, my Helen. I acknowledge all the stupidity and wickedness and darkness of the past. The light came into my world, and I was blind to it. I had eyes that saw not, ears that heard not, a heart that responded not, for my senses were steeped in a witch's glamour, my will was crushed beneath a siren's foot. But now, blessed woman, I am awake. I see, I hear, I feel, and the rich vision of the spirit seeks reality in you."

With slow, persuaded motion his wife had again turned toward him until her face, fair with an inner loveliness which seemed to shine through every feature, looked sweetly in his own.

" Let me woo and win you," he went on, gathering her hands close against his breast, and dropping kisses on them, " let me show you that this late love, coming after so strange a passion, is.no dishonor; but a royal

tribute of awakened manhood to the queen of womanhood, an outburst into bloom of all the finer issues of
life which had been saved and concentrated in their
essence, even amidst the soil of earthly passion.   Let
me give you my whole long life of earnest endeavor, not
to atone, — for you would not subject me to punishment,
but to improve and progress under the lovely influence
of a genuine affection.   Helen, be my wife.   Give me
the assurance of your confidence."

"The moment that you told me that I could securely
trust you, thrust away the last barrier, Ralfe," said she.
"There has been no moment since you first came into
my presence that I have not loved you.   My love seemed
hopeless; but I did not try to quench its flame.   It was
beautiful and holy, because it was true and right, and,
dearest, now that for the first time you claim it, take
it, take it with all my being, all I am!"

With tears in their mutual eyes, but unspeakable joy
in both their hearts, their first fond kiss was given and
taken.

Kiss of the union of man and woman, the mating for
all eternity of wedded spirits.   Kiss of the harmony
of all that is natural and all that is supernal in the
history of human existence.   A vision of some brighter
sphere, some heavenly paradise of promise, hangs over
the joining of two such beings, and the chrism of God's
purpose toward His children crowns the marriage of two
such souls.

It was amazing to both Helen and Ralfe when they
thought of it afterwards, how freely and eagerly and
earnestly they had conversed, when once their tenderer
mood had passed.   Each poured forth to the other the
whole hidden history of the past few months.   Their
reserve was forever broken toward each other, even as

the ice in a great river under the warm and the glow of a golden sun, parts, breaks and sweeps down the current, leaving a wide, free passage for every passing thing that floats toward a boundless sea. They talked as if they had been old friends, just met after a long and painful absence. They revealed to each other every trifling point which had either puzzled, pleased or pained them. They rushed through the strange incidents of the Visonti's sojourn with mutual surprises, explanations and interpretations, until not a foible or freak of hers remained, that they had not canvassed and understood. Even the general chatter of the place took on a new and absorbing interest, for now they saw things not apart, and from different standpoints or with divided opinions, but from a partnership of feeling and a companionship of thought.

The fascination of thus rediscovering each other, the magic transformation of motives and meanings, now that with absolute frankness they confessed their inner secrets, was almost maddening in its delicious and growing sense of mutual possession, unchecked, unlimited. It was a drama of delight which held them enthralled in each other's presence until gray day began to dawn, and a warning streak of rose told them that another morrow had arisen.

"Come!" said Ralfe, drawing his beloved one to the open window, "Come and look out upon our new world. See! over the mist of the ocean and the darkness of the night, rises the sun of life and beauty, the glory of a new day. So, dear wife, over the mist and darkness that has so long kept us moving strangely apart, yet ever truly seeking each other, rises the sun of love and righteousness, to make for us a new existence of faith and sacred joy. Oh, Helen! here in the early dawn of our sweet union, promise to be gentle with me.

I am not as noble and pure as you are, but I will be as worthy as I may."

While she, leaning on his arm and looking with perfect tenderness into his face answered, " My hus band has my whole respect. I honor him above all men. He is my king. He has no faults in my eyes. I have given him all I have, and I trust him with my whole happiness now and forever."

CHAPTER XXXV.

ALMOST A TRAGEDY.

> " Where peace
> And rest can never dwell, hope never comes,
> That comes to all! "
>
> *Paradise Lost.*

SEVERAL days passed with little to excite apprehension in the patient. The physicians had reported that she had become quite lucid, but was astonishingly weak.

Although answering questions rationally, Miss Visonti had made no conversation with her attendants until one afternoon, when she began to beg to see some one she knew. " I am so lonesome, shut up here," she pleaded. " I feel quite strong enough to go down to dinner. Do let me go down and see Helen, doctor ! I am sure I am quite well enough. I shall die up here, shut away from everybody."

Although her physicians feared it would be a dangerous experiment, thinking that any excitement might send her quite back to her strange delirium, she begged so passionately that they finally spoke of her request to Ralfe and Helen. She instantly gave her consent. Her pity overcame any abhorrence she may have felt, and her generous desire to do anything whatever which might aid in restoring her to strength and reason, actuated a quick and eager compliance.

Ralfe demurred, however. He feared the repetition of a scene, and again, he could not endure the thought that his wife would again be brought into close contact with a woman he now felt unworthy to breathe the same clear air. But he gave his consent as soon as he saw a soft, reproachful look glance from Helen's eyes.

"We will both dine with you if quite convenient," said the colleagues, as they thanked Mrs. Fielding for her kindness. "We can be seated on either side of Miss Visonti, and should she suddenly show the least inclination to violence or excitement, we can take her away at once. Shall you have guests at dinner, madam?"

"None save those who know her quite as well as we. Madame Menshikoff and Signor Zante take a farewell dinner with us, and Sir Sardia, as they sail to-night for India. There will be no one else."

"We will have her nurses in the hall, so that should there be the least disturbance, if all the party will remain perfectly quiet, we will not permit it to last a moment."

"How pitiful, how horrible!" said Helen when they had gone. "This brilliant, beautiful woman to be guarded as if she were a wild beast! Who could have dreamed a fortnight ago that we should fear to be alone with our most fascinating and charming guest? Ralfe, when I think of this amazing change in so short a time, I believe it is only the climax of a long series of causes. How she seems to hate the moon! Her women say she seems to fear and hate the moon as if it were alive. They have been obliged to close the shutters and hang heavy curtains over the windows the last two nights. To-night it will be full. I hope nothing will happen."

"Well, dearest, if there does we must keep perfectly calm, and not add to any noise by so much as a word. I am assured that however rational she may be at times, she will never fully recover. Her memories will ever goad her to madness."

Helen shuddered and walked slowly out into the

garden, turning her face up to the sunny sky, as if drinking in its assurance and comfort.

When they had all assembled in the drawing-room, Sybil came slowly down the stairs, escorted most cavalierly by the two gentlemen, who were chatting with her with all the nonchalance of old friends.

"We have persuaded Miss Visonti to come down, so as to give you a little surprise," they said. "Come, congratulate us. Have we not quelled the fever quickly ? And does she show illness in the least ? "

All surrounded her with smiles and welcoming speeches.

"How nice," said Signor Zante kindly, "that we really have a chance to say our good-bys in person ! Had that envious disease kept you a prisoner we should have been desolated."

She received their compliments and courtesies with her usual languid grace, answering with the half-bantering, half-cynical speeches which distinguished her conversation, and was seated so quickly at table that she took no note that her physicians were beside her. Flattered and delighted that she seemed to be the centre of attraction, she flushed with pleasure, and her melancholy speedily yielded to the gay chaff with which she was constantly assailed. Through course after course of delicious dishes the repartee was kept up, and the laughter which rippled out of the broad windows made it seem once more as if the summer guests were making merry. Coffee was at last finished, and Sardia strolled out on to a broad piazza, lifted several feet from the stone walk which encircled it, and edged by a fancy balustrade on which he lightly leaned. The others following, leaned or seated themselves in a group and would have continued conversing while the gentlemen smoked, had it not been for little Ralfe, who, according to his royal rights, ran in to claim a pocketful of nuts and a bunch of grapes from dessert. He had become, in all these quiet days, a source of pleasure to every inmate. Sweet-tempered, jolly, and beautiful as a dream, he had made friends of every one and already asserted himself as the privileged darling of the household. To Ralfe he had always paid the compliment of his outspoken preference. He followed him about and persisted in making himself agreeable in such a delightful baby way that he had won a place in his heart deeper than either knew.

Helen, however, was to him a "mamma." All his baby trials and troubles were soothed by her, all his particular wishes were made known to her in softest confidence. It was to her he ran when hot and tired, and into her arms he crept when sleepy and cross. The little fellow had begun to form a chain of strange, thoughtful tenderness between husband and wife. Even from the first, and now, they seemed to feel in him a wonderful link that had been the means of bringing them closer to each other — in mutual charity.

At the first sound of the childish voice Helen became pale with apprehension. She had given strict orders to have the little one kept in the nursery. Of course she was well aware that the sight of her child might awaken in Miss Visonti intolerable emotions. How had he escaped ? Before she could make a step forward from the balustrade on which she was half-sitting, half-leaning, with a gay laugh the boy danced through the long window and sprang up to be taken, and she involuntarily lifted his feet so that he stood on the edge.

"Mamma," he cried, "nuts, nuts, mamma !" and flung his chubby arm across her shoulder. But before she could clasp him, with a fierce cry, sharp and sudden as some frenzied tiger, Miss Visonti leaped forward and struck her a violent blow, at the same time trying to tear him away. But it was too late. He had stood so

unsteadily that letting go his hold, he fell to the stone
walk below, and lay there stunned and white, his face
silvered into snow by the moon which beamed upon him
in fullest radiance. Sybil cried out with exultation,
leaning over and looking down on him with wild
laughter.

"Oh, at last, at last I have you !" she cried. "Dead,
dead on the earth and never to rise again ! You round,
white face that has stared and stared at me all my life !
You haunting, hideous, mocking moon that has followed
me so ! Now I've dragged you down. Now I've got
you in my power. Lie there, you white-faced devil.
I'm glad I've killed you too, you spy, you watcher !"

The scene had been so totally unexpected, that even
the alert physicians were taken aback, but in the midst
of scornful, derisive laughter they led her away between
them, and in a moment the house was again still. Sardia
had leaped over the balcony and taken up the little lad,
who made no sign nor motion, while Ralfe escorted
Helen around to the front hall, where, in spite of the
pain in her shoulder caused by the thrust Sybil had
given her, she insisted upon carrying him at once to the
nursery, where one of the doctors almost instantly
joined her. Comment by her guests was needless.
They had all understood the natural fury that arose in
Sybil's soul at the sight of her son in Helen's arms, and
while they deplored the inapropos appearance of the
child at that moment, they were but confirmed in the
opinion that Sybil Visonti was hopelessly insane.

CHAPTER XXXVI.

THE CROWN AND CROSS.

O love, what better proof have I for thee
Than this : that I can put thy love aside,
And seeing plainly all that is to be;
How time and space shall make the gulf so wide
That even this perfect hour thou mayst forget,
Or growing weary, turn to other things;
Still can I praise the Lord that we have met.
Gathering the strength renunciation brings,
With sense of finer ends, my life shall roll
In sweeping currents of the tenderest faith
'Till it shall join those calm waves of the soul
That break upon the silent shore of death.
Then, having gained our freedom, should we meet,
Thy heart shall know how I have loved thee, sweet.

C. L. D.

HELEN remained in the nursery more than two hours. It seemed impossible to calm the little fellow, who, after being restored to consciousness, complained of headache and nausea. But soothing him sweetly on her faithful breast and singing him soft little lullaby songs, remembered from her childhood, she finally had the gratification of seeing him lie in his crib-bed, his cheeks once more delicately rose-shaded and his face moist with the fresh dew of slumbering content. When she came down the stairs, she felt the strain of that terrible incident tell upon her strength, and her steps were slow and unsteady, as she clung to the balustrade, not trusting herself to put down one foot after another from step to step, but both feet on each stair, after a little rest. It took her some time to go down, and she stopped on the broad landing in the middle, her heart sinking into nervous dread. The house was absolutely still, — and now she noted, brilliantly lighted. From the three doors opening into the hall from drawing-room, library, and reception-room, came a great stream of light, as if every chandelier was fully blazing. The nursery, situated in the wing, had been closed to prevent the least disturbance of the child, and she had heard no guests arrive. What could it mean ?

She gave a little exclamation, as she gazed around, when instantly Sardia drew aside a portière and looked up. Standing in the brilliant light, his face turned to hers with an almost seraphic smile, his grand beauty held her gaze in admiration. The strength and sweetness and light of his spirit beamed upon her with a visible good will, as if she had come to her best wish realized at last, out of great tribulation. He came up the steps remaining, and supporting her with an arm at once tender and vivifying, led her into the drawing-room and seated her by a little table, on which was spread a delicate repast — a bit of salad, a slice of dainty bread, an olive, a bunch of grapes, and some rich wine which sparkled in its decanter like a topaz.

"Refresh yourself," said he gently, "let me see you eat." Yielding to his tender command she ate and drank, almost heartily, with a feeling of growing satisfaction and relief. "You ate nothing at dinner, I noticed," he said, "and I was sure in all this time you would be hungry."

"Why, yes," she replied, glancing at the clock, "it is ten. I had no idea of it. Where is every one ?"

"The princess and Signor Zante have gone down to the yacht, and Ralfe went with them. Everything was packed and on board this afternoon, and I will join them there. There are still two hours before we sail."

Helen leaned back with a deep sigh, looking at him with an expression of sorrow which thrilled him with its intensity.

"She will miss me," he thought, "she will miss me. Come, dear," he said aloud, "I am going to take you on a pilgrimage. I am going to show you a sweet home, in which a sweet woman may live a happy life." And drawing her from her chair, he again put his kind arm about her and began to walk along. "This, dear heart," he said, "is the drawing-room, and this the smoking-room, and this the dining-room," as they went along into each. "Here is the music-room, this is the breakfast-room," and so on, through all the spacious and beautiful apartments of the lower floor. Then, mounting the stairs, he opened the doors of two or three chambers. Every room was in perfect order, lighted brilliantly and garnished with flowers. Helen said not a word. She looked at Sardia in a sort of maze, as if she believed him bewitched, yet leaned on him with a trustful anticipation of his meaning which she knew would be given her in the end. He now flung wide the door of Ralfe's apartment. "This is your room," he said.

"No, — no, Ralfe's," she answered, hanging back a little, but in the full glare from the gas, both caught sight of a ripple of soft silk and laces carelessly flung across a chair, and on the toilet-table a jewel and ribbon which unmistakably proclaimed a woman's presence. He pressed her hand with a warm strong pressure, and said again, —

"This is your room," while a clear, modest blush spread sweetly over her fair forehead, as she dropped her meek eyes. Sardia led her along, still opening doors to show fresh bright rooms where her happy guests had so enjoyed her hospitality, and then paused before that of Sybil Visonti.

"No, no," gasped Helen, "don't, Sardia, don't. I cannot see her. I can never see her again. Please don't make me go in there. I fear her. I shudder at her."

For answer, he flung wide the door. The room was not lighted, save by the full moon, which streamed in silvery radiance through the open casements, which formed nearly one side of the delightful chamber. The bed, no longer tossed with the rich crimson hangings and covers of satin which pleased the Visonti, was made up in its cream white laces and looked like the couch of a maiden bride. On the table, a great bunch of mignonette, a flower beloved by Helen, and detested by Sybil, sent out its delicate fragrance. Not a trace, not a sign or token of Miss Visonti remained. Sardia turned up the gas and said smiling, —

"Look in the closet, dear. There is no skeleton there," and timidly Helen peeped in, to find it stripped and empty, — not so much as a veil remaining to remind her of her whom she almost feared would leap upon her again from its recesses. "Listen," said he.

The servants, who had been ordered to keep as silent as possible during Miss Visonti's illness, had collected on the laundry steps, not far from this part of the house, and were singing a jolly tune in chorus, laughing and chatting and "fooling" as servants will, when free to do so.

"She has gone!" exclaimed Helen, looking about with an air of one who has received a gift of unexpected value. "She has gone."

"Yes," replied Sardia, "you will never see her again. Come, let us go and sit in the moonlight, and I will tell you about it."

On the little balcony where so many happy talks had almost made its stones historic to the inmates of Spray View, seated at her feet, Sardia told her how, when she had gone to the nursery with the boy, Dr. Davis had immediately requested Ralfe to send the close carriage around to the door.

"'The young woman cannot remain in a private house another hour,' said he. 'She is a maniac, dangerous, and I believe, incurable. I will drive her at once to Dr. Spiers' private asylum, where the very best care will be given her, but where she will be properly restrained.'

"The nurse and he accompanied her, and in fifteen minutes they were gone. Ralfe and I then ordered Jeanette to pack and the other servants to put the house into the perfect order you have seen it, and then Ralfe himself left it to me to tell you, — and to bid you good-by. He felt that you would not be able, as proposed, to go down to the 'Uarda' when we sailed, so he took all your messages for you, and will bring back their farewells. Is the little boy all right?"

"Yes, he was only stunned. We shall keep him always, Sardia."

"Ralfe said so," he answered quietly.

Helen sat in silence a few moments, bending over Sardia, and caressingly moving her hand over his curls, looking down into his face with the gentle tears dropping on her hand, and once even on his cheek. She stooped to brush it off, but he stayed her hand.

"No, dearest, it is precious. Let me wear it."

"They are tears of joy and sorrow mingled," she murmured. "Who ever had a friend like you? What woman has ever known a love and loyalty like yours? Sardia, I am to lose you. Ralfe is to lose you. Can we

bear it ? But yes, to ask you to stay would be too much.
Oh, believe me, you do not go alone. In those far lands
when on some lonely night, you stand with longing eyes
turned westward, believe me, you will then be not alone.
My heart has been bound to yours by bonds that no time
nor space can alter. I shall surround you with my
prayers, I shall enter into your work, I shall aspire with
you, suffer with you, wait with you, until that hour when
all shall meet as the angels do, in an ineffable union
which is bound by no conventions, prevented by no ties.
If you have given me my soul's desire, if you have given
me to rest in peace upon the heart I love, you have won
from me for yourself a feeling indescribable, — but not
of earth. Be blest by it, Sardia, even to the end of your
whole life."

"My saint," he murmured, as they both rose, and
moved by one impulse, drew together. Their lips met
in one long kiss, a kiss which pressed by lips so pure on
lips so brave and true, is the seal of eternal chivalry and
honor among men; the sign of perennial righteousness
and faith among women, while human hearts shall abnegate themselves and human souls shall burn with grateful love. With one more strong clasp of her clinging
hands, one more look into her sad face, Sardia smiled
cheerfully and sweetly. "It will not be many years,"
said he, "Life flies swiftly," and walked away.

She watched him until he turned into the path that
would lead him out of sight. Then he paused and taking
off his hat, stood and looked back at her for a full minute. Then with one grand gesture of farewell, he disappeared. She sat hiding her face in her arms, for a
long time, thinking over the events of this strange, sad,
sweet summer, and seeing everywhere Sardia's quiet,
perfect devotion. She was awakened by Ralfe's voice,
whose gentle cadence broke her reverie.

"Dear wife," he said, lingering on the word as if in love with it, "I have come to bring you the last message from our friends. The princess, when I left her, was rolling a cigarette as comfortably as if she were merely bound on a trip across the bay. Her cabin is a dream of luxury. Satan was lying asleep at her feet. Signor Zante is in a hammock on deck, his face serene and filled with a grave sweet joy. He believes they will do wonders in lifting the poor natives out of their misery. As I hurried back, I met Sardia. He was walking slowly, his hat off, and the wind blowing his hair in a sort of halo about his head. It looked golden in the moonlight, —I could not help noticing it. When I came up to him, he looked at me long and steadily. 'Yes, I can trust you,' he said, and then he uttered slowly, 'We have kissed each other.' And do you know, Helen, I put my arms right around his neck, then, and we kissed each other too. He then gave me a little box, and said, 'Here is a jewel that I wish Helen would always wear, in remembrance of me, if you are willing. Are you quite willing? Will you take it to her?' I told him, 'Yes, I am more than willing. Whenever I see her wear it, I shall feel you are near us, my best friend.' So then we shook hands, and I have brought it. Let us go into the house and see what it is."

Leaning gently against her husband, Helen went with him beneath a chandelier, and they opened the packet. On a snowy satin bed, rested a cross of sapphires, encircled by diamonds white and glittering as some star that studs the northern sky. The fine chain which held it was clasped with another sapphire, so perfect, large and luminous, that its glory seemed to reveal depths ever receding from the eye. Across the back was a little band on which was chased as if in his own handwriting, the one word: Sardia.

Ralfe clasped the royal gift about his wife's neck, where it rose and fell with her true heart beats, and would lie there even when her white bosom was motionless beneath the grasses.

"Purity and truth," he said, looking at the blue and white, "they are fitly placed. They represent you both. But oh, dear Christ, how have I deserved it! For me the crown, — the cross for Sardia!"

THE END.

NARRATIVES · OF · NOTED · TRAVELLERS

GERMANY SEEN WITHOUT SPECTACLES; or, Random Sketches of Various Subjects, Penned from Different Standpoints in the Empire

By HENRY RUGGLES, late United States Consul at the Island of Malta, and at Barcelona, Spain. $1.50.

"Mr. Ruggles writes briskly: he chats and gossips, slashing right and left with stout American prejudices, and has made withal a most entertaining book." — *New-York Tribune.*

TRAVELS AND OBSERVATIONS IN THE ORIENT, with a Hasty Flight in the Countries of Europe

By WALTER HARRIMAN (ex-Governor of New Hampshire). $1.50.

"The author, in his graphic description of these sacred localities, refers with great aptness to scenes and personages which history has made famous. It is a chatty narrative of travel." — *Concord Monitor.*

FORE AND AFT

A Story of Actual Sea-Life. By ROBERT B. DIXON, M.D. $1.25.

Travels in Mexico, with vivid descriptions of manners and customs, form a large part of this striking narrative of a fourteen-months' voyage.

VOYAGE OF THE PAPER CANOE

A Geographical Journey of Twenty-five Hundred Miles from Quebec to the Gulf of Mexico. By NATHANIEL H. BISHOP. With numerous illustrations and maps specially prepared for this work. Crown 8vo. $1.50.

"Mr. Bishop did a very bold thing, and has described it with a happy mixture of spirit, keen observation, and *bonhomie*." — *London Graphic.*

FOUR MONTHS IN A SNEAK-BOX

A Boat Voyage of Twenty-six Hundred Miles down the Ohio and Mississippi Rivers, and along the Gulf of Mexico. By NATHANIEL H. BISHOP. With numerous maps and illustrations. $1.50.

"His glowing pen-pictures of 'shanty-boat' life on the great rivers are true to life. His descriptions of persons and places are graphic." — *Zion's Herald.*

A THOUSAND MILES' WALK ACROSS SOUTH AMERICA, Over the Pampas and the Andes

By NATHANIEL H. BISHOP. Crown 8vo. New edition. Illustrated. $1.50.

"Mr. Bishop made this journey when a boy of sixteen, has never forgotten it, and tells it in such a way that the reader will always remember it, and wish there had been more."

CAMPS IN THE CARIBBEES

Being the Adventures of a Naturalist Bird-hunting in the West-India Islands. By FRED A. OBER. New edition. With maps and illustrations. $1.50.

"During two years he visited mountains, forests, and people, that few, if any, tourists had ever reached before. He carried his camera with him, and photographed from nature the scenes by which the book is illustrated." — *Louisville Courier-Journal.*

ENGLAND FROM A BACK WINDOW; With Views of Scotland and Ireland

By J. M. BAILEY, the "'Danbury News' Man." 12mo. $1.00.

"The peculiar humor of this writer is well known. The British Isles have never before been looked at in just the same way, — at least, not by any one who has notified us of the fact. . Mr. Bailey's travels possess, accordingly, a value of their own for the reader, no matter how many previous records of journeys in the mother country he may have read." — *Rochester Express.*

Sold by all booksellers, and sent by mail, postpaid, on receipt of price

LEE AND SHEPARD Publishers Boston